'I ⟨...⟩ ⟨...⟩le to
pu⟨...⟩ ⟨...⟩so a
poi⟨...⟩ ⟨...⟩ting
loo⟨...⟩ ⟨...⟩eart-
sto⟨...⟩

⟨...⟩*wins*

'In⟨...⟩ the
different timelines, whilst simultaneously unpicking the nature of
women's relationships. Chamberlain is a brilliant storyteller and
this tightly-plotted tale of tough choices and hard truths doesn't
disappoint.'

Sonia Velton, author of *Blackberry and Wild Rose*

'No one honours the hidden stories of women who've lived
through wartime like Mary Chamberlain. *The Lie* is a testament to
all those who've had to hide their truth – a compelling, poignant
and heartfelt tale about the quiet devastation that is caused when
the secrets of the past surface in the present.'

Lianne Dillsworth, author of *Theatre of Marvels*

'A gripping, absorbing mystery about the true meaning of family, and
a fascinating exploration into the huge social changes that impacted
ordinary lives, particularly those of women, during the 20th century.'

Sarah Day, author of *Mussolini's Island*

'Not only is *The Lie* a fascinating and deftly-written novel of
sisterhood and secrets exploring women's untold stories, but it's
the first book I've read in which Rick Astley is thanked in the
Acknowledgements.'

Anna Mazzola, author of *The Clockwork Girl*

Praise for *The Forgotten*

'*The Forgotten* is an utterly absorbing novel... The devastation of Berlin in 1945 is powerfully portrayed through the eyes of the women who are caught between the conquering forces, trying desperately to survive and to protect one another... The plot twists kept me riveted.'

Jennifer Saint, author of *Ariadne*

'Mary Chamberlain... has written another fine novel about lives shaped by the Second World War... A moving story of two people discovering the power of past trauma to intrude on the present.'

Sunday Times

'Engrossing, heartbreaking and eloquently written, *The Forgotten* left me breathless. Chamberlain offers readers new perspectives on war, women, espionage and what it takes to survive.'

Lara Prescott, author of *The Secrets We Kept*

'Beautifully crafted, elegantly written, with characters to root for – I loved this heart-stopping tale.'

Saskia Sarginson, author of *The Bench*

'Through a cast of memorable characters, [the novel] reveals the difficult choices faced by ordinary people, and their aftermath. A compelling work of fiction that's grounded in real events.'

Choice Magazine

'Mary Chamberlain's moving novel is a vivid and immersive exploration of the lasting impacts of war and how love can rise from the ashes.'

Woman's Own

'A masterclass in immersive wartime fiction. While Chamberlain is characteristically unflinching in her portrayal of the grim realities of war, *The Forgotten* is so much more than a catalogue of brutality. It is a pacy and compelling story of intrigue and espionage, and of how people can survive and love can endure. I loved it!'

Sonia Velton, author of *Blackberry and Wild Rose*

'Beautifully written, realistic on the human impact of war, with characters I fell in love with.'

Louise Hare, author of *This Lovely City*

'Mary Chamberlain brilliantly explores the devastating toll of war on every side, the price paid by women for survival, and the impossible choices ordinary people were forced to make, reminding us that history is never really in the past.'

Sarah Day, author of *Mussolini's Island*

'A riveting drama in the lingering shadows of the Second World War: the inherited, the lived, the choices made and the secrets they bring.'

Cecilia Ekbäck, author of *The Historians*

'*The Forgotten* is a triumph, the kind of novel you hate to finish.'

Carmen Callil, author of *Oh Happy Day*

ALSO BY MARY CHAMBERLAIN

Fiction
The Forgotten
The Hidden
The Dressmaker of Dachau
The Mighty Jester

***

Non-fiction
Empire and Nation-building in the Caribbean:
Barbados, 1937–1966
Family Love in the Diaspora: Migration and
the Anglo-Caribbean Experience
Narratives of Exile and Return
Growing Up in Lambeth
Old Wives' Tales: The History of Remedies, Charms and Spells
Fenwomen: A Portrait of Women in an English Village

THE LIE

Mary Chamberlain

MAGPIE
BOOKS

A Magpie Book

First published in Great Britain and Australia
by Oneworld Publications, 2023

Copyright ©MsArk Ltd, 2023

The moral right of Mary Chamberlain to be identified as the Author of this work has been
asserted by her in accordance with the Copyright, Designs and Patents Act 1988

ISBN 978-0-86154-358-8
ISBN 978-0-86154-359-5 (ebook)

Typeset by Geethik Technologies
Printed and bound in Great Britain by Clays Ltd, Elcograf S.p.A.

This book is a work of fiction. Names, characters, businesses, organisations, places and events are
either the product of the author's imagination or are used fictitiously. Any resemblance to actual
persons, living or dead, events or locales is entirely coincidental.

Oneworld Publications
10 Bloomsbury Street
London WC1B 3SR
England

Stay up to date with the latest books,
special offers, and exclusive content from
Oneworld with our newsletter

Sign up on our website
oneworld-publications.com

PROLOGUE

March 2008

'Music was my first language,' she was saying. 'The land surrounds you in music, in song. The wind, for instance.' She was centre-screen, mid-shot. 'Those fen blows. *Whee, whaa*.' She lifted her arms, swinging them from side to side, her body flowing and fluid. 'It sings from Siberia, picking up notes like an Aeolian harp.' She tilted her head to one side. 'It can be sad and mournful, a lament. Fast and furious like a shanty. Tense and blustery.' She flung up her arms, clicked her fingers, arched her back. 'Like a tango.'

'I loved the sounds, the rhythms,' she went on. 'Did you know grass wails when the cow pulls at it, sings its funeral song? Or that dying birds flap their wings, *ker-tum, ker-tum?* Even agony has a beat.' The camera closed in on her face. 'People think the countryside is quiet, peaceful. But it's not. It's jazz, polyphonic, syncopated, beating its way from the heart of me to the heart of the earth and the heart of you.'

'Do I detect a nostalgia here?' the interviewer said.

'No.' The camera panned out, dissolved into a long shot of the fens, heavy slate skies over thick, yellow wheat pleating in the breeze. 'Look at that sky. It makes you small, insignificant. I suppose that appealed to a certain low-church mentality.' She laughed, her face once more in view. 'But it wasn't for me.' She furrowed her brow. 'There's a small-mindedness about village life. A fear of difference, and if you don't fit...' She paused as the camera closed in on her fingers, opening, folding. 'Life can be hard.'

'And you didn't fit?' the interviewer said. 'Why?'

'I can't tell you.' She was looking down, scratching at her thumbnail.

'How do you feel when you sing?' the interviewer asked. 'Are you conjuring those childhood sounds? Those demons, perhaps?'

'Maybe,' she said, in shot once again. 'When I sing it's as if I break outside of myself, become more than myself, become everyone. Perhaps song came before stories. I don't know. But there's a dishonesty about stories, isn't there?' she went on. 'The writer hides behind a character, whereas a song has a truth about it, a directness.'

'And yet,' the interviewer said, his voice slow, deliberate, 'yet you hid behind a pseudonym. Was that truthful? Were *you* hiding something?'

JOAN

Damp armpits and clammy palms. Joan clenched her fists, opened her mouth, sucked in the air. It stuck in her windpipe, a ball of gas. Her lungs deflated, tightened in her chest, knotted fast. She tried again. *Breathe in.* She grabbed the chair, her face stiff, frozen. She began to pant. Panic attacks. Soldiers had them, she had learned, after a battle. Post-traumatic stress disorder. It had a name. Everyone she knew said it was stage fright, and dead common. *Break a leg.* That's what they used to say. *Break a leg.* But what did they know? They weren't inside her head.

She could see the hall through the wings, daylight pouring through the windows, could hear the hum of the audience. Was it better at night when all you saw was a black hole, the pit of hell rising towards you?

The pianist struck up the opening bars of the music and she saw the MC clapping his hands and beckoning her on. She let go of the chair, stepped through the wings and onto the platform. She walked, jelly steps, to centre stage, lifted the microphone from its stand, took a deep breath and opened her mouth.

'*When the columbine and dog rose start to flower, and the pitch-black ravens in the princes' tower*—' It would be all right. It always was. In all the years, she'd never failed. Her voice was still clear, but

3

then she practised, every day, breathing deep from the diaphragm, running through her scales, C, D, E, F, G, A, B. Major, minor, trilling her tongue and lips. *Do re me fa so la ti do.*

This song was in a major key, though she preferred minor. It suited her voice better. She added a quaver, like a folk singer, took another deep breath, from the belly, raised her arms, gestured to the audience, *join in, sing along.* She paused a beat. Hung on to the last note, air in, voice out, on and on, until the audience had stopped singing. She dropped the microphone back into its stand, bowing as she took in the applause.

It was a themed contest. Songs from the Second World War. It was between her and that woman from Mill Hill with her Vera Lynn tribute act. She'd dressed in period, Joan would give her that, with her wrap-bodice tea dress and hair in a victory roll, but her voice was so-so, had never been trained, not like Joan's. The other finalist was a man, a wannabe Arthur Askey, with his 'Hang Out the Washing on the Siegfried Line'. He was good, and shared Askey's impish face, but she knew, she just knew, that her song hit the right notes of nostalgia and bombast, of whimsy and grit.

She joined the other finalists on the stackable chairs placed in a row to the side of the stage and waited for the judges to pronounce. It wouldn't take long. They had to be out of the hall by six so the caretaker could sweep and lock up, and everyone wanted a cup of tea before they left.

The judge walked to the centre, took hold of the microphone. 'Ladies and gentlemen.' He raised his hand for silence. 'We had three talented artistes who were all equally deserving of winning.' He paused. 'It was a truly difficult choice. But the rules don't permit the prize to be divided.'

Joan knew not to get agitated. Five hundred pounds were still five hundred pounds.

'However,' he went on, 'my fellow judges and I felt that there was one person who stood out for the clarity of voice and the sheer passion of delivery.' He beamed and Joan began to sweat again. She hoped the arm shields wouldn't leak and the perspiration marks show.

'So the winner of the Senior Singing Competition of 2004, with a rendition of that splendid hit…'

He paused, milking the drama, and Joan edged forward in her seat. She'd had by far the loudest applause, but things could be unpredictable. They could feel sorry for the Vera Lynn lookalike or, heaven forbid, the Arthur Askey impersonator could have slipped a tenner to one of the judges.

'"Ravens in the Tower".'

Joan breathed out while the MC clapped, microphone in one hand so it crackled with the pressure.

'Please, everybody, a big hand for Joan Spalding.'

Joan nodded at her fellow competitors, smiled in empty sympathy. It was hard living on a state pension, and what she'd put aside over the years was dwindling. She wanted little luxuries from time to time. Nice soap, a gin and tonic. They sold those ready measured now and she'd treat herself when she did the food shop on pension day. She'd like to go on a holiday, meet other people. She wasn't meant to be lonely. She'd been on her own too long.

She walked towards the MC, arms outstretched. He took her hands, lifted them to his lips, kissed her on both cheeks and, producing an envelope from the inside pocket of his jacket, pressed it into her hand. Her eyes glistened and she wiped away a theatrical tear before turning to the audience and smiling. 'Thank you,' she said. 'Thank you. This means so much to me.'

A chair fell over at the back of the hall, a metallic clatter on the wooden parquet. A tall man stepped out, lifted the chair and put it upright, limbered down the aisle, lithe and hip. He swung a painted cane in one hand, was carrying a bunch of flowers in the other, and as he came closer she saw that the flower stems were wrapped in crinkled tinfoil. He stopped at the foot of the stage and looked up at her.

'Madame,' he said, holding out the flowers towards her and tilting his head to one side. 'A bouquet for you.'

Joan bent over and took the posy. The asters were purple, her least favourite colour, looked half dead. She wondered whether he'd lifted them out of a vase on his kitchen table, or from a grave in West Norwood Cemetery.

He pulled himself to his full height. A tall man, slender, elegant even. He had a presence about him, the air of authority. 'I'm Harry Bowen.' His voice had a Caribbean lilt. He took the steps to the stage two by two, circled his arm and bowed.

He was about her age. A beautiful man, she thought, and pushed the posy to her nose even though she knew there'd be no scent.

'Imagine,' Harry went on. The audience was silent. He was addressing them now, arms outstretched, embracing them all. 'You are at the Palladium. The spectators are in raptures. You have been given the biggest bouquet you have ever seen.' He smiled as he turned and faced her. A winning smile, a melting one. She'd always been a sucker for those. 'How would you accept it?'

She hesitated, wondered what he knew about her. This had always been the way she'd signed off. Lies play dead, snap back into life, she thought, though he looked genuine enough. She cradled the flowers as if they were peonies, shut her eyes and hummed to herself as her feet began to tap out the rhythm. They weren't tap shoes, but the heels were sharp and made an impact on the wooden platform. *Shuffle, tap, toe drop, paradiddle, ball change.* Muscle memory, that's what it was. And daily exercise, like her singing, *keep up, keep up.* The neighbours complained, all the time. Caterwauling, they called it, banging their party walls with the broom handle. *Will you stop your caterwauling, woman?* Or thundering at her door, *stop that bloody racket*, as she danced her way across the piece of hardboard she laid out over the carpet, *ripple, slurp, cramp roll, toe, step, stomp*. She did a final pullback, lifted her skirt above the knee, then slipped into gracious splits.

Harry stood open-mouthed. There was a pause before the audience clapped and cheered. 'You've knocked the words clean out of me,' he said. 'Joan Spalding, you are a force of nature.' He bent over and hooked his hand under her elbow and she allowed herself to be helped to her feet, brushing the wilting flowers against his sleeve so that a couple of petals fell to the floor. 'Will you teach me how to do that?'

Smiles flirted round Joan's eyes and mouth, the habit of a lifetime. 'How long have you got?'

He roared with laughter, and the audience joined him. 'Ma'am,' he said, 'this is the seniors' competition. Nobody's got that long.' He lifted her hand, kissed her fingers. 'Wasn't that the most amazing performance?' His voice thundered across the hall. 'Can you believe this woman?' He was taking over the show, and Joan could sense the MC and the judges getting restless. This wasn't part of the script, and she wasn't sure she was happy with his intervention either. This was her moment, not his, charming though he was, and flattering with it. It had been a long time since she'd had an admirer, mind.

The MC moved towards them, clapping his hands, mouthing *Get off* at Harry. 'Ladies and gentlemen,' he said, picking up the microphone, 'if we are to enjoy our refreshments, I'm afraid we need to call this part of the event to a halt. But I'm sure Joan will be happy to talk to everyone about' – turning to her, beaming – 'the secret of her eternal youth.'

She could do with a cup of tea, but the last thing Joan wanted was to mingle with these pensioners. Her heart was pounding, adrenaline raging too much for relaxation, or chit-chat, but she knew she had to do it, love those people in the audience even though, seconds before she'd step out, she'd hated them, wanted them all to go away.

'A final round of applause for our winner today. Joan Spalding.'

She bowed, looked up. Was that Kathleen at the back of the hall? Her eyes were bad these days and she couldn't be sure. If so, she'd taken her time to arrive. Had she missed the competition? Joan could use her as an excuse, get away early. She hoped Kathleen had her car. She couldn't face the bus, not now. These things took it out of her. There was a time when she'd go out after a show, the Café Royal or the Chelsea Arts, unwind, champagne and home at dawn and sleep it off in the day. But that took its toll, too. Still, even now, she could pull a performance out of the bag if she needed too. A performance was a kind of lie, she thought.

She was aware of Harry by her side and wished he'd go away. 'Next time,' he said, 'you'll get a bouquet the size of Kew Gardens.'

'Next time?'

He pulled out a card and gave it to her: HARRY BOWEN, MBE. There was a telephone number, an email address and a website URL. 'Ring me.'

He turned, and Joan watched as he threaded his way through the people wandering towards the tea urn and the ranks of green Beryl Ware cups stacked three deep on the trestle table.

Well, Joan thought. Well.

She balanced her biscuit on the saucer, sipping her tea. It hadn't been Kathleen at the back. It had been some other woman with the same build and colour hair. She'd left already, anyway. That old emptiness returned, that crater hollowed by the thump from her heart. And the fear. Joan turned to replace her cup on the table, to reach for another biscuit, but there were only broken scraps left. She turned and walked towards the back, inclining her head as she went, grace and artifice and smiles along the way. She lifted her coat off the peg by the door and slung it over her shoulders, dumping the bunch of wilted asters in the waste bin as she went. Thought again, retrieved them. It had been years since anyone had given her fresh flowers, and though these had seen better days, they'd last for a few more, remind her of her victory, of the stranger who'd thought enough to give them to her.

§

Joan stabbed the lock with her key and opened the door, flicking on the light switch. Why hadn't Kathleen come? She could have given her a lift, at the very least. She'd had to sit on the bus for over an hour as it forced its way through the rain and rush hour. She tugged off her damp coat, hung it on the peg by the door. It was an old, misshapen thing, with sagging pockets and a torn lining, but it was still warm and she'd been glad of it walking to the flat. She went into the kitchen, filled the kettle, slammed it on the gas, rummaged around for a cup and saucer. There were a couple of gin and tonics in the fridge, and she'd defrosted a ready meal for two. She couldn't afford that kind of waste. It was typical of Kathleen not to turn up, not to let her know she couldn't come. Always the big I am. Always something more important to do. She unwrapped the tin foil from the asters and put them in a tumbler of water on the windowsill.

The ceiling lamp cast a cold lemon glow. She'd never expected to live here. It had only ever been a temporary retreat. She could sell it, she thought, live on the capital, take out an annuity, rent somewhere better, but what better could she rent on that money? Nowadays it would be called a studio flat, but really it was nothing more than a bedsit with a kitchenette and bathroom, albeit with a tiny balcony overlooking what had once been the swimming pool but was now a car park. Joan pulled the flimsy curtains, unlined fabric in orange polyester, which muted the sodium lights from outside. She looked around her, imagining how the seasoned eye of an estate agent would see it. Against the far wall of the room was her single divan bed covered in a gold candlewick throw, and either side of the beige-tiled 1930s fireplace were two easy chairs covered in a threadbare brown moquette. There was a built-in cupboard in one alcove, an old-fashioned radiogram in the other. Above the mantelpiece was a bevelled mirror, the only thing of any beauty or value. Beneath the kitchen hatch was a small Formica table with folding flaps and two kitchen chairs with plastic seats. A vase of artificial flowers was on the table, waxy chrysanthemums, too big for the jug that held them.

Autumn colours had been fashionable once, and the tenants over the years had never complained. It looked tired now, dated. She'd watched every episode of *Property Ladder* on the television and knew she'd have to paint the walls something nondescript, take down the curtains and put up blinds, throw out the bed and buy a sofa bed or one of those that folded into the wall. Original period features, she'd say, pointing to the fireplace, the built-in cupboards, the kitchen hatch and – she'd lift up a corner of the fitted carpet – the parquet flooring. After all, the block of flats had been Grade II listed, though when she'd bought this place decades ago, it had been a run-down development scheduled for demolition.

She propped Harry's card on the mantelpiece. Why had he given her his card? Perhaps he was a talent scout. She snorted. Talent scout. At her age. He seemed nice though. Perhaps money wasn't everything now. Companionship, someone to laugh with. She knew Kathleen would say she reaped as she sowed, but she'd always hoped one of her lovers would stay the course. *Rolling stone*, Kathleen would say, *no moss*. Kathleen could talk. Pots and kettles. Where had the years gone? The worst about living alone was having no one to share in the humdrum of life, putting out the rubbish, shopping, cooking. That's what brought people together, that's what made them happy.

Perhaps something had happened to Kathleen. It had always been difficult with her, tiptoeing round her to keep her on her best side, a prickly love, pushing them apart as often as it drew them together.

She pulled out her scrapbook, laid it out on the small coffee table. She'd always loved Kathleen so much, had so little to show for it.

The kettle screeled and Joan made the tea, passing the pot and a single cup and saucer through the hatch. She sniffed, pulled out her handkerchief from her sleeve, blew her nose. She poured herself a cup, lifted it to her lips, but it shivered in her hand and tears began to trickle down her cheeks. Grief played dead too, could snap back to life when it was least expected.

She replaced the cup and stood up, looking into the mirror above the mantelpiece, mascara running like silt into the open sea of her face, plastered in five and nine, with greasy eyeshadow and orange lipstick ranging over the wrinkles around her mouth, water in a delta.

The dress was shabby, looked cheap. Black lace. There was a time when she wouldn't have been seen dead in lace, *tarty*, she always said, *common*. Perhaps she'd quibble now. *It's broderie anglaise, can't you see?* Either way, it was ill-fitting, fell off at the shoulders and sagged in the middle. Where had she bought it? A discount store? Or a charity shop? Her memory was playing tricks these days. Perhaps she'd fished it from the back of her cupboard. She looked a mess. No wonder Kathleen hadn't come. She was ashamed of her.

Joan opened the album, ran her finger over the photo of Michael. It was the only one she had of him, cut from a poster all those years ago. It had yellowed slightly. She faced it to the light. If she looked at it sideways, she fancied his eyes followed her. Where was he now? He'd never returned, had never sought her out. Had he been killed, mowed down on the Omaha beach, his perfect body rendered and washed up on the shore? Or was he alive? Did he ever think about her? Did he feel her loss, the way she felt his? A membrane of memory covered her wound, but she could still feel it, as if it were a keloid scar on her flesh. She wondered what he looked like. Was his hair white, still wavy? Or had he lost it along the way, his pate now round and shiny as a conker?

Memories. Dreams. They were no more than stagnant pools where mosquitoes bred and dragonflies hunted.

She closed the scrapbook and wandered off into the bathroom, staring at herself in the mirror as she pulled out the combs and let her long hair hang loose. She looked like a witch with it down, white and straggly, could see herself with a pointed hat and a black cat, the nightmare of a child's story, poking sharp fingers, *what have we here, little girl?* She scooped her hair back, tucked it into her shower cap.

Propped on the edge of the bath was the old cigar box with its kohl eyeliners and grease sticks, and a small piece of natural sponge stained with make-up. Slap. She smiled. That's what we used to call it. *Give me a moment while I put on my slap.* She lifted a powder puff from the sill of the basin and wiped away a film of pink dust. She replaced it in the box and fished for the cold cream, lathering it on her face, wiping off the make-up with sheets of loo roll. She washed her face and hands, drying them on a grubby towel draped over a rail on the side of the bath, slipped out of her dress and reached for the dressing gown, which hung behind the bathroom door, wrapping it round her as she went back into the sitting room.

She picked up Harry's card with one hand and her phone with the other.

Just as it rang.

KATHLEEN

Kathleen drove into the car park, stopped. She pulled down the vanity mirror, squinted into it, running her fingers through her bob, flicking it behind her ears. It was overdue for a cut and colour. Now the blonde had turned to mouse, it needed an uplift every couple of months. It had been her crowning glory once. Joan used to say how envious she was, how Kathleen's long, fair hair turned heads. Like Marianne Faithfull, she used to say, or Françoise Hardy. *Pity you don't sing.* She rummaged in her handbag, pulled out her lipstick, dabbed some on, smacking her lips together, pinching her eyebrows into a neat arc and, delving again, found her perfume and sprayed a little on her wrists. Her sister made her feel old and frumpy, like she needed to tidy up, present herself. Silly, when she was the sister with the prestigious job and steady salary, but that counted for nothing compared to Joan's glamour, faded though it might be.

She stepped out of the car, opening her umbrella and running across the tarmac, skipping the puddles, hoping the rain wouldn't splash too much on her new suit, which Joan would think dowdy, headmistressy. *Liven it up*, Kathleen could hear her say. *Make a statement*, ferreting in her drawer for a brooch or a scarf, draping it over her shoulder. *There.* She wished Joan would stop patronising her, as if appearances were the only thing that mattered. Maybe they were, in Joan's world.

The doors were locked. Kathleen had the right address, but the place was in darkness. She'd set off later than she wanted, and the traffic was a nightmare. Rush hour was bad at the best of times, but these damned bendy buses made it ten times worse. She hadn't meant to be so late. She checked her watch. It was 6.45. The competition couldn't be over. These things usually took a couple of hours at least. Had she got the wrong day? She ran back to the car, switched on the light, pulled out Joan's letter from her briefcase. She shut her eyes, slammed her head against the driving wheel. Such a stupid mistake: 15.00 was not five o'clock. It was three. Of course the show would be over.

She didn't mean to mess up, and it only ever happened with Joan. Kathleen was never late for a work meeting or a professional appointment, but Joan always wanted to see her at awkward times, and running a research institute was more than a full-time job. It seeped into her life, clogged up her plans, flooded her time. There was always one crisis or another that kept her late or required an emergency sticking plaster. She'd never thought of scientists as prima donnas until she took on this job. Sulks and slights and tantrums and politics. Sometimes it was like being in the middle of a Victorian melodrama as hearts were savaged and ideas ravaged. She was supposed to find solutions and compromises, a satisfactory denouement, like some born-again *deus ex machina*. Funding cut to the bone, all the stresses of the RAE, and now the uncertainty of the future. She'd thought of taking early retirement more than once, but the nature of her work, its potential, pulled her back in. Of course, she wasn't indispensable. Nobody was, but the institute gave her a platform to speak out and she had a responsibility to use it while she could, until proper retirement cut her off like a guillotine. And that, she knew, was galloping towards her.

Kathleen checked her phone, pressed Joan's number. No reply. Perhaps she wasn't home yet. She'd drive over, try and make amends. Joan had wanted her to be there today, though Kathleen couldn't see why. Joan was an old hand at this competition malarkey, why did she want her backing? She was too needy these days. Ever since Bill's funeral, she'd rung at least once a week, if not more. Or so it seemed.

Bill's accident had been the catalyst. Only two years Joan's senior, falling off the barn ladder, which he should never have climbed at his age, breaking his neck. They carried his coffin on bales of straw on the Ifor, took him on a tour of the village before the service in the church. Their other brothers, Fred and Jimmy, Alf and Denis, and her nephews carried the coffin, and Bill's oldest sang 'The Lincolnshire Poacher', which made everyone laugh, considering, and the wake was in the village hall. That had been two years ago. No. Double that. Four years ago. She couldn't remember the last time she'd seen her brothers. It had been at their mother's funeral, she guessed, and that had been a good thirty years past and Joan hadn't been able to come. Said she was on tour, but there was little love lost between Joan and Mum and Kathleen knew she'd stayed away on purpose. If she'd had more guts, Kathleen would have done the same. The family thought her a snob as it was. Their father had died when she was in America and Kathleen hadn't been able to fly over for that. What a pair, missing one or other of their parents' funerals. Little wonder their brothers were so angry.

Their brother's death had disarmed Joan. Reminded her of her own mortality, Kathleen supposed. Joan was the next in line, and who would come to her funeral? Kathleen could sense she was lonely and knew she was hard up. She'd never asked what she'd done with her money. Easy come, easy go. Frittered it away, she guessed, without a thought for the future. But that's showbiz for you.

Kathleen had helped Joan move into that dismal little dump in Streatham Hill which she'd owned for years but never lived in.

When was that? Five years? Ten? Fifteen? Fourteen. God, time flies. It was the summer after she'd returned from Stanford, she recalled. She always made an excuse not to visit. It was all too depressing. When they met, it was in town. Joan liked the restaurant in Heal's, and that suited Kathleen. It was near her work and she could slip out for a quick lunch or, on occasions, afternoon tea, though she was invariably late.

'Doesn't matter,' Joan would say. 'I know you're busy.' There was always a hint of Eeyore with Joan, *thanks for noticing me.* 'Gave me a chance to look around. Such beautiful things.' There was a time, Kathleen knew, when Joan lived in apartments furnished from Heal's. Or Liberty's. Her flat now looked as though it was filled with handouts from the local furniture scheme.

They'd never really been sisterly. The age gap between them had been too much when Kathleen was a child, and their lives too divergent once she'd grown up, with Joan always away on tour in a world Kathleen had no inkling about, and she'd focused on her university career, which she knew was as opaque to Joan as a stone wall. They had nothing in common, just blood, an odd sort of pull but real nonetheless. What ran through Joan's mind? It was closed tight as a tabernacle, as if there was some sacred, secret script within.

Kathleen always paid for lunch.

She pulled out her *A–Z*, checked the route and set off. November, drizzle, traffic. Damn it. She turned on the radio for the news. There was talk about the government banning smoking in public places. About bloody time, she thought. More devastating news from Iraq and the kidnapped Westerners. She'd marched against the war along with the whole of London but it had made no difference. She felt so helpless. Why bother with politics, she thought. She could understand the young. *What's the point? They don't listen.*

The buzz of a text came through on her phone. It wouldn't be Joan, as she didn't have a mobile. Didn't even have a computer. Kathleen nagged her. *For your own sake,* she said, *in an emergency.* Besides, if Joan had a mobile Kathleen could text her, which was an easy way to stay in touch. She didn't always have time for long telephone conversations. The phone pinged again and she sneaked a look. *When can we meet? David x* She waited until she'd stopped at some lights, tapped in, *Please stop texting. It's for the best.*

She'd ask the IT wizards at work how to block his number.

Kathleen had other things to concentrate on. Retirement, for instance. This was not something she had planned, but it had sneaked up on her. It was unfair that she had to go at sixty. Doubly unfair now, when the retirement age was due to change in a few years. She could still be productive, capable of innovative research, had dreams for the Institute that she'd never be able to realise. Although of late she'd been thinking a sabbatical might not be a bad idea, recharge her batteries. She'd begun to draw up, in her mind, a list of things to do. Cross the Andes by bus. Sail through the Panama Canal. Chase the Northern Lights. Go on a safari, walk in the Himalayas. Spend the year travelling, rent out the flat. Perhaps it could be a gap year, between work and worse. Relive her youth. Become a hippy. Dig out her old cheesecloth skirt and platform shoes. She was, after all, a child of the sixties.

She'd have to reconcile with spending her retirement in professional limbo, the ageing academic hanging round the fringes of the conference circuit. Coming home to an empty house. She was used to that. *Spinster of this parish.* Had science desexualised her, working in a male environment, bowing to its norms? Is that what had happened? Aping male behaviour? It clearly hadn't been alluring enough to tangle a man in her web long enough to make it last. Except David. She gripped the steering wheel so the bones of her knuckles glowed white, blinked hard to swipe the tears. It was for the best. She told herself that. Every day.

She slowed down to let a young man cross the road, his jeans slung low so the waistband of his underpants showed. What a curious fashion, she thought.

Stop, start all the way down Streatham High Road, wipers on slow, scooping away the drizzle and the grime. She hated this weather, the endless grey days, the cold, damp air. Perhaps she should move back to California. Could she take up another fellowship at Stanford? There was no retirement age in America. She could rent her old apartment in downtown Palo Alto with its communal swimming pool and view of the mountains, its neighbourhood restaurants and organic food stores. Happy days then.

Joan's building hove into view, a striking white modernist structure. She crossed the lights, turned immediately right into the car park, switched off the ignition and dialled Joan's number again.

§

Joan looked older than Kathleen remembered, standing there tired and drawn in a shabby quilted dressing gown, her hair loose, resting on her shoulders. 'I'm sorry,' Kathleen said. 'Were you on your way to bed?'

Joan shook her head. 'No, I just got out of my things, took the make-up off.'

Kathleen walked past her, into the sitting room. It was as dreary as she remembered it.

'I bought us a couple of gin and tonics,' Joan said.

'Just what the doctor ordered,' Kathleen said. 'Do you have any nuts?'

'No,' Joan shook her head. 'But I've got a shepherd's pie for later.'

Kathleen smiled. 'That's nice. But why don't I nip out and get some nuts? Can't have gin without them. It'll take me five minutes. Give you time to get dressed.' She nearly said *in privacy*, but thought that would rub it in. Joan had fallen a long way in the world. Kathleen could sense her sister's mood, flat, deflated. She must have come second or even third. 'You'll feel better,' she added.

'There's a shop on the corner,' Joan said. 'Take my key. It's by the door.'

Kathleen bought a family pack of cashews and a small cyclamen as a peace offering, and a couple of bottles of red wine while she was at it.

Joan had pinned her hair up into a pleat, put on a pair of slacks and a black cashmere jumper Kathleen recognised as one of hers. She'd hesitated offering Joan her cast-offs at first, but she had seemed grateful. 'At least I know where these have been,' she'd said. 'You never know with charity shops. I got bedbugs once from them.' She'd shivered, pulled a face.

Joan still had a good eye and could make herself look more than decent when she needed to. She'd draped a scarf around her neck, a rip-off Hermès in polyester, had made an effort. She'd put on some lipstick too, and foundation so her face was less pallid. She was still a pretty woman, Kathleen thought, still an impossibly glamorous older sister despite her surroundings. Joan fetched a couple of glasses, poured out the drinks and emptied some nuts into a bowl.

'It's not often I have company,' she said. 'Thank you for coming.' She lifted her glass. 'Cheers.'

'You still haven't told me,' Kathleen said, taking her glass and going to sit on the easy chair on the far side of the electric fire. A card propped on the mantelpiece caught her eye. She twisted her neck to read it. *Harry Bowen, MBE.* 'How did you do?'

'I won,' Joan said.

'Well done.' Thank God. If she'd have lost, that would have been the pair of them mired in gloom.

'I practise.' Joan shrugged. 'That's why. I take it seriously.'

'Always the pro,' Kathleen said. But really, she wondered, what does Joan do all day? There wasn't a book in sight, though there was one of those new flat-screen televisions on the old radiogram behind her and a scrapbook on the table.

'How are you?' Joan said.

'Busy.'

'And your fancy man?' It was an old joke between them, but Joan was tilting her head to one side, raising an eyebrow. Had she guessed something was amiss? Joan leaned forward. 'Don't tell me he was another philanderer,' she said. 'I can spot them a mile off, you know.' She rustled her fingers in the bowl and took out a couple of nuts, shoving them in her mouth, catching a crumb as it fell from her lip. 'I've been at the other end of their attention too many times.'

'We don't have much choice at our age,' Kathleen said. 'Let's face it. Most of them are married.'

'What was his name again?'

'David,' Kathleen said. 'David Lambe. He's a journalist.'

Kathleen recognised the pain balling its way into the back of her nose, making it run. Just the mention of his name. Each affair started with hope and ended in desolation, a hurricane of desire leaving a trail of damage in its wake. She took another sip of gin, swilled it around in her mouth, feeling the warmth of the spirit filtering into her blood. She'd almost finished the glass. There was nothing in these pre-measured cans.

She nudged at a smile. 'It wasn't that,' she said. 'Well, it was. His wife has terminal cancer. I'd become a kind of emotional doss for him, somewhere to flop while he licked his wounds.'

'Or a comfort?'

Kathleen shook her head. 'His wife needed him. I told him that, said he couldn't distract himself with me.'

'That was very high-minded of you.'

'Not really. It was self-preservation.' She stared into her empty tumbler, the landscape of the room reflected and refracted in its glass, its optics creating fresh worlds from the tired, domestic elements.

'It's strange, isn't it, how neither of us married,' Joan said.

'Would you have wanted a family?'

'I suppose,' Joan said. 'If I'd met the right man.' She gave an anxious titter, caught her breath as if she was about to say something. Silence. Added, 'Well, it's too late now. No point crying over spilt milk. What will be will be, and all that.' She smiled at Kathleen. 'And you?'

Kathleen shrugged, stared at the remains of her drink. She wasn't sure. She was used to being on her own, making her own decisions, ensuring her life was on an even keel, hand on the tiller, steering through the waves. She wasn't sure a family would have fitted in.

'Well, perhaps David wasn't the one for you,' Joan went on. 'You're probably better off without him. A needy man is a controlling man. What happened to all that high and mighty right-on women's lib stuff you used to spout at me? Smash the patriarchy and all that. Your words, not mine.'

There was something of their mother in Joan. She could have a nasty tongue when she chose, knew how to taunt and needle, point the stiletto in the soft spot and turn it so it stung. Still, she could do without Joan's advice. What right did she have to lecture her? Joan had never managed to make a relationship last more than a few years, if that, and her career had long since run into a dead end.

A police siren screamed, and another. Joan's flat was on the corner of two busy main roads. Kathleen didn't know how she put up with the noise. She stood up and went into the kitchen, bringing back a bottle of wine. It was a Beaujolais, nothing fancy, but she'd bought it for its screw top, not its quality. She couldn't be sure Joan had a corkscrew.

She poured two glasses and leaned forward, picking up the scrapbook, opening it. There was a series of picture postcards, of grand liners, the *Queen Mary*, the SS *United States*, the *Empress of Britain*, of foreign cities shimmering under blue skies and bright sun. *Saludos desde Valparaíso*.

'You used to send me these cards when I was at Miss Loughton's,' Kathleen said.

'Did I?' Joan said. 'I've forgotten. Were you happy there?'

'I didn't really think about it, to be honest. I don't think you do, if you're content. It's misery that scars your memory.' She turned a page, staring at a photo of Joan as a young woman, with a sparkly evening dress and long gloves. 'Is that Frank Sinatra?' Kathleen said. 'I didn't know you performed with him.'

Joan was smiling. 'London Palladium. 1950.'

'Wow,' Kathleen said. 'I was only six then. You really were quite somebody once.'

'Once.' Joan leaned back in her chair.

'Look,' Kathleen said. 'Tony Bennett, my God. And Frankie Vaughan.' She pointed to an advertisement. 'Equal billing.'

'That meant nothing,' Joan said. She laughed. 'He always had the biggest room when we went on tour. I had to make do with a garret, or over the kitchens.'

'"Twas ever thus.' Kathleen shrugged, flipping the pages. 'And is that you? In uniform? I've never seen that one before.'

'ENSA,' Joan said. 'In the war.'

There was a picture of an American GI, a portrait cut out from something, on a page by itself. 'Who's this?'

Joan craned her neck. 'Oh, him,' she said. 'Some Yank I knew once. He was a singer.'

'Was he famous?'

'I don't know what happened to him,' Joan said. Her face clouded with sadness for a split second, long enough for Kathleen to see it. There was something cagey in Joan's reply, her response too casual, dismissive. It didn't match up with her expression.

'If he was a singer, surely—' Kathleen said.

'I'm glad you came,' Joan went on, cutting her off. 'I really am.'

'So am I,' Kathleen said, closing the scrapbook and leaning back. Her sister wasn't all bad, even though they were chalk and cheese.

JOAN

Aitham, Cambridgeshire: November 1943

Sitting on the pew in the Pit Lane Baptist chapel, Joan tried not to catch the elderly minister's eye, but he was walking towards her.

'While I'd be the last person to stop you singing praise to Jesus,' he said as he drew close, his horn-rimmed glasses resting on his fleshy cheeks, 'He isn't deaf, and nor am I.' He pulled himself to his full height, peered down at Joan. 'Sing softly, please. Or not at all.'

'I can't help it,' Joan said. Singing was the only part of chapel she liked, toccatas of sound, cascades as deep as a wave. 'It takes me to heaven.'

'Heaven?' the minister said. 'More the work of the Devil. It's unseemly.'

He turned on his heel. *Blessed are the meek*. Singling her out, humbling her. If she didn't think it would get back to her mother, she'd a mind to walk out and never come back. Her mother had religion, forced it down her throat. Religion slithered like a greedy eel. They had teeth, eels. She had no truck with Jesus, Sunday services or otherwise, women in cloth coats shiny with age, children, cross-legged on the floor. Unwashed hair, hand-me-down shoes. Dirty socks and impetigo, sticky eyes and snot, the stench of poverty. What had Jesus ever done for them? Seemed to Joan he was tin-eared as well as deaf.

§

There was an icy wind that day. It blew the clouds so the sky became a marbled sheet, and it sucked the earth so it hovered over the fen like a coarse grey blanket. Joan folded her arms around her body, glared at the black earth. Dad was driving the horses. She could hear his gentle orders, *whoa girl, get up, girl.* Bill was behind, lifting the beets as they fell, laying them out for Joan and her mother to knock off the soil. Alf and Denis were still at school, got off scot-free for now but they'd be leaving soon enough, once they were fourteen, like Jimmy. She turned, watched Jimmy forking the beets into the cart.

'Keep going,' her mother yelled. 'Why are you stopping? Stoop your lazy back.'

Never had the plain of the land seemed so endless, or the sky so close it crushed the earth and pushed out the air between. One day she'd leave this behind, go to a place of song and dance, music and happiness. Wouldn't tell a soul, would slip away before the sun came up, leaving no trace.

Joan went with Bill when he took the beets to the factory in Ely. She could smell the sugar miles away, that sickly, cloying stench of boiling juice. Bill said it made a syrup that turned into crystals. 'A kind of magic,' he said.

Joan didn't see what magic there was in the factory belching out black smoke and pouring out sludge into the settling ponds, what magic there was for her in her brother's cast-offs, padded with newspaper against the wind, even though Bill said once he thought she wasn't bad-looking if she did her hair nice and stopped trying to look like a scarecrow.

'Where would I get the money to buy nice clothes?' Those land girls got paid for what they did, and they got work clothes and all. Joan had been working for two years, with barely a shilling to show for it. Bill had left school at fourteen too, but he'd manned up. Farm work had built him muscles and strength, his body had shaped up like their father's, tall and big. He could swing a fist like the best of them if he had the inkling. She'd grown skinny and scrawny, with calloused hands and wind-burned cheeks. Bill favoured their mother with his tight mouth and mousy hair, but Joan took after her father with her thick chestnut locks and neat, even features.

'That's why you're so good-looking,' her father had said. 'Chip off the old block.'

'You'll give her airs,' her mother said. 'There's nothing special about that girl.'

Bill had taken to smoking, paying for the cigarettes with the money he earned. It didn't seem fair to Joan that he got paid and she had nothing, but he said he did a man's work and she didn't. He fished in his pocket, pulled out the pack, offered one to Joan. She shook her head. She'd never liked the smell of them. They were almost as bad as the stench of smelting sugar. Joan watched as his breath formed a long plume of vapour.

'I'm going to ask Mum to let me take you to the Yankee hop tonight,' he said. 'Will you cover for me?'

'What do you mean?'

'I'll take you there and leave you while I go and see Aggie. I'll pick you up when it ends. Take you home.'

'And what am I supposed to do there by myself?'

'Dance,' he said.

Joan heard the music drifting in the breeze on a Saturday night, would tap her feet to the tempo. She'd never been to a dance, wanted to go with a longing so sharp it spliced her heart. 'Why?' she said.

'I want to meet Aggie, make hay while the sun shines, before my call-up.' He turned and winked at her. 'So will you cover for me?'

What harm could there be? She got to the dance, and Bill got to see Aggie. 'All right.'

'Thanks.' He drew on his cigarette, tapping away the ash over the side of the cart.

A teal flew out of the reeds by the ditch, a rhomboid of green on its wing. *Rhomboid.* She hadn't thought about words like that since elementary school.

'Now, give us a song,' Bill was saying. 'I love to hear you sing.'

Her stomach felt nestled, happy. She'd wear her best frock. Pin her hair up nice and scrub her hands so the dirt was faint and grey. Nothing she could do about the chapped skin, but then everyone had that.

She sat up, breathed in, opened her mouth, filled the echoing cupola of universe. *What a friend we have in Jesus.*

It was a bitter night, with a sharp frost and a clear sky, stars aligned like sparklers at Guy Fawkes. The farm was a mile and a half from the village, a good walk at the best of times. The Prickwillow road was black, the bulrushes and the hedgerows silhouettes against the sequined sky. She had bare legs, and her flimsy cotton frock was no match for the chill, even underneath her old cloth coat.

'Wait up, Bill,' Joan said, grabbing her brother by the sleeve of his jacket. 'I've got a stitch. You're walking too fast.' They were almost there. 'So where will you be?' Joan said. 'It's cold outside.'

'Never you mind where I do my courting,' Bill said. He stopped outside the village hall.

Even though the doors were shut, and the blackouts held firm, Joan could hear the music pulsing through, loud and fresh, making the ground vibrate. There was a poster outside. MAJOR EDDIE MARTIN AND HIS ALL-STAR BAND. FEATURING MICHAEL O'DOYLE,

VOCALS. She checked no one was looking, unpinned it, folded it and put it in her pocket. She looked up at Bill. 'A souvenir.' What with the war and all, what chance had there been for fun? She wanted to remember this night.

'You're still stealing it.'

'Souvenirs are different,' she said.

'Ten o'clock sharp.'

Joan felt a tug of anticipation as Bill bought her a ticket. She hung up her coat on the peg, opened the door, battled through the curtain and entered the hall. Hesitated, tempted to run after Bill, *you've got to stay with me.*

There was a line of young women along one side of the hall. One or two she'd seen before, though she'd never been friendly with them. Most of the girls she didn't know. They looked older, worldly, a little bit flashy, Joan thought, with stocking seams painted up their legs and pin-ups and topknots, puffed sleeves and cleavages.

Perhaps some were land girls. They kept to themselves, that's what was said in the village, like they were ashamed to show their faces since most of them didn't know a pitchfork from the back end of a cow. Perhaps some were WAAFs from Mildenhall. Some looked like Soham girls, rough as hell.

Opposite them were the men in their khaki uniforms, neat creases down the trouser leg, boots brushed and polished. And in the front, on the raised dais, was the band, in the same smart uniforms of the USAF. There was the singer, a young man with a voice rich and golden as a summer oriole, and the men were real musicians with trumpets and God knows what. Joan didn't know half the instruments, but she knew a thrill when it came. This music spoke to her gut and to her senses, the percussion of its beat and the percussion of her heart one and the same, alive. Whatever happened tonight, whatever happened in her life, this music would be at the heart of it. Her destiny. The minister would call it the Devil's music. She liked that idea.

She stood by herself, swaying with the rhythm, looking at the men lined up as if for battle or a firing squad, the women opposite them pretending to be oblivious, chatting and smoking, worldly wise. She looked down at her own dress, shabby, ill-fitting, a hand-me-down. She'd had to wear her chapel shoes too, with ankle socks.

Behind the dais was a sign with an arrow that said REFRESHMENTS. Bill had given her some money and she thought she'd buy herself a drink. It would give her something to hold, something to do while she waited for him to pick her up. She crossed the floor, went into the room. Bottles were lined up on the table, drinks she'd never heard of, Coca-Cola, cream soda, 7 Up.

'Can I buy you something?' a voice behind her said. She turned. It was the singer. He stood, smiling, his USAF khaki clean and crisp, his cap folded and tucked under his epaulette. She'd never been that close to any man she wasn't related to, but he looked kind, a soft and sensitive intelligence in his eyes. His hair was curly, the colour of autumn, faded freckles across his nose. 'Soft drinks only.'

Was it all right to accept a drink from a strange man?

'I don't bite,' the singer said. 'Come. Have you ever tasted Coca-Cola?' Joan shook her head. He paid for the drink and the soldier serving at the bar opened it up and poured it into a glass, the clear brown liquid frothing like water through a sluice. He handed it to her. The bubbles burst and tickled her lip as she sipped.

She winced, shivered. 'I don't like that fizziness.'

'It's not everybody's taste.' He was laughing, swigging his drink straight from the bottle. He looked troubled. 'Try another sip,' he said. 'It's not foaming quite so much.'

Joan looked at the drink, raised it to her lips and took a gulp. This time round, it wasn't so bad, although its sweetness made her shudder. 'What's in it?' she said.

'That is a closely guarded secret,' he said. He put his bottle back on the table. 'What's your name?'

'Joan,' she said. 'And yours?'

'Michael. Michael O'Doyle.'

'I liked your singing.' Was that brazen of her? She didn't know what to say, standing here, side by side with the singer.

'You look kinda young to be at a dance.' He smiled at her, hazel eyes flecked with green and gold, the kindest eyes she had ever seen.

Joan pushed her shoulders back, lengthened her neck, raised her head, stared him in the eye. She'd done her best to look grown-up, practising a knowing air in front of the cracked mirror in the bathroom, looking down through half-closed lids, pinching her lips so they were red. 'Oh?' She swallowed. 'I'm not as young as you think I am.'

He smiled again, his eyes crinkling at the corners. He was older than her, older than Bill even. 'I haven't seen you here before.'

She wanted to bluff, to show him she was wise in the ways of the world, but her nerve failed her. She shook her head.

'It's a bold young woman who comes alone, without a friend,' Michael went on.

'I came with my brother,' she said.

'And is he here?'

'No,' she said. 'Not at the moment.'

'Ah.' He nodded. 'Do you like dancing?'

'I don't know,' she said. 'I think so. I'm not sure what to do.' She peered through the door into the hall. Two of the young women were on the floor, and she could see the airmen milling around. It struck her it was like the cattle market in Ely, the animals in a pen, picked off by the farmers, one by one. She wasn't sure she had the nerve to go through with it. Yet the music beckoned her. 'Would you dance with me, Michael?' He raised an eyebrow and she knew she'd stepped across a line into a world whose rules she did not know. Added, 'I may not be any good.'

'There's no such thing as a bad dancer,' Michael said. 'If you can walk, you can dance.' He took her glass and put it on the table next to his bottle and ushered her into the hall and the ranks of soldiers and women standing on either side, the stiff formations of earlier breaking down. He turned to face her, placed her hand in his, and his walk transformed into rhythmic steps she couldn't help but follow, hips and turns and fancy feet. He took the next dance with her, and the one after. One or two other couples were now on the floor, and Joan sensed the evening livening up. 'Thirsty?' Michael said.

She nodded. She was hot too, could do with some fresh air.

He led her into the refreshment room, retrieving their drinks from the table. The Coca-Cola was nothing like as fizzy and Joan gulped it down. Michael watched her, smiling. She wasn't sure whether she was supposed to dance with him all night, or whether she should dance with other people. This was new to her. She felt happy, released, and that, too, was new to her.

'I could do with a breather,' she said.

'Good idea.'

There was a door to the outside in the refreshment room, so he led her towards it, and they stepped out into the crisp night air.

'You're not really dressed for this,' he said. 'We'll go back in if you get cold.'

'That's nice of you,' she said. No one in her family would dream of saying something like that.

He shrugged. 'What do you do, Joan?'

'I work on the land,' she said. 'On the farm.'

'I guessed so,' he said.

'How?'

'Hands.' He laughed.

Joan felt a hot flush of shame. She hated her hands, the way the earth seeped into the swirls of her fingertips and lodged under her nails, the way her skin was rough and chapped, her knuckles creased like an old woman's. She felt him run his thumb over the skin of her fingers.

'Beautiful hands,' he said. 'You know they're the most expressive thing about a person?'

'I know your palms can tell your future if you know how to read them.'

'That's as may be,' he said. 'But almost everything you know passes through your hands. You wave your hands, or ball them tight, you point and you hold, you stroke and you strike. You eat and work. You love through your hands. They hold your life and its story.'

The night was dark. A chink from the blackout curtain cast a triangle of light on Michael's face. She tried not to shiver as he caressed her palm, his fingers soft and warm. He spoke with an intensity she'd never encountered before, found herself thinking in ways she never knew were possible, because when he said that, she thought, yes, he's right.

'Do you like farm work, Joan?'

She shook her head. Nobody had ever asked her that, either. Farm work. That's all there was round here. 'I hate everything about it,' she said. 'The earth bites and gnarls your hands, the work destroys your body.' She looked at him, his soft, attentive eyes. 'It's relentless. Season after season.' She paused. 'Except when the wind sings and brings its music. I stop and listen then. It takes me away, to where it came from, where it's going to.'

He was listening, she could tell, taking her words and chewing them over. Nobody had ever done that.

'What would you like to do?'

'I've never had an option to think about that,' she said.

'What do you like doing, then?'

'Singing,' she said. 'I like to sing.' The only songs she knew were hymns and the minister said she sang too lustily, like it was a sin. 'Nothing else.' He'd understand that. 'Did *you* always want to be a singer?'

'I'm not a professional.' He laughed. 'I'm a writer.'

'Oh.' Joan wasn't sure what to say, couldn't understand why he'd want to write when he could sing. 'What do you write about?'

She saw his breath in puffs against the dense, black sky. 'Men and women no one else writes about.' He paused. 'People like you. And me. All the poor immigrants to America. The Poles. The Irish. I want to write stories ordinary folks will read,' he said. 'In their own words, through their own eyes.' She could see, in that small triangle of light, how his face lit up. 'Hey. That's too serious for a dance night, and you look cold.'

She was cold, but she was with this man and she wanted to stay with him, to be alone with him, hear him talk. He was unbuttoning his jacket, slipping it off. He wrapped it round her shoulders.

'Don't want you catching pneumonia.'

She felt him shiver, his body tremble cold against hers. 'You're getting frorn,' she said. 'We best go indoors.'

'Yes,' he said, but he made no effort to move, as if he wanted to stay outside forever with her. He moved close to her, and she thought he was about to put his arm around her waist. She hoped no one could see, would think her fast, tell her mother. 'What was that word you used?'

'Frorn?'

'Yeah.'

She shrugged. 'It's what we say when we're frozen. We should go inside now.'

He stepped aside, reached forward, opened the door, ushered her into the warmth. She slipped the jacket off, gave it to him. He led her back into the hall and into the centre of the floor. The dance, she learned, was called the Lindy Hop, and it seemed to her, as she held Michael's hand and twisted round and away, close and far, as her feet tapped and pranced, her hips swayed and whirled, that this dance was a kind of freedom, that her body was in a trance, her mind soaring into the unknown.

§

Joan didn't complain about the cold once, nor her aching back, nor having to wait hand and foot on her brothers at night when she'd been working as hard as them all day. Nothing would give her mother cause to stop her going to the dance on the next Saturday, and Bill kept his word and promised to take her so long as he could slip away with Aggie and no one was the wiser.

She had to wear the same dress and shoes, but she'd washed her hair the evening before and the weather wasn't so raw and bitter, though the wind blew like a raging bull. Michael was already there when she arrived, crossed the floor to greet her, leading her into the refreshment room and buying two Coca-Colas. There was a table and two chairs in the corner and they went over and sat on them. She wanted to stroke his skin, feel its silk. *You love through your hands.* She didn't know what it was, this urge, didn't know if he felt the same.

'I've got a present for you,' he said. A flush began to climb her skin, smouldering welts round her neck. Presents were only at Christmastime, and even then nothing much more than a walnut or two. He fished into his pocket, handed her a small tube.

'Lipstick?'

He smiled. 'Go on, put it on. I've got something else for you too, when you come back.'

'Thank you,' she said, standing up, heading for the ladies. She didn't know how to put a lipstick on, but it couldn't be too hard. She peered into the mirror, pulled the bright red lipstick out of its case, held it in front of her mouth.

A cistern flushed, a bolt was drawn and a young woman came out of one of the cubicles. 'That's a nice colour,' she said. 'All right if I borrow some?'

Joan held it out to the woman, who leaned forward, drew round the outline of her lips and filled in the rest with short dabs. She smacked her lips together, smiled at herself.

'Thanks,' she said, handing the lipstick back to Joan, who leaned forward, copied the woman's actions, not so assured, she knew, but practice would make perfect. She stood back, smiled at herself. Made all the difference. She pushed open the door, returned to the table and sat down opposite Michael. He nodded, *nice*.

'I've been writing.' He fished in his breast pocket and pulled out a piece of lined, yellow paper, folded in four. 'For you.'

She opened it up. 'Joan's Song'. Her skin prickled with the rush of another blush. This was not a world she knew, this torrent of emotion, this awkwardness she had no words for, no way of understanding except that deep down she felt an overwhelming passion for this man, an excitement she never knew possible. She'd never known this need to touch, to caress another's body, to desire another flesh so thirstily.

'That's very nice,' she said. 'You wrote that for me?' She read it again, the words brushing her mind like a soft eider feather. 'I'll keep this forever,' she said, looking up at him. 'I have nothing for you. I'm not clever with words.'

'You've made a mark in my memory,' he said. 'That's indelible. That's enough.'

She smiled, sipped at her drink. 'It says it's a song. Is there music to it? Only I could sing it, if there were, if you taught me the tune.'

'Well now,' Michael said, 'as a matter of fact…' He winked and Joan watched as he walked across the floor to the band, signed to the leader, who signalled to a man playing the trumpet to move up front to beat time as he stepped down and followed Michael into the back room.

'So this is the lady,' he said. 'Pleased to meet you, Joan. I'm Eddie.' Joan could feel the sting of a blush. Major Eddie Martin himself.

There was an upright piano in the corner draped under a canvas cover, which Joan hadn't noticed before. She stood back as Eddie went over to it, pulled off the cover, adjusted the stool and spread his hands over the keys. She felt Michael nudge her forward.

'You have to listen real good,' Eddie said, cupping one hand to his ear, pointing to the doorway with the other. 'Those boys make one hell of a noise, if you'll excuse me, Joan.' She smiled, looked at Michael nodding, *go on, don't be afraid.* She stood next to Eddie, listening hard for the tune against the noisy brass and jittering tempo of the band. The melody was slow and simple. As he played, she read the song, matched the words, married the words, one flesh, one blood. It was pure, beautiful.

'Thank you,' she said. She'd never been the centre of such attention before, of a man who wrote her a poem, another who set it to music.

'You want to try it?' Eddie said.

She nodded, smiled at Michael, waited as Eddie played an introduction, before he looked at her and she opened her mouth and sang.

'Oh wow,' Eddie said. 'That's something, Joan. You don't want to do it tonight, with the band?'

What if it got fed back to her mother that she'd stood up and made a spectacle of herself in front of all those Americans? Her words had drained away, but her skin was flushing with the thrill of it all. She gripped Michael's hand by way of a thank you, said in a small voice, 'Yes.' To hell with the consequences.

Michael led her to the dais, humming Eddie's tune as he went. She joined in with him, began to sing, and he sang with her, his voice deep and true, in perfect harmony as the band played behind her, kept time, beat by beat, and Michael stopped singing and she was on her own, her voice gaining strength with each bar. She swayed with the rhythm, watched Eddie as he signalled, beckoned her on, until he lifted his hand and paused the music. She hadn't noticed what was happening as she sang, but now she saw the dancers standing still in clusters, like larks on the corn stubble.

There was a moment's silence before they began to clap and stamp their feet. She could feel the dais vibrate, could hear their whistles, their calls.

'Always sing.' Michael had come up behind her, was whispering in her ear. 'That way I'll hear you forever.'

She touched her face. It was warm, flushed.

KATHLEEN

Aitham, Cambridgeshire: August 1960

The Bakelite shell of her pen lay kinked and misshapen on the table, the nib spliced in two. It was the Burnham Joan had given to her when she passed her eleven-plus. It was part of a set, with a propelling pencil, marbled blue, green and black. They had come in a box with a white satin lining, only the pen had leaked a few years ago, stained it blue.

'Who did this?'

'Alf needed a sharp point to unscrew something on his crystal set,' her mother said.

'But this is a nib. Why didn't he use a screwdriver?'

'Said it wasn't fine enough.'

'He's ruined it,' Kathleen said, fighting back the tears. 'Look at it.' She waved it at her mother, then threw it on the table. 'What's he done to it? Why's it all twisted like that?'

'The plastic melted.'

Her pen was precious. Everyone knew that. She sniffed, her lips quivering. 'Didn't you stop him?'

'You won't be needing it,' her mother said. 'Not now you're leaving.'

Mum had said all along that she had to quit the grammar school as soon as she got her GCEs, but Kathleen didn't think she meant it.

'But what'll I do?' It wasn't what she wanted to say. Her brain was moving fast, tripping up her thoughts. School was the only thing she cared about.

'What will you do? You'll earn your keep here, on the farm.' Her mother set her mouth, two hard lines of discontent. 'Stay here until you marry.'

Kathleen picked up the mangled pen. She didn't have many treasures, but this had been one of them. She looked across the table at her mother, at the thin, taut lips, the furrows of her scowl, the hard grey eyes.

'Look sharp, my girl,' her mother said. 'There's the pig to feed and the vegetables need doing. You haven't got all day.'

Kathleen threw the pen across the room, picked up the bucket with the peelings, swung it so it crashed against the table leg.

'Stop that mood right now, do you hear me? Unless you want to feel the weight of my hand.'

Kathleen stomped out, slamming the door behind her, stormed across the yard, bucket clanking. Alf was in the barn, fiddling under the bonnet of the tractor. 'I hate you,' she shouted. 'I hate everyone here.' She tipped the peelings into the sty, watched as the pig lumbered forward, snout in the air. Threw the bucket on the ground and ran through the yard and out onto the drove, as far as the clearing by the willows. She sat on the ground, her chin on her knees, staring into the still deep of the dyke. Bill said this clearing was used by the poachers, in the old days, for catching eels, but Bill fished here at night, so what did that say about him? In the distance, a car was chugging on the Prickwillow road. Kathleen heard it slow as it turned into the drove, listened as the sound grew louder. She lifted her head. A small, grey Morris Minor, with the hood rolled down. Nobody had a car like that round here. It passed her, stopped, reversed.

'Kathleen, what are you doing out here?'

Joan was taking off her sunglasses, unwrapping the scarf round her head. Kathleen leaped up, grabbing the handle, pulling open the car door.

'Let me get out first,' Joan said, stepping onto the drove, her high heels sinking into a crack between the stones. 'Damn.' She tugged her shoe free, turned to Kathleen as Kathleen flung her arms around her sister's waist.

'Take me back with you,' Kathleen said. 'Don't leave me here.'

Joan kept her arms round Kathleen, holding her close. 'Don't be daft.' She unhooked herself, stepped back.

'Why not?' Kathleen felt the drag of disappointment.

'You're being silly,' Joan said. 'You can't come and live with me.'

'Why? I'm sixteen. I can still go to school.'

'Oh, sweetheart.' Joan grabbed Kathleen's shoulders, pulled her close again. She felt Joan's chest rise and fall. 'It's hard, Kathleen, and I'm away most of the time, on the liners.' Joan lifted Kathleen's head, finger under her chin, smiled. 'What are you doing here, though?'

'I come here sometimes,' Kathleen said. 'If I'm sad. I sit here and look at the water.' Feeling the cool of the earth and the wings of damselflies, sitting by trees glistering in yellow and jade, crooked from the blast of the fen, listening to the rustle of the rushes, smelling the dank of the marsh, its peace and solitude submerging her.

Joan took Kathleen's hand, stepped close to the water's edge. 'It's a nice spot,' she said, pulling her skirt tight, sitting down.

'You'll get your dress dirty,' Kathleen said.

'So what?' Joan said. 'Come.' She patted the earth next to her.

Joan not worrying if her dress got soiled. Nothing mattered to Joan. Kathleen wished she could be the same.

'Why are you sad?'

Kathleen scooped up her knees and leaned forward, picking at the hole in the toe of her canvas plimsolls. 'Mum's making me leave school.'

'Is she now?' Joan said. A sharpness to her voice made her sound like Mum. 'And how do you feel about that?'

'She says I've got my GCEs and that's enough. I don't want to leave,' Kathleen said.

'I don't even have GCEs.'

'But you're a singer,' Kathleen said, lifting her head, eyeing Joan. 'I can't sing. All I could do is work on the farm, and I don't want to do that.' She paused. 'Can you talk to Mum?'

'She won't listen to me,' Joan said.

'Why doesn't Mum like you?' Kathleen said. She saw Joan's lips begin to quiver.

'Don't believe everything Mum says about me, Kathleen. I'm not all bad.' Joan pushed herself up, brushing down her skirt. 'I've got to go.'

'You've only just arrived.'

She shook her head. 'I'm not welcome.' Joan was trying to smile, make light of it, but Kathleen could see the effort. 'I only came to see you really. And that I've done. I've got other things to do now.' She pulled her keys out of her pocket, stepped towards the car.

Kathleen rushed forward, clasped her arms round Joan. 'Take me away.'

Joan shook herself free. 'Stop it.' She opened the car door, jumped back in, turned the ignition, revving so hard thick black smoke belched from the exhaust as she wheeled round, Kathleen running after her.

'Please, Joan. Please.'

The car turned the bend, out of sight, its engine fading into the day. Kathleen stood, her breath in light, gulping motions. Joan didn't care about Kathleen, didn't care about anyone. If Joan wouldn't have her, she'd run away. Joan had done that, when she was Kathleen's age.

JOAN

London: November 2004

Joan stood on the balcony in her dressing gown and slippers, waving until Kathleen turned the corner and disappeared down the stairs. She waited till Kathleen came out again, crossed the car park and started her car, watched as it crawled towards the exit, indicator light blinking right.

The man from five doors down walked towards her on the balcony. She didn't know what he did for a living, but he wore jeans and a waxed jacket, carried a bulky computer case. 'Good morning,' he said. 'You're up early.'

She nodded. 'I'm saying goodbye to my sister.'

Standing in her night things in the dawn of a November morning, saying goodbye to her sister when everyone knew she rarely had a visitor from one day to the next, let alone anyone stay the night. Did he think she was doolally? Joan leaned over the balcony wall. She had lost Kathleen in that trespass of vehicles stalling and tailing on the South Circular, back lights and headlights, red and white streaks in the damp, grey morning.

'Oh, by the way,' he said, 'there was a man here yesterday afternoon, ringing your bell. Said he was looking for Joan Spalding. Wanted to know if you lived here.'

Joan looked at her neighbour. 'Did he give a name?'

'No. Scruffy chap. He said you were a family friend. Something to do with his mother.'

She turned back into her flat and shut the door, muffling out the sounds of other people's lives, the revving of lorries and cars, breakfast television from her neighbours, the fractious baby two doors along.

Family friend?

Joan felt the blood drain from her head, a tide of nausea rise up, her limbs soften. She sat down, head between her knees, waiting till the sensation passed. The empty bottles lined the hall passageway. They'd drunk too much last night, like a pair of lushes. That's why she felt sick, had come over faint. Too much alcohol. She wasn't used to it anymore.

Queenie. Dear God.

§

Joan had only been sixty when she'd moved back into this flat. Only sixty. Kathleen's age. She touched her face, feeling the grooves that criss-crossed her skin. A wash of unhappiness flooded through her and all she could hear was her own silence, the sound of loneliness, a throbbing, vibrating emptiness.

Kathleen had stripped the mattress and helped her push it back under the bed.

'Leave the sheets,' Joan had said. 'It'll give me something to do.'

But they'd only had one use, and it seemed a waste to go to the launderette for that, so she folded them carefully, corner to corner, and put them back on their shelf in the cupboard. She made herself a cup of tea and a slice of toast, turning on the radio to hear the voices even though she never listened to the words. She was up earlier than usual. It would be a long day.

She chopped up her time, made chunks of it, targets. Wake up, breakfast, bath. Sing, dance, dress. Those routines came first, every day, then a walk down Brixton Hill, shopping in the market, pausing in the library on the way back to read the newspapers. She'd been on courses there, *Introduction to the Internet* and *How to Use Your Email* and had opened a Hotmail account. She should have given Kathleen that address before she left, showed her how she kept up with the times too, though to be honest, she wasn't sure if she could remember what to do.

She'd made a busyness in her life so she didn't drift, and if she did drift, it looked as though she had a purpose. Was she drifting? Whiling the time away? Building structures on sand? One day, tomorrow, next week, something would come to turn her threadbare life into a coat she was proud to wear. Until then she had to hold herself together. It hurt, those man's eyes, *you're up early*, as if it was odd to be standing in your dressing gown waving your sister goodbye. What did he know of her life? Did he know what it was like to live day by day with nothing more to pull her through than routine? At least she had the competitions, but even those were hard these days. Stepping onto the stage now was as bold a stride as any she'd ever taken, with a cloak of courage that masked her terror.

Joan peered at herself in the mirror above the mantelpiece, pulled the skin back at the base of her ears, tightening the sagging jowls and the crease lines in her skin. But the face reflected could never be the face of youth again. She let go of it, watched it pucker back like a balloon losing air, picked up Harry Bowen's card. She'd forgotten about him. She'd look him up when she went to the library on her way back. With an MBE he was probably in *Who's Who*. And if not, perhaps the nice librarians would help her use the internet.

KATHLEEN

London: November 2004

Meetings all day, a revolving door, in one, out the other, sandwich lunch, coffee in a flask with chocolate biscuits, management stuff, a disciplinary issue, postdocs to supervise. Kathleen looked at the clock. 6.15. Her PA would have left by now, and it was about time she went home. She was tired, couldn't be bothered to cook. There was an Italian by the station, and she had plenty of reading matter to occupy her while she ate. Order some wine, let someone else prepare the food. She was used to eating by herself in a restaurant. Rather liked it, if she was honest. It gave her an air of mystery, all Celia Johnson and *Brief Encounter*. She slipped an interim report from one of her teams into her briefcase, locked her own papers away in the filing cabinet, glanced around her office to make sure she had everything.

The phone rang. Kathleen placed the briefcase on the top of her desk, swung into her chair, picked up the receiver.

'Please hold,' an American voice said. 'I have Professor Brunning from the University of California, Los Angeles on the line for you.'

Susan Brunning. Her oldest friend. They never rang each other at work, only at home.

'Kathleen.' Susan's voice, so familiar, with its East Coast twang. 'How are you doing?'

She leaned back in her chair. 'I'm fine. Just fine. And yourself?'

'Hunky-dory. But listen,' Susan said, lowering her voice. 'We'll talk later. I want the latest on David. But right now this is official business, on the university line.' She paused, and when she spoke her voice was raised, normal. 'I guess you know Professor Fryxal is finally retiring. Moving back to the East Coast.'

'So I heard.'

'I know there wasn't much love lost between you.'

'You're right there,' Kathleen said, picking up a pen, fiddling with it. The memory still had the power to disturb. 'He must be well into his eighties. It's about time he went. Isn't that what everyone's saying?'

'I couldn't possibly say,' Susan said in a way that suggested she not only agreed but had probably started the rumour. 'But that means the directorship of the Grant Institute has come free. I'm chairing the search committee for his successor.'

Kathleen leaned forward.

'The committee was asked to put preliminary names in a hat, and yours came up every time.' She paused, and Kathleen held her breath. 'Would you consider being put forward?'

Why not? May as well be alone in LA with Susan than in London with nobody. It would help her forget David. She'd have work. Resources were plentiful in the States, funding unlimited, or so it seemed. She could feel her heart beating double time. *Yes*, she wanted to scream, *yes, yes*.

'We'd want you to lead by example,' Susan went on, her tone professional, as if the search committee were listening. 'Your work on human immunologic genomics is an area we very much want to develop...'

Kathleen sat still, her breath sharp, short, excited.

'Of course, you'll need time to think about it...'

Three to five years. That's all she need do it for. Five years in the California sunshine. House in Santa Monica. Build up her pension pot.

'Yes,' she said. 'Please put my name forward.' She'd negotiate the terms and the salary later, when they offered her the job. She stopped herself. *If* they offered.

'I'll have to recuse myself from the process, because of my personal interests here, but if you're shortlisted, the committee will do the preliminary interviews via video link,' Susan was saying. 'Probably in the new year, then fly you over for the second round. We hope to have it stitched up by March, with an August or September start date. How does that timetable suit you?'

'Perfect,' Kathleen said. 'I have to retire at the end of August, though you know that.'

'Of course,' Susan said. 'You don't by any chance have a green card? I can't remember.'

'No,' she said.' I've only ever worked on a J1 visa.'

'No problem. It can be arranged,' Susan said, adding in a hushed voice, 'I'll ring you at home. About, you know, other news.'

Kathleen replaced the receiver, shut her eyes. It was by no means in the bag, but top of the list was a good start. She ran through the likely competition. For the first time, she realised, being a woman was an advantage. And a finger to Chuck Fryxal.

Los Angeles: March 2005

Kathleen let herself into her room in the UCLA guest house. The maid had switched on the lights, turned down the bed, placed a single square of chocolate on the pillow. She looked at it, the brown wrapper sparse and stark against the starched white of the bed linen. The enormity of the job, its sheer prestige, hit her like a full-force gale. In the event, the decision to appoint her had been unanimous. The committee had taken her to dinner afterwards, in a fancy Los Angeles restaurant that spoke to a certain West coast pretentiousness.

Whatever made her think she could do this?

She looked around her room, the minibar and the coffee machine, the oversized television and the queen-size bed. She'd come back to an empty apartment at the end of each day. Being the director was a lonely position at the best of times, junior colleagues too in awe to invite her to their homes. Contemporaries too jealous. How would a woman her age make new friends? Where?

It would be daunting, pulling up old roots, putting down new ones. Did men ever have second thoughts? Or contemplate a life of solitude and celibacy? The thought probably never crossed their minds. Had she made the right decision? Was she even up to the job? Her position in London was high profile, but this post was off the scale.

She opened the minibar, pulled out a small bottle of Cabernet Sauvignon and unscrewed the top. Only a few months ago she'd been arguing that sixty was still young, and now here she was thinking she was too old.

She slumped on the sofa, switched on the television, controls in one hand, flipping channels. She'd make friends. She always did. On her salary, she could afford a nice apartment. Beverley Hills, perhaps. She had a fleeting glimpse of Joan in her bedsit in Streatham Hill. Was she just a more affluent version of her sister, but deep inside a dried, brittle bulrush woven into the basket of her past? Chaff blown in the wind of men's affairs? She should ring Joan. Ask her opinion. She could hear the disappointment in Joan's voice. *Los Angeles? So far away.* Kathleen was sure Joan hadn't thought that when she went round the world on the liners. *I'll never see you.*

Kathleen flipped the channel again. The phone by the bed rang. She turned down the volume on the TV and reached over to answer.

'A quick call,' Susan said. 'About the papers you gave me, for the green card.'

'Yes?'

'Your birth certificate. It's a short-form version. We need the long form.'

'It's all I have,' Kathleen said. 'All I've ever used. It's a perfectly legal document. What's wrong with it? Our passport office accepts it as valid.'

'Don't shoot the messenger,' Susan said. 'I'm not privy to the inner workings of the USCIS. But you need to issue them with a long-form birth certificate. I'm sorry, Kathleen. Can you look into it?'

She'd get her PA to do it as soon as she was back in the office. She looked at her glass, at the gory red of the drink. She stood up, went to the bathroom, turned on the tap, swilled the wine down the drain, watching its colour fade from blood to rose until it was as clear and empty as the water.

JOAN

Aitham, Cambridgeshire: March 1944

Her back was hurting from all that stooping and sowing, she had stomach cramps and her breasts were tender. It seemed a long trudge home across the fields. Mum was waiting for her by the kitchen door.

'I want a word with you, my girl,' she said, stomping back into the room and thumping the kettle on the range. Joan knew that tone of voice, though she couldn't for the life of her think what she'd done. Gave Joan the runs, her mother's tongue, frightened her so much it griped her guts. She didn't know why she got picked on and not her brothers, why she was the problem and not them. She didn't want to work the land and made no secret of that, but that was no reason for her mother to hate her.

Her mother pulled out a piece of paper from her apron pocket and waved it at Joan. 'I found this filth under your mattress. "Joan's Song" indeed.'

'Give it here,' Joan said. 'That's mine.'

'There's no "mine" in this house, my girl. So who is he? Writing dirt like this.'

'It's not dirt,' Joan said. 'It's beautiful.'

'Beautiful.' Her mother spat the word like it was a dollop of pig shit. 'There's only one place for this.' She opened the door of the old kitchen range, embers glowing white and red.

Joan ran towards her mother, arms stretched to grab it, but her mother screwed the paper up and threw it into the fire. Joan would have plunged her hand into the furnace, only her mother pushed her back and Joan watched as two orange tongues curled round the paper, biting the edges, turning them black, before Michael's words were tempered by the smoke then swallowed by the blaze until all that was left were fine flakes of carbon.

'So where did you get it?'

'One of the Americans gave it to me,' Joan said. Added, 'He wrote it for me.'

'Did he indeed,' her mother huffed, arms akimbo. 'I should never have let you go to those dances. Don't know what came over me. All those Yankee soldiers. Mature men.'

Joan looked over at the range, as if it could spit out Michael's song, blow it back to her intact. But she had the words in her head. No one could ever destroy those.

'A little bird told me you were carrying on,' her mother was saying. Joan hated this place, with its tittle-tattle, its nosy parkers. They policed the village more vigorously than any constable. 'And you made an exhibition of yourself,' she went on. 'Singing. In front of all those Americans.' She spat the word out.

So what? Joan wanted to say. *What was wrong with that? It made me feel alive, for the first time.*

'Is there something else you should tell me?' her mother said. 'Because if you're hiding something and I find out later...' She stopped, the threat hanging.

'What are you talking about?'

'Don't play the innocent with me. I'm not going to beat about the bush. Did you let him have his way?'

They'd stopped by the banks of a dyke, the water silent as it slept. He'd taken his jacket and laid it on the ground, pulling her down alongside him, holding her tight and it felt right and normal when he kissed her deep and their fingers began to touch and intertwine and she felt him enter her and it hurt only a little, but he knew and kissed her and she swore he said, in a moth's wing breeze, *I love you, Joan. I shouldn't, but I do.*

'I don't know what you mean,' Joan said.

'Don't lie to me. Are you going to have a baby?'

'How should I know? Nobody ever told me these things.'

'You are, aren't you?' her mother said, fluttering her apron. 'I haven't seen your rags hung out since Christmas.'

Joan's belly clammed shut with a painful spasm. Her monthlies hadn't come, but she hadn't thought twice about that. Nobody had ever told her how a baby got to be a baby.

'Never did I think a daughter of mine would bring such shame on the family.'

The kettle began to steam and whistle. Her mother lifted her hand with its leathery palm and corrugated fingers, shifted the kettle off the hob, let it rest on the side.

'I heard he was Irish and all.'

Joan was trying to take it all in. Her expecting a baby, her mother burning his poem. That was unforgivable. And who'd told Mum about her and Michael? Or that he was Irish? He wasn't Irish. He was American.

'You'll have to marry him,' her mother was saying. 'And God help that child. Don't think the two of you can move in here neither. I'm not having no Irish under my roof. You'll have to clear off somewhere else. America.' She lifted the kettle, pulled a saucepan closer, filled it with the boiling water.

The back door opened and Bill came in dressed for the Saturday night hop. 'Nearly ready?' he said.

'She ain't going nowhere,' their mother said. 'I thought you were keeping an eye on her.'

'Why, what's she done?'

'Only got herself in the family way.'

Joan stared at Bill. He sat down at the table, reached over for the bread, cut himself a slice. 'She ain't the only one,' he said, calm as anything. 'Me and Aggie are getting married, soon as we can.'

'Oh no.' Their mother flapped the skirt of her apron. 'Oh no. This is too much.' Reached over to the table, pulled out a chair, sat down. 'Wait till your father hears this.'

'Seems to me,' Bill said, 'that things have a way of coming round full circle.'

'And what's that supposed to mean?'

'You got married in a bit of a hurry too.'

'How dare you,' she said. Joan kept quiet. She'd have got the belt if she'd been as bold as Bill. 'It was different then,' her mother went on.

Bill pushed himself upright. 'Lay off Joan,' he said. 'And let her come with me tonight.' He looked over at Joan. 'She'd best tell the father, at least.'

Their mother sat at the table, mincing her lips. Bill indicated the door, pointed to his wrist as if he had a watch. Joan rushed upstairs, pulled off her work clothes, tugged down her best dress, grabbed a cardigan and her church shoes. She daren't go out through the kitchen, so drew back the bolts on the front door. They were stiff and rusty, never used, but she worked them loose, slipped out.

KATHLEEN

Ely: September 1960

The home bus left at a quarter to four, though some of the girls
stayed on for orchestra or netball practice. She could hear them
in the cloakroom next door as they changed out of their sweaty
clothes, dancing around, *itsy bitsy teenie weenie yellow polkadot bikini.*
Gosh, she thought, they're taking their time. She'd have to wait
until the building was silent before she could come out of hiding.
She wished she had whiskers like a cat, could sense danger like
them. Now they were singing 'Cathy's Clown', laughing, hand-
jiving, she guessed. The gym storage room was dim, smelled of
coconut matting, of leather and sweat from the pommel horses and
vaulting boxes and the old, shiny netballs. The new ones, she knew,
were kept near the courts.

Kathleen needed to do her homework. She was behind as it was.
And there was the business of the note. She should have brought
one from her mother, explaining why she'd been absent from
school the first few days of term. Well, that wouldn't be too hard
to forge.

The singing was fading away. Thank goodness.

She pushed herself up and cracked open the door wide enough
to see the gym clock. The school was mute, a solid, muffled silence,
the kind she heard when she wrapped her head in a pillow. In the

distance, the bells of Ely Cathedral struck. She counted. Six o'clock. It must be safe to come out now. The matting was uncomfortable, prickly. She gathered up her bag, opened the door. Although it was a while to sunset, the brightness had drifted from the sky and the dark was gathering outside. The light in the gym was grey, dense. She listened. Nothing. The building was locked up for the night. She crept out, pulling the door shut behind her. Waited. No sound. She tiptoed across the floor, slipped into the corridor. It felt different in the half-light, as if the walls were crowding in, poised to crush her. She ran to the small stone staircase leading up to the sickroom, stumbled on the step, banging her shin, letting out a cry. Stopped. Had someone heard?

A machine was humming in the distance. Was it in another part of the building? No. The school was empty, vacant, everyone had gone home. She crept up the stairs, turned the handle to the sickroom. It was locked. *Locked.* She froze. This was not what she'd expected. She'd pictured herself curled up on the bed, the sickroom a cosy, makeshift home with its warm blankets and comfy pillow, a basin in the corner with running water, hot and cold. They didn't have that at the farm. Water was pumped from the outside, warmed in the copper for washday and a weekly bath, one after the other. By the time it was her turn the water was lukewarm and full of scum.

She slumped down to the floor, back against the door, not sure what to do. None of the classrooms had a bed, though the sixth-form common room had a couple of old easy chairs. Perhaps she could pull them together, make something to lie on. Or go back to the gym cupboard. At least there was matting there. If she left the door open, the smell wouldn't be too bad.

Now the humming sound was getting louder. A light went on, illuminating part of the stairwell. Someone was in the building. Her heart began to race, a bitter metal taste flooding her mouth. She had to hide. The only other room on this staircase was the music room. *Think*. There was a cupboard in that room where the music was kept, and the records and instruments. She scooped up her things, tiptoed to the door.

The blinds had been pulled down and the room was almost dark. She had to wait for her eyes to adjust. The cupboard was in the far corner of the room but the chairs were laid out higgledy-piggledy, not in neat rows like in their musical appreciation lessons. There was no clear way through them, she'd have to zigzag this way, that. She wove her way, one chair, another. The strap of her bag caught across the back of one, tipping it over. It fell with a clatter, catching another in its wake, metal legs crashing on the hard wooden floor. Kathleen froze, tugged at the strap, but it was jammed. She bent down to try to free it up, heard footsteps up the stairs. The lights in the music room flashed on. There was a soft whimper she knew came from her.

'Well, what do we have here?'

It was Mr Howgego, the caretaker. She and the other girls saw him around school all the time, replacing light bulbs, adjusting door handles. He always made a joke when they passed him, tried to make them laugh.

He walked towards the centre of the room, flipped the strap free, set the tumbled chair upright with one hand, did the same with the next. Kathleen stood, nerves and sinews trembling, unsure whether to run or stay.

'What you doing here then?' he said. 'You should be home.'

Kathleen tilted her head up, willing the tears which had filled her eyes to roll back where they'd sprung from. She didn't want to cry. She was in the sixth form, for heaven's sake. *Young ladies now*, Miss Loughton had said. *Adults*. She sniffed hard. 'I can't go home,' she said, hoping she sounded assertive.

Mr Howgego pulled out a chair, sat on it, pointed to another chair, opposite. 'Why don't you sit down here and tell me why you can't go home?'

Kathleen shook her head, stood her ground.

He was filling his pipe, tamping down the tobacco, lighting it with a match. 'Let's start at the beginning,' he said. 'Where do you live?'

'Aitham.' She hadn't wanted to say a word, but it was hard.

He gave a low whistle. 'That's some distance. You come on the bus then?'

She nodded.

'And you missed the home bus? Well, that's easily sorted. We can ring your father, and he can come and fetch you.'

'We don't have a phone,' Kathleen said. 'Or a car.' She hoped he wouldn't press her more.

'So what were you going to do? Sleep here?'

Kathleen nodded. 'I know there's a bed in the sickroom, so I thought I'd hide there. But it was locked.'

'Yes, it is,' he said. 'For good reason. There's lots of medicines in there. Only the nurse has a key.' He puffed at his pipe, little putting sounds from his mouth. He kept his eyes on her, narrowing them as he considered. 'Seems to me you thought this one through. Planned it, had you? To stay the night?' Bubbles of saliva burst from his lips as he spoke.

Kathleen nodded again.

'I don't rightly understand,' he said. 'Why? Was it a dare?' He tutted, shook his head.

'I've run away.' It came out, just like that.

Mr Howgego sucked on his pipe, a soft, fruity gurgle. 'Well now, that's a serious matter.' He puffed, circles of pipe smoke drifting in the air. 'I'll have to call the headmistress.'

Kathleen wanted to say, no, please.

'Miss Loughton isn't the Wicked Witch of the West I know you girls think she is.' He smiled, winked, took the pipe out of his mouth and damped out the smouldering tobacco with his thumb. 'In fact, I'd say she was a very kind lady. Are you hungry?'

Kathleen nodded.

'Why don't I take you home and my missus can rustle you up something to eat while we wait for her.'

There was, Kathleen realised, no way out of this.

§

She heard voices outside in the hallway, the latch on the door open, and there was Mr Howgego with Miss Loughton. The headmistress always wore a dark suit at school, straight skirt, matching jacket, but now she was wearing a pair of brown slacks and a soft pink jumper. She looked a different person, less forbidding, gentler in some way. Perhaps Mr Howgego was right, she was a very kind lady.

'Don't get up, Kathleen.' She was smiling. Miss Loughton walked over to the other fireside chair, sat down, her feet in their brown spinster shoes square to her knees.

'I need to get back to the school,' Mr Howgego said. 'If you don't need me, that is.'

Miss Loughton nodded, smiled, turned to Kathleen. 'Sometimes,' she said, 'things can be hard, I know.'

Although she was in the sixth form, and they had their own common room, Kathleen had never sat so close to a teacher before outside a classroom, let alone the headmistress, and it felt strange, as if she'd entered another world where the rules were muddled and out of sight, like Alice in Wonderland.

'Mr Howgego said you'd ran away from home. Was there a particular reason?' She said it like it was the most normal thing in the world. She added, 'I won't tell your parents if you don't want me to.'

Kathleen sat in the chair, crossing her feet, uncrossing. She'd never spoken to anyone about what went on at home. Miss Loughton was smiling, nodding, and Kathleen saw a soft, caring woman, not the dragon who stood up at assembly and conducted the morning prayers. Apart from Joan, she didn't know any other women like that. All the women she knew in the fens were large and tough and loud, handy with their fists when it came to children, tempers as fiery as a summer's storm.

'Take your time,' Miss Loughton said.

Kathleen took a deep breath. 'I don't fit in at home,' she said. 'Simple as that. Mum doesn't believe in educating girls. Says there's no point.' She had to do things like reading and thinking on the sly so they didn't find out, say she was daydreaming, wasting time. *Get your nose out of that book. There's enough to do without you sitting on your backside all day.*

'So she forced me to leave school,' Kathleen said. 'After I did my GCEs. Wouldn't let me go into the sixth form.' An old chilblain on her knee began to itch. She scratched it hard. 'I ran away,' Kathleen went on. 'My sister ran away when she was the same age as me. I thought I could too.'

'What happened to your sister?'

'She's a singer.'

Miss Loughton raised an eyebrow. 'A singer?'

Kathleen nodded. Joan had talent that saw her all right. Kathleen had nothing like that. 'You won't send me home, will you?'

Miss Loughton looked down at her hands and Kathleen heard her breathe as if she was about to speak. 'You can stop with me tonight,' Miss Loughton said. 'I'll let your parents know you're safe while I think what to do.' She stood up. 'Let's gather your things. I don't live far away.' She smiled, held out her hand. 'I have a very friendly cat who likes nothing better than sleeping on your lap.'

A single bed with clean sheets and fluffy blankets and a thick, pink eiderdown, a hot bath in the morning with clean, fresh water. Breakfast of porridge and toast, a walk to school. She was summoned to Miss Loughton's office in the afternoon.

'Sit down, Kathleen,' she said. 'I paid a visit to your parents this morning.'

That tug of worry began to pull in Kathleen's stomach.

'We have agreed…' Miss Loughton went on. Kathleen studied her face, thinking fast. She swallowed hard. If Miss Loughton sent her back, she'd have to run away again. Go to London this time. Hitch a lift, find Joan. Plead with her to let her stay. 'That you will stay here with me during term time.'

'What?' Kathleen looked up, mouth open. She hadn't expected this, hadn't even dreamed of it, staying here, with the headmistress. The house had a serenity about it, a safety she liked. It was full of books.

'You go home at the weekends, and the holidays,' Miss Loughton went on. 'It'll be as if you were a weekly boarder.'

Kathleen looked down. Her skirt had a gravy stain which she rubbed with her finger. 'Can't I stay here all the time?'

'Kathleen,' Miss Loughton said, picking up a pencil and tapping it on the blotting pad, 'your parents are your legal guardians. I have no choice in the matter.' She had a file open on her desk, began to leaf through the pages. 'Your school work is exemplary,' she went on. 'There may be bursaries I can look into, for boarders, hardship cases.' She looked at Kathleen, a long, hard appraisal. 'Will you leave the matter with me?'

JOAN

London: January 2005

She needed milk, bread, and was low on butter. She threaded her way into the covered market. It was warmer here, and she wondered whether to treat herself to a cup of tea and a toasted teacake. Call it an early lunch. She was peckish. Joan liked that word. She always put out crumbs on her windowsill, no matter that it was the pigeons who helped themselves, but sometimes she saw a blue tit or a chaffinch and occasionally a robin. She'd like to tame them, train them to come every day. She could move her table closer to the balcony, watch them while she ate, peckish creatures together.

'Joan Spalding?' She stopped, craned her neck to see who was calling. 'Is that you?' She sensed movement in the crowd, saw a man waving, before he appeared before her.

'Harry Bowen.'

'What are you doing here?' he said.

'Me? I shop here. Every day.' She smiled, added by way of an explanation, 'I live up the road.' As if she needed to say that. 'And what are you doing here?'

'Same as you,' he said. 'And I live round the corner.' He laughed. 'You never rang me.'

'No,' she said. She shrugged. She hadn't been sure about him when he'd appeared at the competition, had resented that he'd muscled in on her triumph, had no idea what she'd say to him anyway. She'd become timid over the years, not emboldened, as if life and what it brought had sapped her confidence, not built it. Now, wearing a beige polo neck under a smart navy blazer, he looked a different man.

'May I treat you to a cup of coffee?'

Well, why not? He must have read her mind. 'Yes,' she said. 'Yes, thank you. I'd like that very much.'

They threaded their way out of the market, onto Coldharbour Lane, and he led her into a small café with three tables down one side, a counter on the other, which served also as a work surface. They sat down opposite each other. There were bottles of sauces in the centre of the table and a holder of paper napkins, the cheap kind bought in bulk from a cash and carry.

'A classy joint, this,' Harry said. Joan smiled.

'I nearly didn't recognise you then,' she said, for want of something to say. 'Do you often go to those competitions?'

He shook his head. 'I happened to be passing and heard you singing, so I came in to listen.' He waved a long, elegant finger, pointing at her chest, a gesture she found mesmerising, intimate. Seductive. '"Ravens in the Tower". The great Petal Sisters hit.'

Joan stared into her coffee, watching the froth dissolve into a rim of beige scum. She picked up her spoon, dipped it into the liquid, stirring it so it made murky, muddy waves.

'You're Lillie Pettall, aren't you?' Harry went on.

It was years since Joan had felt that hot sting of a blush, but the reflex hadn't gone, not after all this time. She ran her finger inside her scarf, hot and uncomfortable. She should leave, now, not face the humiliation of exposure, the has-been on the circuit. Nobody else had guessed who she was.

'I loved your records. We played them all the time when I was a student.'

'You were a student?' She could change the subject, steer him away. 'Where?'

'Manchester.'

She'd played there once, years ago, the Palace Theatre. Perhaps Harry had seen her there? Heard her sing?

'Why be coy?' Harry went on. 'You should shout it from the hilltops.' He smiled, turning his fingers, circles in the air. She looked at him, his white hair, his brown skin, dark eyes rimed with thick, black lashes. A longing pranged her, a sensation she'd not had for decades, a desire to touch this man, to feel him with her hands, to stroke the finger pointing at her chest, to hold it and pull it close to her.

'I didn't do that recording.' Joan cradled her cup. She saw not her flesh but her mother's, the same corrugations on the knuckles, the liver spots on the skin, veins swimming on the back of her hand like elvers across a marsh. She shuddered, put the cup back crooked on the saucer so it rattled, spilled. She didn't look good. She was old and shabby, a sad has-been.

His sweater looked soft, expensive. Cashmere. How would he understand? Harry put his head to one side, raised an eyebrow.

She could get up and walk away, have no more to do with Harry. But why? Half of her – more than half – was flattered to be recognised. It had been so long since anyone had paid her a compliment, let alone given her any attention. What was the point in denying it?

'I needed the money,' she said. 'From the competition.' Harry sucked his teeth. She wasn't sure whether it was in reproach or surprise. 'Lillie Pettall was my stage name,' she said. 'I'm not proud of the deceit, with the competition. But I'm not proud, either. Can't afford to be.' She tugged at her scarf. 'Well, I am proud. How the mighty have fallen and all that.' She stared into her cup, tilting it back and forward, making waves in the dregs of her coffee. She'd never admitted that, not to anyone, not even Kathleen.

That wasn't the reason. She'd hidden behind Lillie Pettall, a fire curtain against the truth. Lillie Pettall was a mask, a disguise. Call it what you will. A cover-up. Who would understand that? He was watching her, studying her face, fathoming her hesitation.

'You had some big, big hits.'

'A long time ago.' She heard a bitterness in her voice. She wasn't prone to self-pity but sometimes the sheer drudge of her life, of making ends meet, the unfairness of it, got the better of her. She was aware of Harry's gaze, sharp as a laser, measuring her up. She swallowed, needed to say something, anything, turn his attention away from her. 'You have an MBE,' she said.

'Yes.' He leaned back, laughed. 'I was going to turn it down. The British Empire is not something to be celebrated, but my wife would never have forgiven me if she'd missed her turn at the palace.'

'Your wife?' Joan could feel the disappointment, that familiar brick in her gut. Of course he'd be married. She was about to say *Then why did you ask me to ring you?* But she knew, and held back. There was a pause, too long. Joan shut her eyes. Why should she care if he was married? They always were. The pause became a cleft.

'My late wife, I should say,' he added.

'Oh, I'm sorry,' Joan said, and she was, for his face had washed with sadness. 'What was your MBE for?'

'Services,' he said. 'To the arts. Film. The powers that be seemed to think I was deserving of a gong.' He laughed.

She found herself tongue-tied, out of her depth, him with an MBE and all, with the most alluring hands she had ever seen.

'Listen,' he went on. 'I have to level with you.'

His voice had a seriousness about it, an intent. She understood now he had no desire for her, that his interest had been in something else. She wasn't sure whether she was relieved or hurt. Angry, indeed, as if he was denying her a final chance of comfort, even love. He was a stranger, but she found his presence comforting. She sensed an interest, an empathy that was enthralling.

'I recognised your voice. That was the reason I went into that hall to hear you.'

She smiled, but it was an effort. She felt diminished, as if she'd been caught begging on the street.

'As I said, I had all your records. Played them over and over. As a matter of fact,' he said, 'I still do sometimes. I still have my record player. I love jazz, swing, Big Band sound, all that.'

Joan picked up a napkin off the table, wiped her nose. 'Don't tell me you wanted my autograph?' She tried a laugh, this was a joke, but it came out a sob. There had been a time when the queues outside the stage door stretched all round the theatre.

'If it's going,' he said, and laughed. 'No. I'm a film-maker. Documentaries. I'm doing a new series on girl bands.'

'Girl bands?' It was a long time since anyone had thought she was a girl.

'Across time, starting with the Hamilton Sisters, the Boswells, the Andrews, the Beverleys, Martha and the Vandellas, you name it. The Ronettes. The Supremes, the Liverbirds, the Spice Girls. Plus a whole lot more in Europe and Asia. And, of course, the Petal Sisters.' He smiled. 'It's going to be big, a TV series, umpteen episodes. I've already sold it to America, South Korea, Germany and goodness knows where else.'

'Good for you,' Joan said.

'But,' Harry said, 'I haven't been able to track any of the Petals down. Seems like the original members have all gone to ground. Literally, in Rose's case. She died in 1976.'

'I'm sorry to hear that,' Joan said, and she was. Rose had been worldly, self-assured, and Joan had relied on her. Joan still felt guilty, the way Rose had stood up for her with Mr Mac, made sure she came on that German tour. And how had Joan repaid her? A mistake, Joan thought, if ever there was one.

'So what do you say?'

'I'm sorry,' Joan said. 'My mind was wandering. I was thinking of Rose.'

'I'd love to interview you,' Harry said. 'I'd love to do a whole programme on the Petals, trace their careers afterwards. You in particular, as you went on to have a solo career. Your voice,' he added. 'What a rare and magnificent gift.' He paused. 'What does it feel like, to sing as you do?'

She shrugged, embarrassed, fiddling with her napkin, looking away, not trusting her face to show her emotion. And yet it was as if she knew this man, a kindred spirit. 'It's like soaring into a dream.' Her voice was soft, thoughtful. 'Or into my inner yearnings.' She smiled. 'Arpeggios of my soul.'

'Wow,' he said, leaning forward. 'How did you begin your career?'

She paused, wondering how she should answer. She'd always been a singer. But that was just the half of it. The older she got, the harder it became to talk about it. A boulder of a burden.

'In the war,' she said.

He looked at her, face tilted sideways. 'The Petals were there at the start, the first British female harmony singers. Legends. You'd have a lot to say.'

Well, Joan thought, she would, the way the bastards had screwed her, leaving her to rummage around in the dustbins of music to find enough loose wrappers for the small pleasures of life. Or had she let them do that?

'This is a serious documentary, Joan.'

'I don't know,' she said. 'I'm not sure I could. I need time to think.' What if the film unravelled the knots she'd made that held her life together? She looked at Harry. 'Can I let you know?'

'Of course,' he said. 'You have my telephone number. I'll pay expenses. You've no idea where it could lead. Do you have a card?'

Joan laughed. 'A card? Do me a favour.'

'Okay.' He pulled out his phone, tapped into it. 'Give me your telephone number, your address.'

She spelled it out for him.

'You don't have a mobile?'

'No,' she said. 'Kathleen goes on at me about getting one, but I don't see the purpose.'

'The purpose could be now,' Harry said. 'Kathleen's right. Whoever she is.'

'Kathleen?' Joan said. 'She's my—' She broke off, paused. 'She's the only family I have.'

'Well, think about it and let me know.' He signalled to the waiter, made a sign with his hands, *bill please.*

KATHLEEN

London: March 2005

Her PA had arranged for the new birth certificate to be sent to the office.

'Shall I just forward it to UCLA?' she said.

'Let me check it's in order.'

Kathleen slit open the envelope. Sat and stared, reading and rereading. Her breastbone felt flimsy, as if her heart would blast through at any time. This could not be possible. She placed the paper back in its envelope, grabbed her bag and coat. 'I'll be back later this morning,' she said. 'Something's cropped up.'

She rushed out of the building, hailed a taxi, her mind in free fall, thoughts twisting like bindweed round the truth. This changed everything. Joan had never said a word. Never even *hinted*. What did she think she was doing? What did she think she was gaining by lying? Never telling her? What if she denied it now? Against all the evidence, what if she said *No, it's not true*? She'd kept silent for sixty years. Would have gone to her grave with the secret. Her breath seethed, short and fast. She fanned her face with the envelope.

'You all right, love?' The taxi driver said, peering at her through his rear-view mirror. 'I can nip to a hospital.'

Kathleen shook her head. 'Thank you. I'm fine. Just had some unexpected news, that's all.'

'Hope it's not bad.'

'I don't know what it is,' she said.

She fumbled with her purse, her fingers trembling, out of control, pulled out ten pounds, *keep the change.* Paused while she closed her bag, slung it over her shoulder. Took the stairs to Joan's flat two by two, ran along the balcony, tripping on the milk bottle outside her front door so it rolled across the walkway and shattered against the balcony wall, splattering milk on her shoes and legs and puddling on the tarmac, a ghostly albescent sheen. She took a deep breath, rang the doorbell. No reply. Joan could not be out. It was far too early for that. She hadn't even taken in the milk. She looked around her, over the balcony wall, to see if she could spot her. What if she'd done a runner? What if she never saw her again? She'd track her down, she'd find her. She tried to conjure her words, match them to her feelings. Nothing had prepared her for this.

Joan had to be here. Kathleen hammered on the door, leaned on the doorbell, peered through the letter box into the empty heart of Joan's home. A slight movement, no more than a twitch, Joan's foot on the bed. She was lying still, playing dead. She must know it was Kathleen.

'Joan. Open the bloody door. I know you're there.'

She saw Joan slide her feet onto the floor, stand up, pad over to the door. She heard her unleash the bolt, turn the mortice lock. 'Well, there's a sight for sore eyes,' Joan said, her face cracking into a smile.

'What took you so long?'

'You look terrible. What's the matter?'

Kathleen stormed past, unlocked the door onto the verandah, stood under its portal, fanning her face.

'Oi! You're treading milk on—'

'Why didn't you tell me?' Kathleen's voice broke in, pulsing with anger. 'Why didn't anyone tell me?'

Joan was in the centre of the room, her hand on the back of the armchair. 'What are you talking about?' she said.

'You know bloody well what I'm talking about.'

'I don't,' Joan said. 'Truly, I don't.'

Kathleen threw the envelope at Joan. It hovered in the air before it fell. 'Read it,' Kathleen said.

Joan walked over, picked it up. 'I need my specs.' She stepped over to the mantelpiece, took her glasses and put them on, sat down, easing the document out of its envelope, opening it up. Slow motion, Kathleen thought. She's playing for time. She heard Joan take a breath, watched as she folded the certificate carefully, a third, over once more, running her fingers along the creases. *She's bloody playing for time.*

'You're not my sister,' Kathleen said, words blurting free before Joan had a chance to say anything. 'You're my mother.' Her heart was beating double pace. 'Why? Why didn't you tell me?' She was keening like a banshee, the eerie noise of grief. 'I grew up knowing nothing.'

Joan sat, silent, motionless. Kathleen wanted to shake her, force her to react. She made to step towards her, pulled back, not sure if she could trust herself. She watched as Joan slipped the certificate back in its envelope and put it on the coffee table. 'I'll try to explain,' Joan said, cool, calm.

Kathleen pressed hard against the door frame as if it could protect her, stem the unstoppable flood of heartache and anger.

'I was sixteen years old when I got pregnant,' Joan said, twisting in the chair to face Kathleen. 'A child myself. How could I possibly have kept you? How could I have looked after you? Sending you to your grandmother's was the only choice I had.'

'Why didn't you tell me?'

Joan shrugged. 'In those days, nobody spoke about things like that,' she said. 'Adopted children weren't told they were adopted.

And if it got out that you were born out of wedlock, your life would have been ruined.'

'My life?' Kathleen said. 'Or yours?'

'I was working on the farm at the time,' Joan said, her voice calm, reasoned. 'And Mum didn't want the village to talk. Illegitimacy was such a stigma then. For the child, for the mother. I had no choice, Kathleen.'

'Who's my father? It says *father unknown*. Don't you even know?'

Joan paused. She's going to lie, Kathleen thought. She's going to bloody lie again.

'His name was Michael,' Joan said.

'Just Michael? Didn't you know his surname?'

'Of course I did. What do you think I am?'

'Then what's his full name?'

'O'Doyle. Michael O'Doyle.'

'Then why lie on the birth certificate? Why say you didn't know?'

'I can't explain,' Joan said. 'I really can't.'

'Who was he?'

'An American,' Joan said. 'On the base.' Her eyes began to brim. Spare me your crocodile tears, Kathleen thought. 'We were driven apart.'

'By whom?'

'The war.' Joan pulled out a tissue from her sleeve and wiped her nose. 'Believe me, you were a love child. A loved child.' She sniffed.

'What happened to him?'

'I'm pretty sure he was killed. In Normandy.' Joan's eyes brimmed with tears. 'He never came back.'

Kathleen looked at Joan, taking it in. 'You told me you ran away from home. But now I know. Were you kicked out? Sent away? I was spun a cock-and-bull story. I believed everything was true. I was the afterthought. That's what Mum and Dad said. My brothers. Did they know? Did everyone know but me?'

Kathleen stepped back into the room, folded herself onto Joan's bed, grabbing one of the pillows, burying her head in it, her shoulders convulsing. She began to tap her feet, *rat-at-tat*, rhythmically, her anguish, her frustration, her fury simmering through her body from her tears to her toes.

'Have you any idea how miserable I was?' She lifted her face out of the pillow. 'I used to think I was adopted, that one day my real mother would come, take me away.' Her mouth was set, drawn as the threads in the pillow. 'I dreamed of *you* taking me away. I even begged you, do you remember, when Mum made me leave school? If only I'd known. You *were* my mother.' She paused, whimpered. 'I wouldn't have been any trouble.'

'Don't think I didn't regret it,' Joan said. She grabbed the arms of her chair and took a deep breath. 'That I didn't want you by my side. I yearned to have you with me. When you begged me, that time, it broke my heart.'

Joan pushed herself up, walked over to the bed and sat next to Kathleen, placing an arm around her shoulder. Kathleen shook it away.

'It was either that or putting you into an orphanage, never seeing you again. I had to know where you were, watch you grow up.'

'You had to know.' Kathleen said. 'Always you. Did you think about me?'

'All the time.' The bed was dipping, shunting Joan closer to Kathleen.

'I still don't understand why you never told me.'

Joan looked down at her lap, her fingers meshed together. 'It never seemed to be the right time,' she said. 'How do you start that conversation? The longer I put it off, the harder it became.'

'You start that conversation quite simply,' Kathleen said. 'You're a fucking coward.' She was shaking her head. 'You could have told me when Mum died. I know you weren't at the funeral, but you could have written to me, rung me. I'm sixty years old and I wait till now to learn who my real mother is.'

'I never stopped loving you, never stopped thinking about you.' Joan shifted on the bed so the mattress bounced. 'I did as best I could, Kathleen.'

Kathleen blew out, hard and deep, draining her lungs of air, of oxygen.

Joan stretched out her hand, groping for Kathleen's. She smiled, a nod of understanding. If you think that's what passes for maternal feelings, Kathleen thought, you'd better think again. Her fury raged stronger by the minute.

'Look at me. Crying. I'm sixty years old, for fuck's sake. I don't know who I am, or where I'm from. Who I belong to.' Kathleen pulled her hand away. 'All my life you'd tap at my door and disappear, play knock down ginger with my feelings. Peek-a-boo, now you see me, now you don't.'

'I couldn't help that,' Joan said. 'I was working on the liners. I tried to keep in touch. I sent you cards, everything.'

She didn't give a damn about Joan's excuses. Her nose was running and she wiped her hand over her nostrils, spreading her fingers through the candlewick tufts of Joan's bedspread, smearing the plush. Her head simmered, filleting out the bits that made sense.

'I know you had no option.' Her words came slow, deliberate. 'I understand that. I might have done the same, in your shoes.' No, she thought. When I *was* in your shoes, I had an abortion. Didn't give it a second thought.

She could feel Joan's eyes searching for a softening, an opening. A weakness, perhaps.

'You lied,' Kathleen went on. 'The woman I thought was my mother. She lied. Everyone I know. Liars, all of them.' She sniffed, hard. 'Not knowing who my father is. Did he know about me? Did he care?'

Joan fiddled with the hem of her nightdress. 'He called you Kathleen.'

'He knew me?'

'No. But that's the name he wanted for you. That's how you got your name.'

He chose her name, he'd *imagined* her. That was a connection, slender but real.

'Have you thought what it was like for me?' Joan's voice was gentle, coaxing. She was looking straight at Kathleen, daring her to glance away.

'Why should I think what it was like for you?'

'Because, Kathleen, I was destroyed by it too. Every day. Nobody escapes something like that. It affects everyone.' She paused.

And then they came, tears, unstoppable, the grief and untruths of a lifetime. Kathleen sat on the bed, convulsing, felt Joan's arms wrap round her, and they rocked to and fro, tears mingling together, trickling over each other's skin, damp, sticky cheeks bonding.

'How can I make amends?'

'Tell me about my father,' Kathleen said. 'Help me find him.'

JOAN

London: June 1944

Michael was outside the village hall. He waited while she paid for her ticket then led her indoors, women along one side, men the other, only this time Joan saw it differently, like a guard of honour. She'd been thinking as she walked to the village hall. Had it planned. Perhaps the baby was no bad thing. They could marry. She was sixteen, after all. Mum and Dad couldn't object. Mum hadn't been much older when she'd married Dad.

'We've got to talk,' she said. 'Can we go outside?'

They stepped out through the room at the back, onto the broken macadam behind, into the light of the midsummer evening.

'Let's walk,' she said. 'Down the fen.' She didn't care who saw her. She waited till they'd turned the corner and were close to the dyke.

'I'm having a baby,' she said.

Michael breathed in sharp. 'You're what?' He turned away, running his hand through his hair, his shoulders hunched. He stood, his back to her, toeing a pebble, knocking it against another, sharp cracks like falling jackstones. In the distance the music from the hall wafted into earshot, faded out, a world she'd entered once now empty and strange. She could hear his heavy, laboured breathing, as if he was rooting out a tree stump or tossing hay into the loft.

This wasn't how she'd imagined it. She'd thought he'd sweep her up, say *marry me*, take her away, carry her from the fen into a world of music and dance. He'd have to now, wouldn't he? He'd sing with the band, and so would she. He'd write more songs, and she'd sing them all. They'd tour the world, entertain the soldiers. She wasn't sure what would happen after the baby was born, but perhaps the war would be over by then. The baby – their baby – made them whole, made this possible.

'Michael?'

'I'm so sorry,' he said, words thrown across his shoulder. 'I should never have started this, let it go so far.' There was a catch in his voice. 'I should have known better.'

He kept his distance and she felt its vast, flat emptiness. He wasn't going to marry her. That's what he was working up to tell her.

She'd heard about girls who got in the family way, cast out without a penny, not even a farthing of Public Assistance or whatever it was called. She'd had no time to think about a baby, or what she'd do to look after it, where she'd live, how she'd eat. The workhouse had closed. That's where they used to put unwed mothers.

Michael looked up at the sky and she followed his gaze, seeing the thick, grey clouds, still and silent as clods of clay against the gathering dark of the sky. She saw his lips move, as if in silent prayer, watched as he wandered down to the dyke, squatted and plucked at a reed. It was a while before he returned and spoke.

'I have a wife, in America.'

She could feel herself sway, as if the earth was churning.

He turned away again, staring out at the fen, shaking his head.

'What'll I do?' she said.

Michael pulled out a cigarette and lit it, his shoulders hunched against the wind. She wanted to go to him, put her arms round his waist, pull him close, but he stood stiff and apart.

'What'll we call it?' she said, hoping to rope him in, bring him back to her. He couldn't have a wife. He was just saying it. 'Our baby? I'd call him Michael,' she added. 'If it's a boy. After you.' Her words were tumbling, out of control. She had to catch him, this man, hook him to her. 'And what'll you call our baby, if she's a girl?'

He turned round then, his eyes moist. 'Kathleen,' he said. 'Little Katherine.'

'Was your mother called Kathleen, then?' Joan said. He was so sure, so swift with his answer. He must have been thinking about it.

'No. My daughter.' He paused. 'Stillborn.'

She gasped. 'Don't say that,' she said. 'That's awful.' Shivered, him saying that, like it was an omen. His eyes had a sadness, as if he was in two minds, as if he was being torn asunder, his words playing their part, with no true meaning to them.

He stepped towards her, pulled her close, ruffled his fingers through her hair.

'Kathleen,' he said. 'She was a beautiful baby.'

She leaned into him, folding her arms around his waist, feeling the beat of his heart, the soft rhythm of his breath on her head. He loved *her*. She knew it. 'Will you come and find me?' she said. 'When the war's over?'

'I'm married, Joan, I told you.'

'But will you?' she said.

He pushed her arms away, stepping back. 'Sure.' He shrugged, fished in his inside pocket, pulled out his wallet, handed her a couple of bills.

'I don't understand,' Joan said. 'What do I do with this?'

'There's plenty places take dollars.'

'I don't know any,' she said. What could she do with foreign money? 'How am I going to manage a baby with this? That don't put a roof over my head.' The unfairness of it, the terror of it, the truth of it, was forming a ball in her throat. She tried to swallow. 'What am I going to do?'

'Listen,' Michael said. 'Things work out. They always do. But I got to go. I'm real sorry.'

She stood, watched him as he turned and walked back to the village hall. Things will work out. Yes, she thought. He's not leaving, not forever. He'll be back for me. He said so. *Sure.*

§

Joan's father walked her to the station, said Auntie Win was the soul of generosity, said it again, the soul of generosity to take her in like this. 'There's not many as'd do that, in your condition.'

Auntie Win lived in London, worked at Bon Marché in Brixton, pulled some strings and got Joan a job on the shop floor. Joan listened to the chimes of the store clock and the gasp of the pneumatic tubes as they sucked the money with a *shluck* to Auntie Win in finance, where she'd turn it over and stamp the bill and send back the change in a clanging brass cylinder. There was a steady, even rhythm to the sounds of shop work. Indoors, in the warm, in a smart black uniform. Didn't seem like real work to Joan.

Come June, Auntie Win took her holidays in Yarmouth. 'You'll be all right, won't you? On your own? You've got some time to go yet.'

Only she got the sack the day Auntie Win left. Dismissed on the spot, bringing the name of Bon Marché into disrepute, she being unmarried and pregnant. Joan put on her cardigan and threaded her way down the back staircase and out of the staff door. She had no way of getting hold of Auntie Win and had no money, apart from what she'd put aside to pay for the Mother and Baby Home when the time came.

She let herself into the flat. Just two rooms, really. Communal landing. Joan slept on the chair bed in the front room that doubled as the kitchen, wrapped up in her blankets and eiderdown. You couldn't swing a cat, Auntie Win said. The Germans had a new weapon now that put the fear of God into everybody because they came without warning. No sirens, no time to take shelter. Only the dull hum, like a treadle machine, the silence when the engine cut, every fibre in her body on fire in case one dropped without sound and blasted them out. Doodlebugs.

If she was honest, she was feeling a bit queasy. Joan lay down on the chair bed, shut her eyes, dozed. It was around six, she reckoned, when she woke. She listened for the sound of a drone and when it seemed all clear, she padded downstairs to the lavatory at the back, her stomach cramping. She must have eaten something bad, though she couldn't think what. She'd had nothing at dinner time and had barely managed a slice of bread and a cup of tea for breakfast. They shared the lavatory with the others in the building. Auntie Win cut up squares of newspaper and they used that to wipe themselves. Joan like to read the odd snippets of news or gossip, half-sentences that made no sense, but she sat there today fingering the paper. It must be diarrhoea, and she wished it would move itself. She'd feel a lot better if it did.

There was a hammering on the door.

'You've been in there long enough.' It was their neighbour. Auntie Win called her Maisie Piss-Pot on account of her boiling up the beetroots in an enamel chamber pot. Sold them in the market, no one the wiser. 'Give someone else a chance.'

Joan flushed the lavatory, pulled up her knickers, opened the bolt. 'Sorry.'

'About bloody time.' Maisie pushed past Joan, slammed the door shut.

She crept back into bed around nine o'clock, pulling the blackout curtains tight as Auntie Win had taught her. She felt no better, if she was honest, with this grumbling stomach and aches in her back. She lay tense and anxious, her mind racing in circles, listening for doodlebugs or an air-raid siren, not that she'd have the energy to run to the shelter, longing to sleep, to drift away and snore, soft as a cat's purr.

The pain was worse by morning, a dull, steady ache. She made herself a cup of tea, put the wireless on. *Good morning, this is the BBC Home Service. Allied forces have seized the city of Caen...* The day was going to be a scorcher, Joan could tell, beads of sweat on her upper lip and forehead. She sat on the kitchen chair, sipping her tea. It tasted funny. The milk was probably off. Perhaps she should try and visit the chemist, see if he couldn't give her something. Milk of magnesia, perhaps. Kaolin and morphine. In the distance she heard Maisie Piss-Pot shouting at her husband, and the street door slam, and the herd of cattle who lived above them clonking across the wooden floor in their solid Utility shoes. Tiptoe, Joan thought, can't you tiptoe?

Michael. She tried to picture him. He must have been part of the Normandy landings, perhaps was entering Caen this very moment. Was he safe, or lying wounded in some field hospital? Or worse. Not knowing. It ate her away. Michael had said he'd find her after the war, and she had to hold on for that, have the baby, take care of it until his divorce came through and they could marry. Auntie Win said she'd have to put the baby out to foster as there was no room for it here but Joan was sure, once she saw the little thing, she'd soften. Joan had been building up the layette, buying something each week from the pawn shop out of her wages, nappies and bottles and bodices, second- and third-hand, a bit threadbare, washed and folded in the bottom of her suitcase under her own clothes.

Joan lay back in the chair bed, trying to doze, wishing Auntie Win was here, because she didn't feel so well. Around eleven she got up to make a cup of hot Bovril. The pains had changed. No longer did she have slow, steady cramps. Now they came in waves. Perhaps she should go to the Mother and Baby Home in

Dunsfield Street. They'd have a nurse there who could give her something.

She lifted the keys from the hook, stepped outside into the summer heat. Walking made it worse, but at least there was some respite between the spasms. Auntie Win had explained to her a bit what she could expect, but Auntie Win had never had a baby so there hadn't been much detail. Can't be labour, Joan thought. I've got weeks to go. She paused, holding onto a post as she waited for another wave to crest her stomach and subside. Ahead was Brixton Hill. A tram trundled by, an advertisement for Typhoo tea on its side: IT GOES FURTHER. A car passed. A man was pushing his cycle up the incline and she saw him stop and wipe his forehead with the back of his hand. She'd get the 159. That took her all the way to Dunsfield Street, down the hill, past the town hall, past Bon Marché and into that no man's land between Brixton and Kennington Park. She grabbed a lamp post as another wave of pain surged, trapped her breath. She blew out, making her hair flutter.

A policeman was coming up behind her, stopped as he drew level. 'Are you all right, miss?' he said.

Joan shook her head. 'I don't feel very well,' she said, her hand over her stomach.

'Where are you going?' She saw him looking at her.

'Dunsfield Street,' she said. The pain had flattened, released her breath.

'The Mother and Baby Home?' His voice was calm. At least he wasn't judging her.

'Help me, please, to the tram.'

He put his arm around her, supporting her as she walked. She leaned into him, feeling his strength. She paused again as another spasm began to grip, a little tighter than the previous one. The policeman helped her across the road. She was light-headed, her breathing shallow. She shut her eyes as the policeman shifted his position, heard the screel of the tram as it stopped.

The policeman helped her on board, steered her towards a seat, went forward and said something to the driver. Then he turned to the passengers. 'Do we have a nurse or a midwife on board?' he said. 'We have an emergency. The tram won't be stopping in Brixton, so please leave now if you need to get off there.' Joan could sense the murmuring, the movement, as one or two people behind her stood up to get off, footsteps thudding on the wooden platform.

He took off his jacket, laid it over Joan. It was warm from his body, his kindness folded in the coarse serge of his uniform. The tram trundled down the hill, its journey smooth and silent. Joan shut her eyes. It would be all right. The policeman was here and she'd be at the home soon enough. Breathed in sharp, panting.

'Are you all right?' the policeman said. 'Only we don't have a nurse on board.'

She nodded, lips tight. A woman behind her screamed. Joan sensed the rush of people standing up, peering through the window.

'Doodlebug. Bloody doodlebug.' Someone was ringing the bell for the driver to stop.

'Keep calm,' she heard the policeman say.

There was a rush, a roar, as if the earth was opening. The light changed, a luminous white. The tram shuddered and stopped, filling with acrid smoke, thick with dust. She could hear screaming, felt her body jostled as people pushed past her. Her head was swimming, the tram turning and swaying, her ears numbed with the noise of the blast as it echoed and echoed, the aftershocks a low, steady rumble crawling through her body.

'Single file,' the policeman was shouting. He stood with his back to her, his arms outstretched, ushering the passengers out. They were covered in dust and Joan could hear them coughing. Her mouth was dry. She wiped her lips with the back of her hand, stared at the fine powder that coated her fingers, her body gripped tight from the inside. She couldn't walk even if she'd wanted to. Her eyes were stinging, full of grit. Another spasm tore at her guts, the pain expanding as if beating a path inside her. She was helpless, stared with glassy eyes at the ash-filled smoke around her, at the shadowy forms of the other passengers as they clambered off the bus. She felt herself being lifted, carried outside, laid on the pavement, saw the policeman's boots, the blue crease of his trousers covered in a grey film, heard the bells of ambulances, fire engines. She lay back, clutching her stomach as another wave of pain passed through her body. She cried out.

'It's all right, ducks.' A woman's voice. 'He's getting help.'

The policeman lifted her to her feet, half led, half carried her to a car. Her legs were limp, her feet tapping the ground like a string puppet. 'This gentleman will take you to Dunsfield Street,' he said, opening the door, lowering her into the seat. 'The rocket hit the rest centre on Acre Lane. The road's blocked, but he knows a way round.' He shut the door, was gone. Joan leaned back and shut her eyes.

KATHLEEN

Harvard University, Cambridge, Massachusetts: Spring 1967

Kathleen stood on the sidewalk. *Hell, no, we won't go*. Ten, twenty abreast, the protesters blocked the street. The campus police were out, eyes sharp, hands on their belts. Even though she'd been in America for nearly two years now, she still felt she'd been catapulted into modern life, standing there like a medieval nun bedazzled by a modern world. Her adviser for her doctorate was Charles Fryxal. She guessed he was in his forties, though his fine, blond hair still had its colour. To look at, you'd think nothing of him. Average height, average build. Shabby and bespectacled, he blended in with the other academics. But he was the best in the field. She'd been in awe of him at first, but he'd tried to make her feel at home. 'Oxford? Love that city,' he'd said. 'I was in Europe during the war, England. France. Paris. London. Piccadilly Circus. Had some fun. The Trocadero. Do you know it?'

'No.' Didn't like to admit she'd never even heard of it.

The war in Vietnam had barely impinged on her consciousness while she was an undergraduate. Oxford now seemed staid and tame, a quiet backwater in a sea of urgency. But here, so many people, so many encounters, the scream of the freeway, the roar of the subway, day and night merging so the natural rhythms of life, of eating, sleeping, working became a chimera and in its place flashes, glimpses. Indifference. That's how people cope, she thought. Don't give a damn. Anything other would lead to madness.

Except, she now realised, city people weren't indifferent, weren't blasé. They cared for strangers whose lives they could only imagine. It was a far cry from the fear and bigotry, the nosy busybodies that passed for concern back home in the village.

Susan was living proof of that.

They'd met on their first day in grad school, Kathleen holding her Harvard Medical School introductory pack, staring at the ground, at the wave of male shoes surging across the floor, the hoorayed roar of voices, the smell of aftershave and sweat, fraternity brothers, bonding, men only. She'd looked up. A young woman was heading her way, thin, bony, awkward, with the loping gate of a catwalk model and a mass of thick, auburn hair. Not beautiful, not pretty, but striking. She reminded Kathleen of a young, rangy wolf in an expensive coat.

'Hi,' the young woman said, ignoring the glances of the men as if they were her natural habitat. Her voice was low, gravelly. 'I'm Susan, and boy, am I glad to see another woman here.'

They'd been inseparable ever since.

Susan was from New York. Graduated *summa cum laude* with a 4.30 GPA from Brandeis. 'Which,' she'd explained when they first met, 'is equivalent to a first from Oxford.'

She was also, Kathleen discovered, a member of Phi Beta Kappa. Kathleen envied Susan's easy, elegant, New England insouciance, her comfortable liberal values segueing from anti-Vietnam protests to civil rights to women's liberation.

'So what's your story?' Susan had asked. Kathleen wasn't sure she had a story, not like Susan's, with a beginning and end. Hers was a zigzag, up the ladder one day, down the snake the next.

'My people were farmers, smallholders really,' she said. She didn't like to admit how poor they were, or how closed off from the world. The likes of her family didn't get an education, especially not for girls. That was for posh people with televisions and indoor bathrooms. 'I got a bursary to stay on at high school,' she said.

The bursary had paid for her board and lodging and Miss Loughton had squared it with the governors to make sure it was appropriate to accommodate a pupil in her home during term time. She must have put the fear of God into her parents, because Kathleen couldn't for the life of her see how they'd consented to this. She'd wanted nothing more than to live with Miss Loughton, in her house that smelled of wood and centuries, but even so, she'd have liked her parents to have put up a bit of a fight to keep her.

'I grew to love science,' she said.

Every Sunday in term time she'd borrowed Miss Loughton's bike and cycled home across the fens, the reeds burnished red and gold, fronds feathered and gentle. There was a magic in its beauty, and a beauty in its science. Standing by the pools among the bulrushes, watching minnows beneath the water, tiny slivers moving as one, shaping clumps into ribbons, bows into knots, circles into helices, bubbles popping on the surface. She knew now that rotting matter in the water let out gas and this was why bubbles formed. They gave off light at night, little sparks of methane, will o' the wisps, luring travellers to a watery grave. Kathleen liked both ideas, the way they ran together like trains on parallel tracks, the proper explanation science and the other magic. She thought magic was used a lot to explain a mystery, and Miss Loughton had agreed.

'Finding out how things worked, beneath the surface,' Joan said. 'The grandeur of it all.'

There was no magic in science. Just majesty. Zooming in under the school microscope in the biology lab with its stench of formaldehyde and gas, she could study the cells of plants and animals, organelles and cisternae, plasma and chloroplasts, their shapes and colours, structures and frames, could garner their pulsing energy, their infinite mutations. She was in awe of the natural world, felt small and humble beside it, pushing to know its secrets and its energy.

'Science gave me a kind of certainty,' she said.

For all the surprises and mutations, there were rules and laws, hypotheses and results, inner logic and infinite depth. Science was never flaky, never moody, could be measured and tested. It was a world away from people with their ruthlessness and passion, love and treachery.

Kathleen had seen a brutal side to Joan that day she'd abandoned her and left her on the road with no choice but to run away. It set up a barrier to love, so far and no more. Love had no place except in logic, its messy footprints leaving no tread upon the heart. Science had no emotions, no flaws. Science didn't desert and deceive. Science was constant, unblemished, a world of itself in itself, seamless, infinite, intimate. Clean. How could she explain that to Susan?

'My headmistress, Miss Loughton, encouraged me to go to university,' she said. 'I got into Oxford.' She made it sound a small, insignificant step, and she'd let herself be cowed by Oxford, made to feel a servant girl in the halls of the rich, had kept her head down and worked. Graduated with a first. 'And now I'm here.'

'Your parents must be real proud of you,' Susan said.

Don't you put on airs with me, my girl, with your posh talk and fancy words. That don't single a beet or pluck a chicken.

'My sister's proud of me,' Kathleen said. Joan sent her postcards, from around the world. Cape Town. Valparaiso. Sydney. 'She works on the liners.'

§

After the first semester, she and Susan moved out of the dorm into an apartment. It had been advertised as 'garden accommodation' but really it was a basement flat, catching the sun in the front at the start and in the back at the end of the day. Kathleen's RCC scholarship just about covered everything, but she didn't have much money to spare and was alone in the US, so Susan's family had taken her under their wing. Thanksgiving and Christmas, folding her into the comfortable yellow bedroom in their brick and clapboard home on Mercer Avenue in Hartsdale while Susan's father commuted to Manhattan and her mother went to coffee mornings, a world so far from her own it could have been a different planet.

Thanks to Susan, Kathleen had started reading up about America's history, the Civil War, the war against the British, the Declaration of Independence. The words had blown her away, as much by their meaning as by the idea that they needed to be said at all, that before the founding fathers wrote them down, it was not self-evident that all men are created equal. She'd never paid much attention to history at school, but now she was beginning to see how it grew like a rhizome beneath the surface, pushing up shoots and putting down roots. Nothing could be understood without it.

Susan was a leading light in the Harvard branch of the Students for Democratic Society, had given Kathleen a copy of the Port Huron statement. 'Read it,' she'd said. 'But be warned. Tom Hayden's a jock. There's nothing about *women* here.' And introduced her to Emory Kerridge. 'Super clever,' Susan said, stage-whispering in Kathleen's ear. 'He's on the math PhD programme. He won the Putnam competition as an undergraduate.'

Emory looked like an athlete, with the same rangy physique as Susan. His skin was flushed, his mousy hair shoulder-length, his moustache tinged with ginger. He wore a black beret and sported a badge with a clenched fist. There was an intensity about him, an excitement she couldn't help but feel. He had an old East Coast charm like Susan, a gracious arrogance, an entitlement, for all his SDS membership and undisputed revolutionary fervour. She had no doubt he'd been brought up in a large, white clapboard house in Connecticut or Maine.

'You're very beautiful,' he said. 'You remind me of Juliette Gréco, only with blonde hair. Can you sing?'

'I've never tried,' she said. 'But my sister's a singer. Lillie Pettall.'

'Never heard of her.' His voice had a tinge of conceit.

JOAN

London: March 2005

A brand-new Nokia sat beside her on the kitchen table, dark blue and silver. Pay as you go, not as expensive as she'd thought it would be. She'd filed away the instructions in her box of documents along with her passport, her organ donor card, her will, letters and other important papers. Not that Joan had much to leave, but she'd named Kathleen as the beneficiary. She was damned if anyone else in the family was going to benefit from her death, nor the government if she died intestate. She'd bought the form in WHSmith's, had it witnessed by a couple of the librarians. She saw no reason to change it now, even though it was years since she'd drawn it up.

She poured herself another cup of tea and added a second slice of bread to the toaster. She'd been ambushed. And Kathleen was right, she should have told her years ago that she was not her sister. She would have had control of the situation, led the conversation, phrased it carefully, cleverly. She was relieved that this was out in the open now, that there'd be no more barriers between her and Kathleen, but it would be difficult building a new relationship, Joan could see that. She'd never considered Kathleen as anything other than her daughter, but she understood the adjustment Kathleen would need to make, the trust she'd need to foster, the love she'd have to realign.

Joan had Kathleen's mobile number, but Kathleen preferred to text. It was quicker than a phone call, Joan could see, but it was hurtful nevertheless. There were times when she wanted to hear Kathleen's voice and not her answerphone message, *I can't come to the phone right now, leave your name and number and I'll ring you back.* There'd always be a text. *Sorry. Can't talk now.* But she never rang. Texting wasn't the same, but it was better than nothing. Joan had been clumsy with the keyboard at first, but once she got the knack of it – she watched young people on the bus using their thumbs – she marvelled at its immediacy, its speed. Harry had something called a BlackBerry which accessed his email. If she ever made enough money, she'd swap it for her Nokia like a shot. Not that she ever sent or received emails, but she liked the idea.

She didn't like to pester Kathleen about her father, but she wished she'd tell her something. Had she found him? How was she looking for him? The silence worried her. She was sure Kathleen would never discover his whereabouts, but there was a nag: what if she did find him? Some things were best swept aside, hidden from view. That's all a lie was, after all.

She met Harry at least twice a week now. Tuesdays they'd go out for a cake and a coffee, Thursdays to the cinema, or he'd treat her to dinner in a restaurant. He rang her almost every day. They never went to each other's houses, an unspoken pact. It gave their meetings a frisson, as if their assignations were a forbidden, secret excitement, an unexplored future. Sometimes he rang at the weekend. 'It's a nice day. Fancy coming out?' A boat to Greenwich, or upriver, to Hampton Court. Or they'd walk sections of the Thames Path, or take the tube to Green Park and saunter. 'Kennington Park is closer,' he said. 'We should go there sometime.'

'No,' she said. 'Bad memories. The war.' She didn't say more, though she felt his eyes on her, *you can tell me, you can trust me.*

She missed him when he wasn't there, panicked if he didn't ring. She could feel herself drawn to him, to his body, brushing into him as they sauntered, feeling the litheness of his frame, the sinews of his moving. She talked to him in her head, imagining him in the room with her, the two of them, young and agile. Sometimes in her mind he took her hand, and drew her close and kissed her, leading her into his bedroom, laying her on his bed. Did he feel the same? He never let on. She'd played the femme fatale too often in her past, but now that it mattered, she had no courage. Well, she thought, maybe companionship was the best she could hope for at their age. And that wasn't such a bad thing. She'd never had it before. Those other men, none had mattered, and nor had it mattered if they'd ever found out the truth. But Harry was different. She couldn't bear to lose him.

'As a matter of fact,' he said on one of their jaunts in late January, 'my nephew runs the Roxie II in Brixton. Why not do a comeback?'

'Get away, Harry.' She'd laughed. But it was there, in her mind, stuck like a wedge in a door. He was tempting her, luring her.

'Well?' He mentioned it again, two weeks later. 'He's had a cancellation for March. Next year. 2006.'

When Harry had talked about a comeback, she'd thought it would be years away, if ever, not months. 'That's too soon. I wouldn't be ready.' She'd need a band, rehearsal time, a set list, new numbers. She'd need nerve. She wasn't sure she had that anymore. A comeback was a recipe for grief.

'Any longer, you'll have cold feet.'

It was one thing to enter a competition, though that was bad enough, but to perform once again in front of a proper audience, who'd paid real money to see her, standing on a stage, under the spotlight so every stumble would be seen, every waver heard?

'What if I flop?'

'You're a pro. In an ideal world you'd build up a head of steam before your big comeback, but this is a chance to test the water.

Come on, Joan. Chances like this don't happen often. It's a one-off, but who knows where it could lead? Besides,' he added, 'I'd like to film it.'

Joan wondered if that was the real reason. Nothing to do with a comeback. Just a scene for his documentary. 'I haven't said I'll do the film,' she said.

Harry smiled. 'I know. I'm a patient man.' He laughed. 'And an optimistic one. And even if you decide not to do it...well, it would be nice to have the comeback recorded for posterity, don't you think?'

Lillie Pettall, the youthful hopeful, Joan Spalding, the fading has-been.

'You could be big again, Joan,' Harry went on. 'If you want. You could use the film plus the Roxie II gig as your launch pad. Youngsters have their promo videos, but you have a real hinterland. And if people think you still perform, in live shows, well...' He broke off, raised his shoulders, smiled. 'It's a win–win.'

'The Roxie II,' she said. 'Who would come?'

'Leave that to me.'

§

Neal Shepherd was a wiry man in his fifties. Well-used face, long, grey dreadlocks tied in a ponytail. A musician once, he'd told her when they first met. 'But I didn't make it in the business, so did the next best thing,' he said. 'Opened this place.' He called it a *venue*. He wore jeans, a faded black T-shirt and a leather jerkin, a KEEP MUSIC LIVE sticker stuck to its front. His office was small, lined with filing cabinets and posters for past gigs in Roxie II. There was a single window that looked out on an alleyway and cast a dingy light into the room. An old black greyhound with a grey muzzle was curled up on a sagging armchair, the only chair in the office apart from Neal's. 'Tea?' Neal said. 'Or something stronger? Bobbo.' He whistled at the dog. 'Down. Let the lady sit there.'

Bobbo crawled off the seat, walked with stiff legs towards a blanket in the corner, padded round in circles before he lay down with a resentful grunt.

'Rescue dog,' Neal said. 'Poor thing. He was really nervy when I got him, but he's calmer now. Aren't you, boy?'

Neal carried two mugs across to his desk, lifted the cushion from the spare chair, gave it a bang to release the dog hairs and beckoned for Joan to sit. At least, Joan thought, greyhound hairs are short.

She looked at his face, at the grooves either side of his mouth, the scars of age and living. But for all his fading Rasta look, Joan had no doubt he was a ruthless businessman.

'I've been listening to your old vinyls. You're world-class, Joan,' he said. 'I'd like to offer you this gig.'

The blood rushed to Joan's brain so it felt hot and tight.

'Mostly, I spot the youngsters,' he went on. 'Bring them on. Reggae, ragga, rap. Rock, hip-hop, house. Early garage, before it became grime. Funky. You name it, I put it on. Many a young hopeful made his or her name here.'

'I'm hardly a youngster,' Joan said. 'As you can see.'

Neal smiled and his face transformed, its granite lines and grooves giving way to soft moorland. 'There's a retro scene out there, Joan,' he said. 'Think Buena Vista Social Club. Think Little Jimmy Scott. Carlos Santana. I plan to make you a part of it.'

Joan sat, lost for words. Bobbo stirred from his bed in the corner, pushed himself up and lumbered over to her, resting his head on her knee.

'He only does that for special people,' Neal said. 'He likes you. So do I, Joan. What do you say?'

Joan looked into the dog's amber eyes, Neal's offer like a mountain pass. The other side would be a different world, but she wasn't sure she had the courage to attempt it. 'Do you think I could?' she said. 'Honestly?'

'I'm a businessman,' Neal said. 'My bottom line is money. I wouldn't be offering you a gig if I didn't think I could spin a profit. Bobbo.' He clicked his fingers and the dog walked over to his side. 'And yes, honestly, I think you could do it. We'd give you a lead time, work up new numbers, perhaps vary your style, jazz, R & B, rock. Ballads.' He leaned back, laughing, tilting his chair. 'My offer is genuine. I've done some homework, talked to a few people. I wouldn't do it if I didn't think I could make money.'

Joan's breath was coming in shallow puffs, like it did before a performance, those collywobbles, as she called them, the familiar fear, a fresh terror every time.

'Think about it,' Neal said. 'Do you have an agent?'

'I'll do it,' Joan said, the words spilling before she'd had time to think. She missed it, singing, an audience, the live show, the adrenaline rush like nothing else in the world. She could lose her past then, in the present. 'And no, I don't have an agent. Not anymore. I used to be with MacMannon's Talent and Entertainment Agency. Do you know them?'

'MacMannon's? Oh yes. They're part of World Talent now.'

'World Talent?'

'A lot's changed in this industry since you were last in it,' Neal said. 'Very few small agencies now. They've all been swallowed up.'

'Who would you recommend?'

'It's up to you,' he said. 'But I do a lot of business with Music Management Global. They're a big agency, branches in London, the US, Sweden. I could arrange an intro. Though,' he added, 'feel free to use whoever you like.'

Her stomach clenched, her hands felt damp. Nerves, she knew, nerves are *good*.

'Perhaps you can give some thought to the set list. Songs you've always wanted to sing.'

Joan touched her mouth, felt the beads of sweat above her lip, the damp in her armpits. *'Joan's Song'*. A crescendo in her memory, it came from nowhere. 'Yes,' she said. 'As a matter of fact there is.'

The shadow of her smile.

'Do I know it?'

The dapple of her laugh.

'No. But you will.' She could still remember the words, the tune Eddie had composed. 'It was written for me, years ago. But I've only ever sung it once.'

The blowing of the chaff.

Neal twisted his lips, head to one side. Joan opened her mouth, sang, 'She rises like a phoenix cresting from the ashes. And calls my name.'

'I like it,' Neal said. 'Is it a love song?' He leaned back, picked up a pen and tapped it on the desk. 'Any other?'

She thought for a second, nodded. 'I'd like to sing "Don't You Push Me Down",' she said. 'It's a Woody Guthrie song. Do you know it?'

'You mean the Melissa Balls hit? In the fifties?'

'Yes, but I'd do my own arrangement. Not that saccharine baby-doll version she did. Much grittier.'

'That'd be a great finale,' Neal said. 'They'll remember that. What a one to go out on, eh?'

Don't you push me down, Joan thought. Not now. Not ever.

KATHLEEN

Los Angeles: December 2005

Joan rang her as she was getting ready to leave for work. She was sitting in her underwear, pulling on her tights, the receiver wedged under her chin. 'This must be costing you a fortune,' Kathleen said. 'Ringing me across the world.'

'It's a quick call,' Joan said. 'Just to hear your voice. Wish you a happy Christmas and all that. What are you doing?'

'I'm going to Susan's for lunch,' Kathleen said. 'She's off to Seoul for three months.'

'That's nice,' Joan said. 'Don't want you being on your own over there.' As if Joan cared that much.

'And you?' Kathleen said.

'Harry's going to take me out,' Joan said. 'To a restaurant.'

'That's good,' Kathleen said. 'So you won't be alone either.'

She felt a sudden jolt of jealousy. Joan with her new man. This could have been her. What on earth had possessed her to push David away? His wife was dying. Probably dead by now. She could have bided her time, supported him when he needed it. He'd turned to her, after all, and when the going got tough, she'd finished it. She must have been mad. Would he take her back if she got in touch? He'd have every right not to. He could have found someone else. Could have remarried already.

Joan paused and Kathleen could imagine her at the other end, twisting the telephone cord around her fingers. She stepped into her dress, bracing herself for the real reason behind her call, twisting her arms behind her, reaching for the zip.

'I've been wondering…'

The phone sprung from beneath her chin, tumbled to the floor.

'Kathleen?'

'Sorry,' she said. 'I dropped the phone.'

'I was wondering,' Joan went on. 'Have you any news? You know, about your father.'

'Don't keep asking,' Kathleen said. Her mother's lie still stung, anger coming in surges, waxing and waning, a bewildering spectrum of grief and hurt. It was as if she had a black hole at the heart of her, at the *start* of her. A void, like the universe.

'Sorry. Only—'

'Only nothing,' Kathleen said. 'You'll be the first to know if I find him. I have to go. Have a lovely day.' She placed the receiver back in its cradle before Joan could ply her with another excuse. She wanted to scream and yell, found herself clenching and unclenching her fists, to stop herself dissolving into a jabbering shadow, skin floating like a Hallowe'en ghoul.

JOAN

The front of the house lay in shattered bricks, in mortar scree, in splinters on the pockmarked ground. Joan stared at the blasted walls and gaping rooms, wallpaper hanging like bandages, Kathleen in her arms swaddled in a moth-eaten shawl. Rubble, homes. *Her* home. She clutched Kathleen tight, nerves numbed, muscles frozen, began to shake, sat down hard on the broken kerb opposite. Where was Auntie Win? Maisie Piss-pot? The family who lived above them? She stared at the notices. DANGER. DO NOT ENTER. Dust got into Joan's eyes, made them water. The roof had been blasted away, broken planks from the floor above jagged through their ceiling, sharp as teeth. She could see the mirror above their mantelpiece, skewed and cracked, still on the wall, glass glinting in the sunlight. The door was gone. The door to her room. Where was it? Anyone could get in now, murder them as they slept. She stared at the chaos, the confusion, not understanding. The old, brown suitcase with Kathleen's baby clothes had been blown across the room, its lid torn off. Something small and white had snagged on a jagged brick. A baby's vest. Kathleen's vest.

The enormity of it all, the horror, slammed into her. She held Kathleen tight, rocking on her haunches backwards and forwards, keening like the cow when her calf was taken, the loud, anguished bellow of loss. Where was Auntie Win? What would happen to her? And Kathleen?

'Miss?' She turned. It was an ARP warden. He was holding a clipboard, tipped back his helmet with its fading W, scratched his forehead.

'Where is everyone?' she said. She pointed to her room. 'That's my home. The door. Where's the door? Where's my room?'

She saw him brace himself. 'Came down the same time as the flying bomb in Acre Lane,' he said. 'I'm sorry.'

The blood drained from Joan's head and she felt dizzy. That could have been her. Half an hour later, she'd have been inside, pulled from the rubble, laid out on the stretcher. Dead. 'I live here,' she said. She heard a knocking sound inside her mouth. Her teeth. Her teeth were chattering. She was cold. So cold.

'Let's get you to the centre,' the warden said. 'You can't stay here.'

'Auntie Win. Where's Auntie Win?'

'Was she inside?'

'I don't know,' Kathleen said. 'She was away. On her holidays.'

He ran his finger down a list on his clipboard. 'She's safe,' he said. 'What's your name, miss?

'Joan Spalding.'

'Have you been away?' The warden sounded cross. 'Only you should have let us know. Wasting our time searching in the rubble for you.'

'I was in hospital,' Joan said. 'Having my baby.' Joan felt tears prick her eyes. 'There wasn't time,' she said. 'It came on all of a sudden. I was alone.'

'Sorry,' the warden said, shifting his gaze to the pavement. 'I didn't know.'

She had nowhere to take the baby, and Kathleen asleep in her arms, a dead weight. 'Where's Auntie Win?' She pointed at the remains of the house. 'What am I going to do?'

'I'm taking you to the rest centre,' the warden said. 'The WVS will give you what you need for the baby and help find your relatives. Can you walk?'

Joan nodded, tried to stand up, but her feet had no force, no balance, as if the tendons had been ripped away. The warden took hold of a wheelbarrow, helped Joan inside, legs splayed over the rim, wheeled her to the rest centre, Kathleen cradled in her arms.

§

Auntie Win got their clothing coupons and emergency war damage payment and they were rehoused in temporary accommodation near Loughborough Junction, two rooms, one for Joan and the baby, one for Auntie Win, and a shared kitchen where Joan boiled up the bottles and rubbed the teats with salt, and washed the dirty nappies and the baby's sheets and vests and bathed Kathleen in the sink. They'd been given some furniture, second-hand bits and pieces, clothes for themselves and Kathleen. Caring for a baby took her mind off things, didn't leave her time to think about what could have been.

'London's no place for a baby, not right now,' Auntie Win said one evening after tea, four weeks later. 'She'll be safer in the countryside. Besides,' she added, 'I can't afford to keep you and the baby, Joan. Not on my wages.'

'I'll find a job,' Joan said.

'And who'll look after Kathleen while your work? There's no place in a government nursery for—' She nodded at the baby, couldn't say the word. 'Them that's born on the wrong side.'

Auntie Win shut her eyes, and Joan heard her take a deep breath. She knew what Auntie Win was about to say. *Best you let her go into foster care.*

'When I was in Yarmouth,' Auntie Win went on, 'I took an excursion to Aitham.' She looked into the distance, fiddled with the cuffs of her blouse. 'I spoke to your mother.' She took another deep breath. 'And she says she'd look after Kathleen. What do you say?'

'My mother?' Joan said. 'My mother offered to look after Kathleen? She threw me out.'

'She's not that bad a sort, your mother, Joan.' She shifted in her seat. 'Bit old-fashioned, especially about women. Said she couldn't let a grandchild of hers go to strangers. Though there are conditions.'

'Oh?'

'That you pay for her keep, and that you never tell Kathleen you're her mother. No one likes an illegitimate child.' Auntie Win leaned back in her chair. 'You'll say you're sisters. I happen to think your mother's right.'

Kathleen was asleep in the drawer in their bedroom, and Joan could no longer imagine being without her than she could losing her right arm. It was as if Kathleen had always been curled within her, waiting to appear, fully formed, her head nestled into that warm crook between her shoulder and her neck.

'I'll take her to Aitham,' Auntie Win went on. 'You'll know where she is.'

'But I can't be her mother,' Joan said.

'There's different ways of mothering,' Auntie Win said.

They had a clock that chimed every quarter hour. Joan heard its angry *tick-tock*, its springs winding up, its harsh *ding ding* as it struck the half hour.

'You have no choice,' Auntie Win said. 'You can't be her mother anyway, you being unmarried. It's either that or adoption.'

Joan looked down at her lap, her hands held together, fingers intertwined, knuckles jutting like bleached pebbles.

But then.

Kathleen up there, hidden like Moses in the rushes. No one would find her. Not Queenie, not nobody. That would be a load off her mind. She shut her eyes, seeing again the white light of the blast, hearing the roar of the gas as it blew, tasting the dry grit of the air, her body thrown and rocked and Queenie, always Queenie. *They'll put you inside for life.*

Auntie Win leaned over, placed her hand over Joan's. 'Try not to remember,' she said. 'Try to put it behind you. You're shaking like a jelly.'

Joan smiled, nodded. She could send Kathleen little things, treat her to this and that. She couldn't tell her she was her mother, not ever. But Joan would know, would know Kathleen was safe and all, could watch her grow up, a fine young woman. She'd always have her in her life, and be a part of hers. And if a constable came asking questions, her mother would have to say no, she's mine, because that was the lie her mother had agreed to. Kathleen would be safe. And so would she. Might be for the best, all things considered. 'All right,' she said. 'All right.'

'Good,' Auntie Win said. 'I'll book a ticket for Saturday.'

'That's tomorrow.' Joan looked up sharp, cricked her neck, rubbed it hard with her hand. 'That's too soon.'

'Kinder that way.'

Joan rushed into her room, lay on the bed looking at Kathleen asleep in the drawer on the floor, her breath in light, slight flurries, the puffiness of her birth giving way to the fine features of her face. Her flawless baby daughter.

Dusk turned to night and Joan could not keep her eyes off Kathleen snuffling in her crib, mewling for a feed. Joan made up her bottles, gave her one when she woke, cradling the baby close in her arms, watching her mouth clamped around the teat, her jaw muscles working, eyes shut. Her perfect, perfect baby. She leaned forward, kissed her on the forehead. *I love you, Kathleen. I'll always love you and look out for you.* Cushioned within Joan's arms, cooing like a wood pigeon, a pink, plump wood pigeon.

The shadow of her smile, the dapple of her laugh.

Your daddy's song, little Kathleen.

The biting of the earth, the blowing of the chaff.
He'll come back. I know it. We'll be together, a family.
She rises like a phoenix from the ashes. And calls my name.

She changed Kathleen's nappy, *for the last time*, she kept saying, *for the last time*. She wouldn't be there when Kathleen began to crawl, wouldn't hear her first words. Kathleen whimpered in her sleep and Joan took her into her bed, feeling the *tick tick* of her heart, the warmth from her body. She lifted Kathleen's hand and held it in her own, rubbing her thumb against the tiny fingers, so frail and alone, the skin silky and smooth. Perhaps she could visit every weekend, if her mother would let her, if she relented. Auntie Win was right. London was no place for a baby, not with the doodlebugs and all. Kathleen could have been killed the day she was born. Joan closed her arms around her, tight to her chest, one flesh.

The moon was a crescent, the stars glitter balls in the sky. Joan lay awake, Kathleen sleeping in her arms, her newborn scent filling the space around her. Joan would have it with her always, that scent of her baby, of blood and birth.

The dark turned to grey and with it a red dawn, livid clouds scudding across the sky, marks of a storm while Kathleen slept, so still and quiet Joan had to check she was alive, fingers light on her temples, floating across her fluffy, fair hair.

She jumped as Auntie Win knocked on her door. 'It's time, Joan,' she said, quietly lifting the baby out of Joan's arms.

Joan pulled the pillow on top of her, bit into it, her heart gripped by forceps, plucked from her, leaving empty bones in a parched membrane. She was no more than a hollow shell, form without soul. She waited until she heard the front door shut, Auntie Win's steps on the pavement fading as she turned the corner before she opened her mouth and filled her lungs and screamed, an animal howl that came from the hauntings of death and loss and betrayal, from the gut, weeping for the baby she had lost, the cuckoo she'd sent away to her mother.

KATHLEEN

Cambridge, Massachusetts: Spring – Autumn 1967

Emory's apartment on Massachusetts Avenue was small. Sheaves of newspapers were stacked against the walls, bulging ring binders piled untidily on shelves, leaflets scattered on the table. The main room was lit by a neon light and the walls were covered in posters advertising the anti-war march on Washington in April, or the Selma to Montgomery march two years ago. There were pictures of Martin Luther King, of Nelson Mandela, Che Guevara, Ho Chi Minh, Mao Tse-Tung.

'Is this your office?' she said.

'Office, home, sleeping quarters.' He smiled and she saw another room leading off the hall, which she assumed must be the bedroom. She wasn't sure where they were supposed to sit, as there wasn't even a sofa in the sitting room and no sign of any food, much less space on the table to eat it. He walked towards her with a slow, languorous walk of privilege and pulled her close. She returned his kiss with a sudden and powerful ache of desire, longing for his body there and then as they fumbled their way across the floor and into his bedroom, flopping on the unmade bed as their fingers danced and wove from one to the other, their limbs entwined, sweat and juices one and the same, caught in the messy anarchy of love.

He walked her home on Sunday afternoon, the first time they'd stepped out of the apartment all weekend. 'Stepped out of bed, actually,' she said. 'Except to eat and go to the bathroom.'

'Uh oh,' Susan said. 'Are you fixed up OK?'

Kathleen shook her head. 'I never thought I'd fall in love,' she said. 'I didn't think I was the type.'

'Aha,' Susan said. 'Evolutionary genes. You can't snuff them out. The species must go on.' She laughed. 'Listen, I know someone in New York you can go to. She might even be able to give you the pill. You make sure he uses something in the meantime. Any old man can buy condoms over the counter, no questions asked, but if you, unmarried, ask for them you're breaking the law. Fucking. Double. Standard.' She thrust an angry fist into the air.

Most weekends Kathleen went to Emory's apartment, cooking simple meals in the kitchen, windows open to let out the steam. She usually spent the first hour tidying. The messiness of the place upset her. She left his table and desk untouched, but, she'd reason, there was no harm in doing the washing-up, cleaning the bathroom or making the bed, since she'd be lying in it soon enough. More often than not there'd be a meeting in the afternoon and in the evening. She couldn't pretend she understood everything the men were saying. They used words she couldn't understand, *dialectical materialism*, *commodity fetishism*, *revisionism*, *hegemony*, spoke a language she was no part of and had no way of joining in with. Perhaps they mistook that for having nothing to say. They reminded her sometimes of peacocks strutting their learning, vying for dominance, all posture, no substance.

She and the other women would help brew the coffee or stuff the envelopes, make posters or type out stencils for the Gestetner, running off copies of articles on the student syndicalist movement or a worker–student alliance, on feminism and capitalism, Joan Baez playing on the gramophone, a faint whiff of marijuana in the air.

'Why do we women do the shit work?' she said, pointing to stacks of papers she was collating, walking round and round, bending over, picking up a sheet at a time, stapled at the top, folded in two, wedged into the envelope. Her back ached and her fingers were sore.

'Is that what you call it?' Emory said, heaving his long frame off the bed, ambling towards her, pointing to the papers on the table. 'What you do is so important.' He held out a hand, enticing her forward. 'You help by doing what you call the shit work, and that releases us men to think strategically so we can fight for everyone. Women too. It's all of our struggle, equality. From each according to his ability and all that.'

He always had an answer, made her feel a child interrupting grown-up talk. Even her adviser, despite his friendliness, treated her as if her views didn't count, as if her research was tinged with mediocrity because she was a woman.

Emory took a deep breath, shook his head, a slow, deliberate action, playing with her hair, his fingers stroking her cheek so she felt the charge of desire. 'We have to smash the system, to liberate everyone. Black, white, men, women.' His voice turned edgy, angry. 'So don't give me any women's liberation crap. It's a distraction. Division diverts the struggle, dilutes it. Do you see Vietnamese women complaining?' He smiled, pulled her close again. 'Capitalism has socialised women, but come the revolution we'll all be free. Hell, capitalism oppresses us as much as you.'

Perhaps the revolution was more important. The war. She walked over to the Gestetner, turned the crank, watched as the stencils came to life, spewing out more paper that she'd collate and secure and stuff into envelopes. She and the others would distribute the leaflets round the campus, shoving them under the doors of the freshmen and sophomore rooms, in the food halls and grad schools, scattered around communal areas.

If you're for the war in Vietnam, why aren't you fighting it, and if you're against the war in Vietnam, why aren't you in the streets fighting it with us?

Burn your draft cards! Resist the university's cooperation with the military industrial complex.

Close the ROTC programs. NOW!

§

It was early June, the middle of a heatwave. The apartment on Massachusetts Avenue steamed even though the windows were wide open. They'd given up cooking, lived on cold food, salads.

'I'm leaving in a couple of days,' Emory said.

Kathleen was chopping onions. She looked up, her eyes stinging and watering. He hadn't mentioned this before. A knot tightened in her stomach, as if this was an omen, a portent. She'd been so sure of him.

'Why?' she said. 'Where are you going?'

'California. To work with the farm-labour movement.' He sauntered over to the sink, leaned against it. 'The National Farm Workers' Association has accepted me on their training programme, so I can be of real help, you know?' He leaned over and opened the door of the fridge, fished out some ice cubes, ran them over his forehead. 'I mean,' he went on, his face earnest, intense, 'we need to teach the farmworkers to organise democratically, to become politically self-sufficient, engage in political education.'

He thrust a fist into the air, but somehow the words had an abstract quality to them. She wondered if he'd ever had to work on the land, knew what the earth was all about, had ever had to struggle for a living. The farmworkers of her acquaintance would eat Emory for breakfast, but perhaps it was different in California. She tried not to smile.

'Mostly they're Mexicans,' he went on. 'Not organised. We can't just teach their kids or help with paperwork. That encourages dependency. We can't tell, we must *do*.'

Come the revolution, she thought, her family would be kulaks. What would Emory think of them?

'How long are you away?'

'Till school starts again,' he said. 'Who knows? Perhaps I'll drop out.'

She'd had to fight so hard to be here, she couldn't understand how he could be so casual, so blasé, about his education.

JOAN

London: February 2006

There was a practice space at Roxie II and Joan had drawn up a set list of twenty-five songs, more than she needed for her forty-five minutes, but she wanted a few in reserve. Some were her old numbers, some freshly minted. She studied those new ones, lyrics and interpretation, modulation and phrasing, pitch. No time was wasted.

One was special. 'Joan's Song'. Sing it like a psalm, a prayer to love and longing. To loss.

She could see the yellow, ruled paper Michael had written the words on, the slick of the flame as the paper caught, his words dissolving into ash. She was one step away from tears, could feel them welling in her nose. The space was hot, stuffy. She pulled off her sweatshirt, stood in her new tracksuit bottoms and Lycra top, fanned her face with her hand. She hadn't sung the song for sixty years, but now it was demanding to be done, as if telling Kathleen about Michael had unlocked an urgency.

Neal booked the session band for rehearsals a few weeks before the show. They were led by a man called Ted. 'An old pro,' Neal said. 'From my recording days.'

She sung him the words, to Eddie's tune.

'I think we can do better,' he said. 'Let's try a different arrangement. Leave it with me.'

Composing the legend she'd use to introduce it, *The bookends of my life*, she'd say, *from my first love, to my last*. No. That wouldn't do. She'd never told Harry how she felt about him, and he might think she was referring to someone else. More to the point, Harry knew about the song, but she hadn't told him about Kathleen. With Kathleen in America now, there'd seemed little point. And if she told him about her, she'd have to come clean about everything. She wasn't ready for that.

When I was a young girl in the fens, she'd say, *I went to the village hop and a young American airman, the singer, wrote me this song*. No. That would open up questions. *I went to the village hop*. She wrote again. *There was a singer in the band, a young American airman. His name was Michael O'Doyle, and he wrote this song a few months before he died on the beaches of Normandy*. That would lay him to rest, but it would kill the mood. *When I was young I went to a hop in the village hall and there was this singer*. She'd go for humour. *I guess you might say I was starstruck, a groupie before they'd been invented*. She'd wait for the laughter. *Always ahead of the curve*. Laughter. It was all about timing, she knew that. *The singer invited me to sing a song. This song*. She'd pause. *The rest, ladies and gentlemen, is history*. She'd dedicate it to Harry. Perhaps he'd understand how she felt about him.

She pulled on her tracksuit top again. Mutton dressed as lamb, she'd thought as she bought them, paid on her credit card. She'd never dared use the card before, had it for emergencies only, but she figured this was an emergency, a new wardrobe for a comeback, a once-in-a-lifetime opportunity, rehearsal clothes, loose-fitting, comfortable. Evening dresses, diamanté shoes from Bloch's. She wouldn't show poor, and with a share of the takings, she'd pay off the debt immediately.

§

'Full house,' Neal said as he stepped onto the dais. She looked past him, to the body of the club, the brass tops of the tables tawdry in the filtered light, the black walls and ceiling heartless as a pimp. By night an alchemy transformed it into a rich, expectant womb of mystery and music. Nightclubs were her natural habitat. Seedy and glamorous, dangerous and mundane. Her fingers began to tingle, and she started to exercise her jaw, open wide, left, right.

They'd worked out the running order, mixing the tempos between numbers, varying the keys, taking note of the timings, allowing for Neal to DJ, for Joan to introduce, the whole shebang wrapped up in forty-five minutes which, Joan knew, was the max before the audience got restive. She'd start with 'Sweet-hearted Bill', place 'Joan's Song' in the middle, end on her version of the Woody Guthrie song.

There was applause before Neal raised his hand and the clapping subsided. 'Ladies and gentlemen,' he began, 'welcome to Roxie II, and a very special evening it is…'

Zoned out. That's what the young would say. Joan shut her eyes, *zoned out* as Neal introduced her, her mind soaring while her nerves began to fret and her stomach to curdle, mouth dry, throat tight. It would be all right. Deep breath. From the diaphragm.

'…Lillie Pettall.' There were cheers from the audience, and Joan could hear one or two slapping the tables and drumming their feet. The lights were on her. Somewhere out there Harry was filming. She heard Ted strike up the first bars.

It felt different on the stage in a club, surrounded by people, like the old times, and though her nerves were wound tight, when the lights went down and her signature tune struck up, she stepped out from the right and the tremors in her legs spread into her guts and arms and head and that old, familiar vertigo took charge, until she lifted the microphone and held it like a crutch, counting down the beats, breathing deep, waiting for her cue. Hands clammy, sweat on her forehead, trickling into her eyes. She rubbed them with the back of her hand, ran one palm down her dress, then the other, wiping away the damp. She could feel the band watching her, could hear the anticipation in the audience, the weighty, expectant silence. She turned to Ted, smiled, nodded.

Deep breath. She let flow the succulent, seductive rivers of song, her breath shimmering on the notes, unsurpassed.

'This number.' She paused. Keep it simple. Add mystery, not history. 'This was the first song I sang, many years ago. I dedicate it to Harry.' She smiled at him, a silhouette in the dark, behind the camera.

The ecstasy of song, the way her soul became her voice, as if a spirit had entered her body and she spoke in tongues. *Can you hear me, Michael?* Because now he was a breath away, behind the door, beyond the ocean. Singing. Soaring. Herself once again, the numbers segueing seamlessly, theme, rhythm, mood. Her voice had changed over the years, had mellowed into a contralto, better suited to the jazz and swing of her repertoire.

Listening as she sang, the timbres of bronze and copper reverberating in her head, the modulations of tone, the harmonies with the band. She shut her eyes, lifted her head, the frequencies of the music vibrating through her body, soaring into a world of tone and touch, of texture and tempo. She stopped singing, the band silent, and all she could hear was the percussion of applause, the stamping of feet and the clapping of hands.

KATHLEEN

Los Angeles: March 2006

She'd been at the Grant Institute now for almost seven months, had watched the shimmering heat of summer give way to the burnished balm of autumn, followed by the sober, steady warmth of a California winter. The apartment she was renting was close to the main UCLA campus. It was set in gardens with a swimming pool and garage parking. There were swankier neighbourhoods, smarter buildings, but she hadn't felt settled enough to think into the future. David. She'd hoped the Grant Institute would be a distraction, and it had been, but now she was settled, he was walking back into her thoughts. Well, he could walk back out. He hadn't been in touch for well over a year so had no right to intrude now. Except he did, barging in when she least expected it, leaving her with the whiff of melancholy.

This apartment would do fine for the time being, and it was a safe and pleasant walk to work. She'd look for something better in a few months.

It was early spring, the botanical gardens lush with freshly blossomed cherries and poppies, Phlomis and aloes, the late-afternoon sun warming their cells, bringing them to life. Susan had returned from Seoul and now they were walking, slow, abstract steps, hands behind their backs. They stopped at the bridge, gazing down at the stream below, searching for the flashy piebald marking of an amur carp.

'You're doing a good job,' Susan said, without looking up. 'When I came back into the office, everyone, and I mean everyone, was at pains to point out to me how pleased they are with your appointment.'

'But?'

'But nothing. There's a buzz about the place again. You master-minded a brilliant coup with the university finance people, so not one but three new appointments to come. You're putting in for funding left, right and centre, appointing a press officer was long overdue, so you're raising our profile. Plus you're approachable and human. It makes a difference having a woman at the helm. I could go on. What more do you want me to say?'

'That'll do,' Kathleen said. 'So thanks. I'm glad everyone's happy.'

'But?'

'But it's tough. My mind is elsewhere.'

A dragonfly darted into view, a luminous, electric blue, losing itself in the reeds.

'I know,' Susan said. 'What's the news? Have you heard anything?'

'Not from Joan,' Kathleen said. 'Well, apart from the usual. She seems desperate for me to find Michael, keeps asking, but says she has no details about him. She doesn't know where he lived, where he was born. When he was born. Nothing. I don't know whether to believe her. She could be lying again. She could have given me a false name for all I know.'

'Why would she do that?'

'You ask me. She's devious, in case you hadn't noticed.'

'It was a long time ago,' Susan said. 'She may have forgotten. I mean, we're talking the Second World War here. Sixty-odd years ago.' She stopped, grabbed Kathleen's arm. 'Was she raped, do you think? It did happen, and the Americans were kind of occupying

Britain. Perhaps he was locked up for it. That would explain his disappearance.'

'It was true love, according to her,' Kathleen said. 'But she was only sixteen, so draw your own conclusions. But listen,' she went on. 'I've had a real breakthrough. I wasted months of precious time ringing any number of Michael O'Doyles. Needles and haystacks came to mind. So…'

There was a bench a short distance from the bridge, and they strolled towards it. Kathleen kicked a loose stone on the path, watched it tumble into a flower bed. They sat down. She crossed her legs, half turning to face Susan. The sun was low in the sky, its rays through the trees brindled, shadow and light, dark and gold, its warmth fading as it crept down in the sky.

'I found out it was the 8th Air Force, and some of the 9th, that were posted in East Anglia, and that it was possible to access wartime service records. I mean…' She reached out to a nearby plant, plucking a leaf, pressing it between her fingers, smelling it. Salvia. MEXICAN BUSH SAGE, she read. *SALVIA LUCANTHA.* 'Eureka, or what?'

'And?'

'A lot of the records were destroyed in a fire, but by some miracle these survived.' She stared at the crumpled leaf, began to strip it of its blades, exposing the midrib, naked and sharp. 'There were three Michael O'Doyles in East Anglia in the 8th Air Force.'

Kathleen stood up, twisting the spine of the leaf. She walked towards the bridge, leaned over the balustrade, aware Susan had followed her. A carp dashed into view, then slid out of sight among the water plants. She stared at the mottled fish darting through the weeds, *now you see it, now you don't. In out. On off.* A father, her father. Hidden from view. Like her mother. She threw the remains of the leaf into the water, watched it drift, catch on a stalk, sink out of sight.

'One of them died in the Normandy landings,' Kathleen said. 'Which would, sort of, figure with what Joan said.'

'And the others?'

'One was somewhere in upstate New York, Ithaca I think, but he wasn't living there, had rented out the house. It was the tenants who answered, said they didn't know where he was, couldn't pass on my message. I left my number anyway, but I don't suppose it will do any good.'

A group of students walked by, sophomores, Kathleen guessed, notebooks in hand as a lecturer explained the taxonomy of the gardens. A cool breeze rustled the fern and Kathleen shivered. The day had been balmy, but it was a reminder that summer was not yet here.

'And the third?'

'No reply,' Kathleen said. 'I've tried him several times, I left a message on his answerphone. I'll try again, but it takes a lot of courage. Cold-calling. Wrings me out every time.'

'You could be getting closer,' Susan said.

Kathleen shook her head. 'Perhaps. But, you know—' She broke off, bit her lip. 'To be honest, Susan, I'm scared.'

'With reason,' Susan said. 'You don't know what kind of monster you'll find.' She smiled. 'My doom-laden friend. Or what kind of charmer who's thrilled to discover an unknown daughter.'

'Perhaps,' Kathleen said, looking up, checking her watch. 'We should go. The gardens close in a few minutes.' She stared at the steel gates of the exit and pushed them open.

§

The meeting was tedious. It involved some minor issue which she needn't be involved with. She'd already laid the groundwork of another meeting so she could leave this one early. It was a common enough trick. How many times, in her teaching days, had she scooped up some papers on her desk and brought a tiresome tutorial to an early end with that excuse?

Kathleen stood up and waved her phone at the chairperson, as if an urgent call had come through. She slipped out of the door and into her office. That had taken some getting used to. Open-plan but not open-plan. She saw no point in transparent partitions except for surveillance, and that was not her management style. 'No one likes to work in a petri dish,' she'd said. She'd ordered vertical blinds for every office, but that was nearly seven months ago and they hadn't been installed yet, despite her PA pestering Campus Maintenance daily. Low priority, she was told. Well, perhaps it was a vanity project. Still. She'd like to check her emails or have a phone call without the entire office watching her.

She pulled out her phone, scrolled through her contacts. David Lambe. She could ring him, for professional advice. He was a journalist after all, was used to tracking people down. There was nothing in the rule book that said they couldn't be friends. And tips for finding people was a genuine enough reason to get in touch, not some dreamed-up excuse. She could tell him everything. She wanted that. She wanted, she knew, to hear his voice.

The sun had already set and the dusk was closing in, the sky a luminous cobalt. The temperature had dropped, another reminder that summer was some time away. Her phone rang. A number she didn't recognise came up.

There was wheezing on the end of the line, the rusty gasp of an asthmatic or an emphysema sufferer. Or a prank. A heavy breather. Her thumb hovered over the stop button.

'Kathryn Spalding,' a voice said. 'Is that you?'

'This is Kathleen Spalding,' she said. 'Who is that?' She knew, before he said it.

'Michael O'Doyle.'

She bit her lip as her heart began to palpitate and a cold sweat gathered round her mouth. 'Thank you,' she said. 'Thank you for—'

'You're looking for me,' he broke in. 'What do you want?'

She hadn't left a detailed message on his answerphone, just her name, her number, and that she was looking for someone called Michael O'Doyle.

'I'm searching for a relative,' she said. She'd decided that was the best course to take as an opener, to test if they fitted the profile, were interested, before she'd admit to searching for a father. *Father* was too loaded, too emotive.

'What kind of a relative?'

'I'd rather not say for the time being,' she said. 'But I received your telephone number and was wondering whether you were in England during the war.'

'Are you from the newspaper?' He was wheezing again, his words smothered in gusts of breath.

'No,' Kathleen said.

'Then what do you want? What kind of relative?'

She sensed she'd get nowhere without admitting her true purpose. 'My father.' She took a deep breath. 'He was in the American Air Force. He and my mother had an affair and—'

'Why d'you say that?'

'She told me,' Kathleen said. 'And she got pregnant, but they lost touch and, well.' She paused. 'I don't know if my father is alive, but I'd like to know, and find him.'

'What d'you want from him?' he said. 'Money?'

'No,' Kathleen said. 'I'd just like to meet him. See what he looks like. Meet my family perhaps. I don't want anything from him.'

'What if he doesn't want to meet you?'

'Then that's fine,' Kathleen said.

He paused again, but she knew he was there, could hear the air squeezing through clogged bronchioles. 'Okay, lady,' he said. 'If there's no obligation. Fire away.'

Kathleen swallowed. No one had questioned her like this. For a reason she couldn't fathom, she felt optimistic even though Joan had told her it was Michael who had named her Kathleen. Her real father wouldn't have forgotten, wouldn't have mistaken her name for Kathryn.

'Were you posted in England during the war?'

'Yeah,' he said. 'As a matter of fact I was. September '43 to June '44.'

'Which part of England?'

'All over,' he said. 'Some time in East Anglia. Some time in Lancashire.'

Kathleen placed a hand on her chest, breathless, light-headed. 'Whereabouts in East Anglia? Can you remember?'

'Lakenheath,' he said. 'Pretty little town. Remember it well.' He spoke slowly, between mouthfuls of air. She wondered if he was on oxygen. It was him. It had to be.

'Does the name Joan Spalding mean anything to you?' Kathleen said.

'Well,' he said. 'It could do. I don't rightly remember. Was she your mother?'

'Yes,' Kathleen said. 'She may have met you at a dance. In Aitham. Does that ring any bells?'

'Sure,' he said. 'We danced all the time. Plenty of girls. We kind of ran through them all.'

'Do you remember a Joan in particular?'

His breath was soft, squelching. 'Can't say I do,' he said.

'Please try to remember,' Kathleen said.

'I told you, I don't recall the name. Besides, we weren't in Lakenheath all the time.'

'When did you leave?'

'I don't rightly recollect,' he puffed. 'Around October '43, I guess.'

'But you said you were there until 1944,' Kathleen said.

'I said I was in England.' There was another pause. She could hear him struggling for air. 'Listen, lady, this conversation's going nowhere.'

He slammed down the phone. Kathleen sat still, taking it in. She had a gut feeling that he was her father. Perhaps he'd made a mistake with the dates. It wasn't October when he'd left but March, that's what Joan had said. She'd give him time, let him get used to the idea, ring him later. She'd come this far. She wasn't going to give up now.

JOAN

London: July 1944

Joan wasn't sure she'd ever get used to London, the way it crowded in with its rows of joined-up houses, jagged chimneys serrating the sky. The air was yellow, left grit in the handkerchiefs, motes on the curtains. She hated the sandbags and bomb craters, the rubble and wreckage, the soot and the shadows, the way the buddleia and dandelions colonised the ruins, the way children with grubby knees and festering scabs played among them. She wanted to get away, smother the past in a thick fleece of forgetting. But she had no future that wasn't coated in a lie, no dreams that wouldn't bring her down again. She wanted Kathleen, to smell her, feel her, hold her, to spread out her fingers one by one, cradle her in her arms, rock her as she sang.

'Should I write to Mum?' she said. 'Ask her how Kathleen is?'

Auntie Win shook her head. 'Best leave it alone,' she said.

Joan got a job in the canteen at the NAAFI in Vauxhall. Long hours, on her feet all day, hair wrapped in a scarf knotted at the front. Listening to the drums of conversation, the snippets and noises of war, the fragmented blasts of *Workers' Playtime* on the Home Service, *good luck, all workers*, as she doled out ladles of boiling soup, cabbage and pork, sheep's head and turnips, or portions of suet dumplings, trench-meat pudding, clumping it on the plates. *Here you are, sunshine.*

Half of what she earned went to Auntie Win. It wasn't much, but it helped. They went equal shares on a second-hand sewing machine, as Auntie Win could get Utility cloth remnants from Bon Marché. It wasn't much but helped supplement the clothing coupons, gave them something to do in the long, empty evenings, running up an apron or, if there was enough, a blouse, nerves tensed for the siren or the flash and rumble of a doodlebug, poised to run for the shelter. Sometimes the doors and windows rattled, the ceiling spitting chunks of plaster, cracks along the walls, and Joan knew it was close. Only a matter of time, she thought, before one of the rockets fell on them. They'd been homeless once. Fear and running were no life. Her nerves shook at the memory, muscles trembling.

'It's all right,' Auntie Win would say, holding Joan's hand or stroking her back. 'Try not to think about it.'

She felt sorry for the soldiers and sailors and airmen she met in the NAAFI, not knowing which mission would be their last, making jokes about German Fokkers and NAAFI food as she dolloped out a plonk of blancmange, *wot no sugar?* She wasn't sure how much longer she could stand it here in London, and what if Queenie found her? She worked with two women who lived in the same buildings as her, after all, though she never let on she knew their neighbour. Queenie was a bit too close.

She sung 'Joan's Song' under the covers at Auntie Win's, other songs too that she picked up from the wireless. Michael had said she must always sing, paint horizons in tones of colour, rhythms and harmonies pumping through her veins.

'Don't think I can't hear you at night,' Auntie Win said. 'Your Uncle Ernie had a good voice, did you know that?'

Joan shook her head.

'Beautiful tenor. Sang all the popular tunes. Life and soul of the party, was your Uncle Ernie.'

Joan found it hard to think of anyone in her family being the life and soul of a party. Perhaps that's why he'd left home too, gone into service as a groom, met Auntie Win skivvying in the big house.

'Evening classes,' Auntie Win said. 'Learn a trade, Joan. Better yourself. Look at me.'

'I only want to sing.'

Auntie Win looked up from her darning. 'Anybody else, I'd say they were dreaming. But you know, Joan, I think you've got it in you. Get some schooling. Morley College. Borough Polytechnic. City Lit. See what they can offer. Make the most of yourself.'

Voice training, it was called. For beginners. The college had been hit in the Blitz, but they'd rigged up stairs to get into the building and crammed the classes in somehow. Joan had been told which room to go to and stood outside, not sure if she should knock or just walk in. It seemed a long time since she'd been in a school, and even though this didn't smell like one, and there wasn't a child to be seen, the building inspired awe. She peered round the open door, backed away as an elderly man in an ill-fitting grey suit with a hand-knitted pullover beneath walked towards it and ushered her in. 'Joan Spalding?' he said, running his finger along a list of names. There were about fifteen others in the class, mainly housewives, Joan thought, old.

'Let us begin. Sing after me, all together, then we'll go round, one by one. *Do re me fa so la ti do.*'

All together, then one by one.

'Good,' he said, lingering by Joan. He turned to her. 'You have a remarkable voice, young lady. Where does it come from?'

'I don't know,' Joan said. 'I'm told my Uncle Ernie was a good singer.'

'No.' The teacher sounded irritable, as if Joan was being cheeky. 'Your voice comes from here.' He thumped the space above his stomach, stalked to a blackboard, fished out some chalk from his pocket and drew a diagram, a face, a mouth, a torso, filling in the parts, labelling them, mouth, tongue, palate. Larynx, lungs, diaphragm. He pointed out the way the air came through the nose and filled the lungs, the way the diaphragm worked, pumping the lungs as if they were bellows.

'And see here.' He pointed at the throat. 'As the air comes out of the lungs, it pushes open the vocal folds.' He closed his hand, opened it, breathed in, and Joan watched as his chest expanded and deflated as he opened his mouth and sang *do re me fa so la ti do*, his voice an organ, echoing round the harsh surfaces of the room and bouncing off the high ceiling.

He drew, with wiggly lines, how that sound was controlled by muscles in the larynx and in the mouth and face. He sang again, loud and soft, long and short. He threw out words such as *pitch* and *tone*, *articulator* and *modulator*.

Joan never knew all this went on when she opened her mouth, or that she could control her voice as if it was an instrument like any other. She was in charge of part of her, at least. Joan laughed, the first time for months.

ENSA was Auntie Win's idea. 'You need to get away,' she said. 'Get your mind off it all.'

'ENSA?'

'Entertainments National Service Association. Every Night Something Awful. That's what Tommy Trinder says it stands for.' Auntie Win laughed. 'As a matter of fact, I know someone who knows Mr Dean's housekeeper.'

'Who's he?'

'Basil Dean. Only the big boss of ENSA. I'll put in a word for you. It's always the way, isn't it?' she added. 'You know someone who knows someone.'

Joan learned the Anne Shelton hit 'Lay Down Your Arms' and the Vera Lynn song 'The White Cliffs of Dover', practised all day and all night in front of Auntie Win so she got her nerves in order, sang them in front of Mr Dean and Mr MacMannon, was signed on the spot.

Jock MacMannon. Variety producer. 'But people call me Mr Mac,' he said. Blood vessels threaded the skin on his nose and cheeks, turning his face choleric, making him look bad-tempered. 'I'm looking for a third singer with a deep voice to make up the Petal Sisters.' Joan's muscles trembled inside and she thought she might wet herself with the fear and excitement of it all. 'Can you dance?'

What was it Michael had said? *If you can walk, you can dance.* 'Yes,' she said.

'Good, because the Petal Sisters will be an all-singing, all-dancing act. Identical costumes, squeaky clean, girl next door. I take it you're intact?'

Joan had no idea what he meant, but she nodded.

'Aye,' he said, nodding. 'Good.' He rubbed his hands together. 'Because there's to be no pregnancies. Am. I. Clear?'

Joan nodded.

'As for your name…' He shook his head. 'Joan won't do. You're one of the Petal Sisters now. How's about Lily?'

'Lily?' She could hear the disdain in her own voice.

'Aye. Lily. I don't take truck with dissent.' His Scottish 'r' rolled like a barrel down a hill.

'I'm not disagreeing,' Joan said quickly. 'Only, perhaps, to make it more special, why don't we spell it with two *l*s? Perhaps an *i* and an *e* at the end?'

'Well,' Mr Mac looked at her. 'You've got a mind of your own, I can see. Have it your own way.' He shrugged. 'You need to get your uniform and kitbag. Give your measurements to Costume. Come back here and I'll introduce you to Rose and Violet.' He beckoned her to follow him. 'You've got five days rehearsal time and then you're on the road.'

Who would ever find her, with a new name? Plying her trade from place to place like a tinker.

Mr Mac chuckled. 'Move over, Andrews Sisters.'

Rose taught Joan the basic dance steps, and, in turn, Joan taught her and Violet how to sing from the belly. The uniform was khaki, a sickly yellow-brown, ENSA in enamel sewn onto the shoulders.

'Jauntier, see?' Rose said, putting on her cap at an angle.

'And how about this?' Joan took the tie, fixed it in a bow, not a knot, made the others laugh. She stood in front of the mirror. 'Much better.'

They linked arms, did as high a kick as they could in their straight khaki skirts with the pleat up the back. They were all the same height and weight, so who would guess they weren't sisters? Until they spoke, of course, but Mr Mac made sure it was only Rose, as the oldest, who gave interviews, so everyone thought they all came from Wigan, which *exuded* stardom, George Formby was born there, after all, he said, so no one would guess Lillie was as exotic as the sedge in her native fens, or Violet as glitzy as a wet London cobble.

Carted around in an army truck, sitting on their kitbags and sleeping bags. Some of the numbers had them come on in cowgirl outfits, or hula skirts, or dressed as mariners with bell-bottoms and sailor hats. Often they had no proper dressing room, especially on the more remote bases, had to hop and duck behind a hessian curtain, slap on greasepaint without a mirror, wait out their turn in a freezing tent.

They spent the months doing the rounds of barracks and bases, hospitals and factories, perfecting their routines and their repertoires. All the hits. The Andrews Sisters. Vera Lynn. Cole Porter. The munitions factories were the hardest to play. Who wanted to listen to them in their lunch hour? Still, Joan thought, it taught them how to pound out the numbers over the clatter of the works canteens. Good training, Mr Mac said. They'd built a name for themselves, were on *Workers' Playtime* twice and even entertained the Yankee top brass in Bedford.

Not a day went by that Joan didn't think of Kathleen, but life on the road with Rose and Violet dulled the sharp edge of loss, reminded her she was young. And once the war was over, Michael would come and find her. It wouldn't be long now, she told herself. Not long now.

KATHLEEN

Cambridge, Massachusetts: May 1967

He sent her postcards from Delano, Oxnard, Yuba City, San José, signed the cards off *a la causa* each time.

Until the postcards stopped. Kathleen had no idea where Emory was, when he was returning. His silence was abrupt, unexplained. Had she imagined the love they felt for each other, that sinewy snake that hugged them close?

She stepped into the bathroom with its mouldy grouting and dripping faucets, vomited. She gargled from the tap, washed her face, dabbed it dry. She was overdue.

'Oh God,' she said, sitting down on the toilet seat. 'Oh God. Oh no.'

She rang his number, on the off-chance he might have come back. There was no reply. Well, she thought. Nothing for it. She went round to his apartment, rang the doorbell. No one answered, but she still had the key so let herself in. There were coffee cups on the table, fresh fruit in the bowl. He was back. Why hadn't he been in touch? Perhaps he'd only just returned, was catching his breath before he made contact. She'd wait for him, *surprise, surprise.* She picked up the coffee cups, took them over to the sink. It was full of dirty dishes. She smiled. Chaos never worried him. He was lucky to have her to help organise this side of his life, make sure it ran smoothly. Doing the shit work, she thought. Remnants of food were stuck on the plates, and the mugs had old coffee stains. It took some work soaking and scrubbing, but she stacked them on the draining board, rinsed and gleaming.

The kitchen clock showed 6.15 when she heard the key in the door. She stood up, forcing a smile, stepping forward in welcome. A young woman walked in wearing a black minidress and knee-high boots, her long, hennaed hair curly and flowing as if she'd stepped out of a Rossetti painting, a confident, imposing presence sashaying to the centre of the room.

Kathleen stared at the strange woman with the key to Emory's apartment. 'Who are you?' she said.

'Ruby.' Ruby sauntered over to the kitchen area, took the bottle of cold water from the fridge, lifted one of the mugs Kathleen had just washed off the draining board and filled it up, ambled over to the table with an exaggerated, entitled slowness, as if she owned the place, and sat down, placing the mug of water before her. Kathleen hadn't seen her around before, not at the meetings nor on campus. She looked too self-assured to be a freshman. Kathleen was wondering if she came from one of the housing projects Emory worked on, if she was the embodiment of the worker–student alliance he spoke so fervently about. 'I'm staying here,' she said. She smiled, but Kathleen couldn't read it as friendly. 'Didn't he tell you?'

'I forgot,' Kathleen said, sitting down opposite her. It was weeks since she'd last heard from Emory, but she wasn't going to let this stranger know that.

'I flew in last week from San Francisco,' Ruby went on. 'Berkeley chapter SDS. I met Emory at the NFWA summer school.'

Kathleen studied her, trying to fathom what she was saying. Emory had every right to let whoever he wanted use his apartment. Except. Except she thought they had an understanding that they were dating. There was only one bedroom, and she thought he might have consulted her before he let another woman sleep there.

She looked at Ruby with her shock of red hair and her miniskirt, sitting cross-legged so the top of her stockings showed. He'd never mentioned Ruby in his postcards, never talked about going with other women. Was she a friend? Or more? Had she usurped Kathleen in his affections?

'That's good,' she found herself saying. There was no reason to think he was dating Ruby, and yet some instinct told her he was. 'How long are you staying?'

She shrugged. 'Till I move on. Why? You have a problem?'

'No,' Kathleen said. 'Of course not. It's just…' She hesitated, groping for words. 'It's just that I'm his girlfriend, that's all. I thought, you know, perhaps you would have—'

'Really?' Ruby said. '*Girlfriend.*' She curled her top lip. 'That's kind of bourgeois.'

'Is it?' Kathleen said. 'If two people love each other—' She broke off. She wished she'd kept her mouth shut, could see the supercilious sneer that had wrapped itself round Ruby's mouth.

'You don't own him.'

'I'm not saying I do.' Kathleen knew she sounded defensive. 'You don't need to own someone to love them.'

'Nor care if they fuck around,' Ruby said. She rummaged in her bag, pulled out a pack of unfiltered Camels, took one out and lit it, creating a haze around her head, filling the room with the sweet smell of Turkish tobacco. She stared, impassively, at Kathleen, her face giving nothing away, a hard, cool anger in her voice. Kathleen felt her bile rising, Ruby looking at her, a cruel sneer playing on her mouth. What had she, Kathleen, done to make Ruby's disdain so palpable? 'Emory was right. You have petit bourgeois tendencies. Like love. Love is petit bourgeois, not for revolutionaries.' She took a deep breath, shook her head, a slow, deliberate action. 'It's a distraction. That and all that women's liberation crap.' She flicked her cigarette and the ash fell onto the floor.

Kathleen turned so Ruby wouldn't see her face, stared out of the window. What other confidences had he shared, what secrets of their pillow had he revealed? She could picture Emory with Ruby, sheets she'd washed crumpled and soiled by them.

'Like I said,' Ruby added, 'I'm staying. If you have a problem with that, the door's over there.'

Kathleen pushed her chair back with a loud screech that raised the hairs on her arm. She was cold inside, as if her skin had been ripped open. Well, she wouldn't stay around to be humiliated. Ruby could be bluffing, the angry lover seeing off her rival. Now *that* was petit bourgeois. She walked past Ruby into the hall. Paused. Let herself into the bathroom. Emory kept a supply of condoms in the cabinet. She took them out of their packaging, stretched them over the taps, leaving the foil wrappings scattered over the floor. Walked out, picked up her bag, shut the door behind her. She wouldn't give Ruby the satisfaction of slamming it.

§

Kathleen felt the mattress shift as Susan sat down next to her, brushing her temple with her hand.

'I'm pregnant.'

A myriad cells within her, anonymous zygotes dividing and multiplying, a hollow blastocyst burrowing into her, a parasite. How could she keep it? What chance would it have? An unloved baby, an unwanted baby. There were too many of those.

'It's all right for the likes of Emory,' she said, her lips tight, angry. 'He can screw around as much as he wants. He doesn't have to face the consequences.'

'You could write to him,' Susan said. 'Tell him. Perhaps he'll want the baby.'

'It's not his choice,' Kathleen said. 'Not any more.' A sob began to swell, a wall of pressure behind her eyes. 'If he doesn't want me, then he can't force me to carry his child.' She sniffed, hard. 'It's my body. I decide. But I feel violated.'

'Oh, honey.' Susan pulled Kathleen close, arms tight round her shoulders as Kathleen buried her face in Susan's neck, her body shaking. 'You need a drink,' Susan said. 'I've got some Southern Comfort.' She led Kathleen into their sitting room, fetched two glasses and the bottle from the kitchen and poured.

'That person in New York, the one you wanted me to see.'

'A bit late now, isn't it?'

'Does she…?'

Susan nodded. 'It is illegal, though.'

'I know,' Kathleen said. 'But I have no choice. Will you come with me?'

'Sure.'

She took a large swig of her drink, feeling its heat sear her throat, its power dazzle her mind. She took another, not caring if her blood turned to alcohol and ran golden in her veins.

JOAN

London: March 2006

They went out for a meal after the show, as if it were the old days, took a taxi home. Harry walked her to her door. 'You know, this time of night. There's sometimes unsavoury characters—'

'Will you come in?' she said. 'For a nightcap?'

'Aren't you exhausted?'

'Yes,' she said. 'But I'm not sleepy.'

'Then let's party on.'

She hesitated, key in the door. 'I don't live anywhere beautiful, Harry,' she said. 'I live very simply.'

'You don't need to apologise.' He placed his hand over hers, taking the key. 'Allow me.'

She let him enter first, followed behind, flicking on the light, scooping up the mail, putting it on the kitchen counter. She'd sort it later. Harry was taking off his coat, hanging it on the pegs by the door.

'Wait,' he said, fishing in his pocket, pulling out a bottle. 'Mount Gay XO. Barbados's very best. Where do you keep the glasses?'

She'd had the foresight to buy a couple of gin and tonics and they sat in the door of the fridge in their aluminium cans. But rum was a different matter. She fetched two tumblers, set them down on the coffee table in the centre of the room.

'Let's have a little music,' Harry said, pointing to the old radiogram on one side of the mantelpiece. 'Does it work?'

'The radio does,' Joan said. 'So I suppose there's no reason why the gramophone shouldn't. I haven't played it for years.'

'Do you have any Lillie Pettall?' He winked.

There was a small cupboard on the right, below the speakers, where she kept her records, some 78s, some 33s and 45s. She pulled out one, wiped it with her sleeve, put it on the turntable, lowered the needle.

'Can we turn down the lights?' Harry said. He poured the rum, handing her a glass, stepping over to her bed with its candlewick cover. 'Let's sit somewhere comfortable. Come.' He beckoned with his finger.

She sat on the bed, feeling it dip beneath her weight, tipping her close to him. His body was warm, electric to her touch.

'Joan,' Harry said. The way he said it, the inflection, made her shiver. It had a portentous tone, a question, a statement, a complaint. She heard him breathe in, waiting for the verdict. 'May I seduce you?' he said. 'I may be rusty and creaky, but I've dreamed of this for fifty years.'

No man had ever *asked* before, not like this. 'Yes,' she said, only this time her body sparked with static. 'Yes. I'd like that.'

§

He went out in the morning, came back with croissants, bustled round the kitchen making coffee. She watched him from the bed, the sun casting a low glow through the French window of the balcony. She listened to the traffic on the South Circular, guessed it must be late, the rest of London going about its business while she lay in bed, warm and content.

Harry's phone rang. 'Bowen,' she heard him say, his voice low. Either he didn't want to wake her, or he didn't want her to listen. 'Yes. Well. That's great news. Yes. I'll tell her.'

She heard him in the kitchen, searching, opening the doors and drawers, the clink of cutlery and crockery, the pull of the tray from the side of the cooker. He came into the sitting room, lifted the coffee table over to the side of the bed, went back to the kitchen and returned with coffee, milk in a jug she hadn't used for years, two plates, two croissants, placed it on the table.

'Breakfast in bed, for the star of the show,' he said, pulling up a chair and sitting opposite her. 'That was Neal. You were a sell-out.' He poured some coffee, passed her a cup. 'He's thinking of inviting you back, for a season.'

A season? She wasn't sure, she wasn't ready, she had no material. 'Why didn't he ring me?' she said.

'He did. But your phone's turned off,' he said. 'I think it's a wonderful offer. He's contacting your agent as I speak. What with this and my film, if you agree to do it, you're poised, Joan. An album, perhaps. *Lillie Come Lately.* I can see it now—'

'Stop,' she said. 'I need to think about it. I can't be bounced, not now.'

He smiled. 'Eat up. Neal's expecting you later today.'

It was midday when Harry left. She gathered up the breakfast things and took them into the kitchen. Yesterday's post sat on the counter, a couple of buff envelopes which she recognised as her TV licence renewal and the gas bill. And another envelope. By hand. She ripped it open, pulled out the letter.

Dear Lillie, or is it Joan? What shall I call you?
   I know who you are, and I would like to talk to you. I really want to meet you. You have no idea.
   Yours sincerely,
   Steve Kingsman

Joan took the letter into the sitting room, sat down on the chair, blood churning like a sluice. Steve Kingsman. Was that Queenie's son? She'd had two boys. One was called Steven, she remembered.

Irene Mildred Kingsman. *Queenie.* The name was a fist in her gut, a haunting from her past, a poltergeist intent on wreckage. He must have been the man her neighbour had seen. Scruffy chap. Scrawny. Unsavoury. Had he taken up where Queenie had left off?

She'd tried to put Queenie out of her mind, but she always came back. That snake.

No, she thought. Actually, *no.* She'd let Queenie derail her once before. She wasn't going to let her do it twice.

Joan fingered the envelope. There was something else inside. She pulled it out. A photograph, of her, entering the block of flats. Why would he enclose that? Proof that he knew who she was? Should she tell Harry? No, she thought. It would be too complicated. She tore it in two, and two again. She'd be sure to pull the bolt on the door at night, look around her before she came home.

She folded the letter and put it in her box of documents. What if he'd been in the audience?

KATHLEEN

Los Angeles: April 2006

Kathleen checked she had everything in her briefcase, lifted her jacket off the coat stand and left the office. The sun had already set and the dusk was closing in, the sky a luminous cobalt. The temperature had dropped but was still pleasant, with the promise of warmth to come. She was passing the mock-Gothic ASUCLA building. Some students were outside, handing out leaflets. She took one as she passed. There was a photo of a man, late middle-age, grey cropped hair, a politician's smile, a studio portrait.

Emory Kerridge. Your next Independent Congressman, talking tonight. Bruin Reception Room. 6 p.m.

Kathleen checked her watch. Well. Why not? She had no feelings for him now, that kind of hurt ran as deep as a culvert, unbridgeable, but she was curious. She'd stay for half an hour, max. She studied the photo. Gone were his beret and T-shirt, replaced by a tailored suit and blue silk tie. He looked like a lawyer, and she wondered whether he'd trained as one. Would he remember her? Life in those days had been peppered with short, intense flings, shiny infatuations that promised to last for eternity but shattered as soon as they were handled, like cheap Christmas baubles. Perhaps hers had broken into sharper shards than most.

'Are you coming to the meeting?

She'd wandered, without thinking, over to the main building and stood poised outside the door.

'Yes.' She followed the signs to Bruin. The room was full but a space was free in the centre of a row, near the back. She edged along, picked up a couple of leaflets off the seat of the chair and sat down, looking around. Most of the people here were young, a smattering of older men and women who, she assumed, were faculty members. She glanced at the leaflet. *Bring Back Affirmative Action! Overturn Proposition 209!* She'd heard that affirmative action had been abolished, but that was some time ago. She looked at the other leaflet. *We have two evils to fight, capitalism and racism. We must destroy both.* Huey P. Newton. *Protest Meeting Royce Hall TOMORROW. 2 p.m.*

She smiled to herself, shook her head. The issues had hardly changed from her student days at Harvard. Whistles and catcalls erupted from nowhere, students stood up, blocking her view. Emory must have arrived. They sat down and he stood on a dais in the front, holding on to a lectern while a young woman read out a résumé of his achievements, from his membership of Students for a Democratic Society, his legendary struggles for justice – she stressed the word *legendary* – his community work, his positions on education and health, same-sex marriage and civil unions, Israel and Gaza, the Iraq War, Robert Mugabe and Louis Farrakhan – some of the audience booed at this – police brutality, slavery reparations. The list was endless, embracing every progressive movement of the late-twentieth century without, Kathleen thought, once mentioning feminism. Well, she thought, that figures. He was standing as an independent in the next congressional elections and, judging from the packed hall and the audience response, could be a popular choice.

'Ladies and gentlemen,' he began, 'I was a freshman at Harvard when I read the Port Huron Statement and joined Students for a Democratic Society. I am still proud to say I stand by every analysis, value and ideal it embodied.' The audience erupted into applause. 'These are as relevant today as they were in 1962.' He paused for effect. 'We don't yet have participatory democracy, nor international peace, nor economic justice.'

The clapping began, cheering. There were cries of 'Fuck Dubya!' and 'Release Proposition 209.' He raised his hand, and the hall fell silent.

'Nor have we ended racial discrimination and human degradation, police brutality and murder.' More cheers. 'I stand to affirm that mankind—'

'And womankind,' someone yelled out from the audience.

'And womankind,' Emory went on, without missing a beat. '*Humanity* is comprised of individuals whose voices should be heard, not silenced, their reasoning listened to, not distorted. Promises of comforts in the life to come must not mask the disfigurements of the present, the migrant workers, the refugees, the lack of civil rights, the victims of our foreign policy, past and present.' He paused. He was a powerful orator, but she had always known that. His rhetoric hadn't changed, even if his appearance had.

It had been so long ago, a bittersweet moment. His presence brought it back, but her desire had long been incinerated by his betrayal, leaving nothing but traces of carbon.

She'd had enough. Curiosity sated. She wished she'd stood at the back, could have sneaked out without drawing attention to herself, but now it would be impossible to leave, stand up and walk out, with all the kerfuffle of crawling along the row to reach the aisle. She hoped he wouldn't go on for too long. She needed the bathroom and, she had to admit, a drink. She'd grown rather partial to chilled rosé.

Ah well. Kathleen leaned back in her chair and shut her eyes, letting his words wash over her.

'Thank you for your time, ladies and gentlemen.' There was an ovation before the chairperson stepped forward, applauding. She took the microphone.

'Thank you Mr Kerridge,' she said, 'for that amazing and inspiring talk.' She turned and faced the audience. 'I'm very sorry, but our speaker has to make his way to another appointment and won't be able to take questions. So please let us once again show our appreciation and thanks.' She raised her hands, clapping hard as the rest of the students followed suit.

Emory stepped down from the dais and pushed his way forward in the central aisle. He paused at the end of Kathleen's row and looked at her. She looked back. *Yes. I am who you think I am.* He gave no acknowledgement. Walked on and out of the room.

§

She let herself into her apartment, went over to the balcony, pulled back the doors. The apartment was built for air conditioning, but Kathleen preferred cross breezes that blew away the frowst, not circulated it. She poured herself a glass of wine and sat on the planter's chair outside, her jacket wrapped around her, listening to the night sounds, the soft, sleepy bass of nature, the gentle rhythm of insects, wind through the palms, the airy bark of a great horned owl.

Emory Kerridge. He'd recognised her, she was sure. She had no desire to renew their relationship. Not even an acquaintanceship. Some things were best left buried.

The light on her answerphone was blinking. She always gave out her landline number as a back-up to her mobile, though most people rang her mobile as a first, not last, resort. She placed the glass on the table, walked over to the phone, pressed play.

'Michael O'Doyle here.' The voice was less rasping than before. 'Give me a call.' She looked at her watch. She'd do it tomorrow. She needed time to compose herself. Excitement clutched at her stomach, trepidation, too. So near, she thought, so far. But he'd contacted her. That had to be a good sign. She'd been sure this

Michael O'Doyle was her father and now, perhaps, he was ready to meet her.

The light was still blinking, another message. She pressed play again. There was a slight delay before it started.

'Kathleen. David here. I'm in LA on business and would love to meet, if you're free. I plan on going to Griffith Park on Saturday, so if you'd care to join me, why don't we meet at the Trails Café at 11.30 and take it from there? I'll be there anyway, so if you turn up, that's great. And if not…' The recording paused a second. 'Well, then. Well. I don't know.' He stopped again and she thought she heard him swallow hard. 'I don't know what that means. You may not be in. You may not get this message even. Sorry, that's a ramble. I hope you still have my number. Perhaps you can—'

The recording ended, mid-sentence. The impossible coincidence of it made her laugh: her first lover, and her last, in the same evening. And her father. She played David's message again. He had rehearsed what he was going to say, or some of it, but then got cold feet, hesitated, unsure. Played it another time. It was good to hear his voice again. Yes, she was free on Saturday. Yes, she'd meet him there. It had been longer than she cared to remember since she'd broken up with him, though he was always on her mind. Now he was here and wanted to see her. There'd be no going back this time.

Griffith Park was not neutral. He knew how she loved nature, would have chosen it specifically. He'd come to woo her, again. She still had the walking boots he'd given her when they went trekking in the Lakes. They weren't glamorous, but he didn't give a damn about appearances. She'd have time to go to the hairdresser's on Friday evening, treat herself to a manicure too. Not that he'd notice, but it would give her courage. *Look good, feel strong.* Perhaps more of Joan had rubbed off onto her than she'd given Joan credit for, Kathleen thought.

§

She caught the shuttle, picked up a takeaway coffee at the café, *no cinnamon, thank you*, stood on the terrace outside, looking at the maps and signposts. There were noticeboards listing the fauna of the park, mammals with identifying illustrations, skunks and squirrels, deer and coyote, amphibians with accompanying images and a short description of behaviour and habitat. Griffith Park was a distance from where she lived and she hadn't really taken in how big it was, how wild, how spectacular the views were or how popular it was. People gathered round the café, groups of friends, families, organised parties. She wandered round, searching their faces for David, checking her watch. She was early, but he was always on time. Always used to be on time, at any rate. Perhaps he'd had cold feet, thought she wouldn't come. She'd left a message on his phone, confirming she'd be there. She'd sent him an email too, but he might not have seen it.

A man and a woman walked past her, ready for a day's hike with poles and rucksacks. 'Wait here, honey,' the man said. 'I'll get the water.' He slipped off his rucksack, put it on the ground next to the woman's feet. She nodded, caught Kathleen's eye, smiled. They were about the same age as her, Kathleen guessed, had the comfortable air of a couple accustomed to each other. She'd never known what that was like. She turned away, *rude to stare*, loneliness, sharp, acute, took her breath, stabbed into her heart. She wanted David to be there. She wanted David. She'd been an idiot. She should have made room for him, loitering in her life, listening to his voice, feeling the imprints of his touch.

He was in the distance, hurrying towards the café, wearing a navy blue jumper. He spotted her, waved, smiled, broke into a trot as he came close, opening his arms, drawing her close. She'd thought he'd be more circumspect, would test the water before embracing, but he was enfolding her and she was hugging him back, needing to touch his face, feel his skin, draw his lips to hers.

She hadn't expected this rush of energy through her body, had forgotten the craving she used to have for him, the yearning as painful as an open wound. Tears were filling her eyes with the sheer joy and relief. And fear. What if he had someone else? Had come to say *let's be friends, you and I?* Friends hugged too. She buried her face in his chest. What was the matter with her?

'Let me look at you,' he said. 'LA suits you.'

'Thanks,' she said, flicking her finger through his hair, which had turned grey at the temples. 'And you. Even more distinguished.' He wasn't a handsome man, no chiselled features and Cary Grant dimple or George Clooney smile, but his face was open and kind and intelligent, wit and humour never far from the surface.

'Let's go,' he said, pointing to the West Observatory Trail. She dumped the remains of her coffee in a litter bin and they strolled down the sandy path, side by side. He walked like a sailor, side to side, couldn't help but knock arms and hips, spiked and electric.

'How did you find me?' She was panting. David had set a fast pace, and the path was on an incline.

'I'm an investigative journalist,' he said. He was looking straight ahead but she saw him smile, sideways on. 'It's not rocket science to track down a world-class scientist.' She'd tried to put him out of her mind but he'd been lurking there all along, hidden in plain sight. 'Even one who doesn't want to be found.' He paused, let her catch her breath. 'If I'd rung you on your mobile, or emailed you, you'd simply have stonewalled me.' He smiled. 'So I thought surprise was the best form of attack.'

'What's your business in LA?'

'You,' he said.

She opened her mouth, lost for words. She hadn't expected that.

He took her elbow, led her over to a viewing point, the white-lettered Hollywood sign nestling at a distance in the mountainside. Chaparral lay between them, rugged hillside with golden earth and scrubby shrubs, sage and brush and barberry, a wild landscape at odds with the iconic sign of celluloid and artifice. She toed the loose earth of the path, turning the red dust into tiny tornadoes, sensed David turn to face her.

'Janice died,' he said.

'I'm sorry,' Kathleen said. 'When?'

'Just over two years ago. It took its time.' His voice was flat, deadened. 'She went into a hospice in the end.'

'Why didn't you get in touch?'

'I wanted to, believe me.' His eyes were searching her face, uncertainty creasing his forehead. 'You were pretty final when you broke it off. I couldn't face rejection again.'

Two young men walked past, a dachshund on a long, retractable leash. They paused, walked on past, tugging at the dog, as if sensing the tension between them.

'It hurt so much when you left,' he said. He breathed in, out.

'It hurt me too, David.' Kathleen's voice was soft, secret. 'I was so in love. Can you believe that?' It was she who breathed hard now, in, out. 'I did what I always did. I pushed you away, in case I got hurt.' She bit her lip. 'I thought you were another philanderer wanting a little outside comfort.'

His face was drawn, his eyes dulled.

'I'm so sorry,' she went on. 'I misjudged you. I never meant to hurt you.'

'I'm not a philanderer,' he said. 'I was the most uxorious man in Europe.'

She smiled. 'And what changed?'

'You,' he said. 'But I was fearful. I couldn't face Janice's death alone and needed to carry you with me. You were right to force me away.'

'I thought neediness was no basis for a relationship,' she said. 'But I was wrong.'

There was a scuttling in the undergrowth. A brown lizard with orange stripes came into view, camouflaged on the soil, almost invisible. 'What's that?' David said.

'An alligator lizard,' Kathleen said.

'Alligator?' He laughed. 'Do they bite?'

'If cornered, yes,' she said. 'But then, who doesn't?'

They watched it, eyes darting side to side, alert for prey, before it scuttled back as fast as it had disappeared. She looked up into David's eyes, green in the sunlight. Green or sage or slate, depending. Light and shade.

'I've been on my own for two years now,' he went on. 'I've grieved for Janice, said my farewells. I want to move on, and I want to move on with you, Kathleen, if you'll consider trying once more.'

He reached for her hands. Kathleen listened, taking in his words.

'Can we make another go of it?' He was looking at her hard, searching, she knew, for clues. 'Or is there nothing left?'

'How?' she said. 'I'm in LA, you're in London.'

'That won't last forever.'

'Nor will we,' she said.

'Don't say that.' He laughed. 'Just think of the air miles.' He pulled her towards him and she felt that old familiar hurtling, that helter-skelter of desire.

'Did you really come all the way to ask me this?' she said.

'Yes.'

Her head rested against his chest. She could feel the gentle pulse of his heart, its steady *dum-dum*, feel the softness of his jumper and the scent of his washing powder, his arms around her. She had a sudden urge to tell him about her father, the quest for him, this missing part of her, her flesh and blood. Strange how powerful that search could be, a hungry, muscled serpent coiled within her. Like love.

'Let's go back to my apartment,' she said.

JOAN

Berlin: August – December 1945

Joan clambered into the back of the army truck and sat on the wooden bench. She hadn't expected it to be hot. She wanted to take off her jacket, roll up her sleeves, loosen her tie, but they'd had the fear of God put into them before they left.

'No disapparel is permitted under any circumstances,' Mr Mac had bellowed, his voice bouncing around the coach taking them to Northolt.

She ran her finger inside the collar of her shirt, easing the tie, hoping to let in a little breeze. Rose sat on one side of her, Violet the other. Violet looked better now, but she'd been as sick as a dog on the aeroplane. Joan wasn't sure she could have stuck it much longer herself, the way the plane had juddered and tilted. She'd sat clutching her paper bag, stomach churning.

Mr Mac had had to wait till Joan was eighteen before he could send her overseas. He'd said he'd get a replacement for her so he could send their act out earlier, but Rose and Violet said they wouldn't work without her. He packed them off to Germany, the first variety show since the end of the war. It was generous of Rose to say what she did, but Joan knew hers was the best voice of the three of them and in most of their numbers she was the lead singer, even though she was the youngest.

She breathed in, looked around her. Tempelhof. Berlin. The city smelled different from London, more pungent, like rotten eggs and dirty drains but much, much worse. She knew it was the smell of death, of rotting flesh and flyblown glands. Some of the airport buildings had been damaged, but the runways had been repaired. The sky was blue, hazy with dust. The engines were still hot, vapours shimmying above the nose of the plane, the blue, white and red RAF symbol gleaming on the tail in the sun. A Dakota, the pilot had said. *This plane's a Dakota.* It was parked next to others, British and American, was being unloaded, boxes and cases stacked on the tarmac.

'Don't worry,' Rose said. 'I've counted ours. Everything's here.'

The band climbed on board the truck, all eleven of them. Joan and the others had never met them before, much less played with them. They were all servicemen, Mr Mac had said, from the Central Pool of Artists.

'Aka Stars in Battledress. SiB. All RAF. They call themselves The Lancasters. Their leader is Reg Berry.'

Joan had to shunt along the bench to make room. Reg himself was in his thirties, Joan guessed, average height, average build, average hair. Nondescript really, apart from his startling blue eyes, pale as a winter sky. She couldn't see him as a musician, wondered whether he played an instrument or whether he was just a producer, like Mr Mac. Reg was the last to climb on board. He squeezed in between two of his players, opposite Joan.

Another lorry drew up beside them and their props were loaded onto it, their costume trunks and greasepaint boxes, along with the band's gear and their suitcases. She kept an eye on hers, made sure it was safe, stuffed as it was with soap and toothpaste, aspirins and sanitary towels, hot-water bottles and candles, pyjamas as well as her smalls and cosmetics, and a couple of frocks for off-duty excursions. Enough for four months, she hoped. They'd been told to take everything they'd need. If the suitcase fell off the lorry, she'd be done for.

A corporal secured the tailgate, pulled out a cigarette, lit it, and climbed into the driver's cab. The truck gathered speed and Joan welcomed the breeze. They passed through the gates of the aerodrome, over parched wasteland, and into a street carved between mountains of rubble. Joan took in a breath. It stood to reason they'd be bombing near an aerodrome, she thought. That's where the bombers most likely took off for England. Though not the doodlebugs. They didn't need aeroplanes. They came by themselves, dropping from nowhere. Still. There was nothing left here.

They drove on, swathed in silence. More buildings stood empty as skeletons, bricks and mortar tumbled on the ground like flayed hides, sockets and chasms where windows and doors had once been. She'd seen the bombing in London, the docks, Woolwich, her own street, her own *home*, but nothing like this. There was hardly a building that stood, and even those that had survived were pockmarked with shell scars and bullet holes. There was a fine dust everywhere that clogged her nose and coated her tongue, and a stench of rot and earth and sulphur. Everyone said the Germans had this coming to them, but even so, she thought, even so.

Through the side streets she could see gangs of women picking at the remains, clearing the devastation brick by brick. Where do they live? she thought. All the people here? Nothing was standing. An old man came out from the basement of a building. There, she thought, that's where they live. In the basement and cellars. She thought of the cellar in her parents' home, its walls dripping with water, the dank, earth floor, the smell of mould and mushrooms. There was no light there, save the sunless beam that came through the coal shaft.

The truck stopped. A pothole the width of the street lay ahead. The driver climbed out of the cab, assessing the road, turned to the lorry. 'Everybody out,' he said. He walked round, opened the tailgate, let the men out first. Reg stood below Joan as she poised to jump.

'Hold on,' he said. 'I'll catch you.' She felt his hands tighten round her waist as he lifted her and placed her gently on the ground. 'Don't want you spraining one of your pretty little ankles,' he said.

She turned, almost stumbled into a baby held in the arms of a bigger boy. Their eyes were hollow, their hair unkempt, their clothes ragged and their faces dirty. Joan knew the face of poverty, the sullen silence of its children. She'd seen it often enough in the labourers' children in the fens. The boy put the baby on the ground and, reaching into his pocket, produced a dirty, bent spoon. He held it towards her. 'Zwanzig Mark.'

Joan shook her head. She had no idea what he was saying. He walked along to Rose, offering the spoon, to the bandsmen handing out cigarettes, stuck the spoon back in his pocket, clambered onto some bricks.

She wished she had some food to give them, or some money. She wanted to reach over and scoop up the baby, take her away from all of this, cradle her tight, her hand around her head, *it's all right, my baby, I'm here.* The baby sat, silent, unsmiling, thick, yellow mucus running from its nose and left eye.

'All aboard,' the corporal said. He'd manoeuvred the truck across the crater and now stood by his cab, waiting for them. They clambered up again, set off, a cloud of black exhaust puffing behind them. Joan stared behind her at the baby. She'd begun to suck her fingers. Her brother was already scrabbling across the rubble. He'd probably found the spoon there.

'Joan.' Rose was shaking her knee. 'Joan. You all right?'

Joan turned back, forcing a smile.

'Only Reg's been trying to get your attention.' Rose nodded towards the band leader opposite.

'Joan?' Reg leaned forward in his seat. 'Joan? I thought your name was Lily.'

Joan shut her eyes, blanking the image of the children. She turned to look at him, shrugging. 'Lillie's my stage name,' she said. 'Spelt with two ells and "ie" at the end.'

'Two Ells Lil, eh?' Reg said. 'That would make a hell of a song.' He chuckled and Joan felt the heat of a blush creep up her neck. She'd made a fool of herself. She insisted on spelling it that way, not common or garden Lily. Everybody said Joan could be a film star, with her hourglass figure and glamorous looks. Well, she'd needed a name to match.

'And you, Rose? Is that your real name?'

Rose was not her proper name, any more than Lillie was hers.

'No,' Rose said. 'But Violet's her name.' She pointed her thumb towards Violet, who hunched on the bench holding her stomach, face pallid.

'Then what's your name?' Reg said.

'I'm not saying,' she said. 'For your purposes, it's Rose.' Rose was the oldest at twenty-one, had a boldness and assurance Joan could only dream of.

'So are you sisters, even?' Reg said.

Rose looked at Joan and Violet, winked. Sharing digs, three in a room and sometimes a bed, made them into sisters of sorts. 'As good as,' she said.

'What's your story, Two Ells?' He leaned forward, tapping Joan on the knee.

'My name's Lillie,' she said, hoping she sounded firm. 'And I joined ENSA.' Damned if she was going to give anything away.

'That don't mean a thing,' Reg said. 'They take anybody.' She smarted. Mr Mac had said she had talent. They all said it. Who did Reg think he was, putting her down like that? Besides, she needed the money. Sent back her earnings regular as clockwork to her mother. She wasn't going to tell him that.

'I think you're hiding a dark secret, two Ells,' Reg went on, lifting his chin, tapping the side of his nose. 'I reckon you're running away—'

'Shut up,' she said. She knew it was rude, but what right did he have to prod like this? What did he know?

'Sounds like I touched on a sore point there,' he said. 'I was only teasing. You know, breaking the ice.'

'Well, don't,' Joan said. She heard him take a deep breath, watched his face tauten.

'Let's start again. You joined ENSA and…?'

She'd rather not talk, but she couldn't risk antagonising Reg. He was the band leader, after all, and his word went.

'Mr Mac thought I had promise. Put me together with Rose and Violet. The rest is history.'

He fished in his breast pocket for a cigarette. 'Do you have a sweetheart, Joan?'

Here we go, she thought. She didn't want his advances, didn't want to encourage him. Why was he picking on her? 'Yes,' she said. 'As a matter of fact I do.'

'And what does he think of you gallivanting round Germany?' His words were muffled as he lit the cigarette, holding it between his lips.

'He doesn't think anything,' Joan said. 'He's an American.'

'And they don't think?'

'He's not here,' Joan said. It sounded pathetic, and she should have told the truth. He hadn't come back. How long do you wait for the return of a soldier? Auntie Win said best forget him, accept the worst. She'd written three times since the war ended to the commandant at the base in Lakenheath, and six times before that, but he'd never replied. He could be dead, but she knew in her gut he was still alive. Wounded. Normandy. She could see him in a wheelchair, legs amputated. *Half a man? I could never make you happy, Joan.* His wife would have divorced him.

'What's his name, this Yankee soldier boy of yours?'

She broke from her dreams, hesitated. It was none of Reg's business. On the other hand, you never know, he might just have come across him. He was a singer, after all.

'Michael,' she said. 'Michael O'Doyle. Do you know him?'

He shook his head.

'And you?' she said. 'Do you have a sweetheart? Or are you married?'

'As a matter of fact,' Reg said. 'I am. Married.'

'Well,' Joan said. 'Let's hope you keep it that way.'

They sat in silence, bones jarring on the hard benches as the truck swerved and bumped on the scarred roads.

'*Sweet-hearted Lil*,' Reg began to sing. '*Just fits the bill*.' Joan took in a breath, looked at him. '*For the girl I'd like to love*.' He smiled at her. She breathed in, a horrid flush rushing up her neck and onto her cheeks. This was too awkward, too embarrassing. He shifted in his seat, winked at her. 'So,' Reg said. 'Lillie with two Ells. Weren't you in *Blighty Parade* last month? Pin-up of the month?'

Joan held her breath, wanting the bench to swallow her, the lorry to stop, the show to be cancelled. The embarrassment. She'd never wanted to do it in the first place and now here she was, face to face with someone who recognised her.

'It's a magazine, for servicemen,' Mr Mac had said. 'Did as much for morale as Vera Lynn. Mainly humorous. Wholesome stuff. Nothing sleazy.' He winked. 'Think Rita Hayworth. Think Joan Crawford. And you. Our very own Lillie Pettall with her film star looks.' He stuck his hand in his pocket, pulled out a cigarette and walked past, giving her a tap on the bottom as he went. 'Give it a go, there's a good girl. Great publicity. You can wear your hula costume.'

'No need to feel embarrassed,' Reg was saying, smiling. He had a nice smile, Joan would give him that. 'It was a beautiful picture. Now…' He pulled out a sheet of paper from his pocket, and unfolded it. 'I've got a new song I'd like you all to do.'

'Oh?' Rose said. 'I think you'll have to run this past Mr Mac.'

'I have,' Reg said. 'Before we left. And he agreed, it's just the ticket for this tour. Called "Ravens in the Tower". Nice victory song.' He squinted. 'Rehearsal tomorrow after lunch.'

'I thought we had the day off,' Rose said.

'Day off? You're in bloody ENSA, not SiB. Now, change to tonight's running order. You'll end with the Hawaii number.'

§

'They've lost our bleeding costumes,' Violet said in the interval.

'Don't be daft,' Rose said. 'They're here somewhere. I counted them all on.'

'The trunk's not here.' Joan said, looking around.

'It can't have gone AWOL,' Rose said. 'I know it was on the lorry.' She leaned over a trunk, as if the missing one was hiding behind. 'Mr Mac will kill me,' she said. 'How can it have gone missing?' She stood in the middle of the tent, scratching her head, face furrowed.

'Knock, knock. It's me. Reg.'

'We're changing,' Violet said. 'Go away.'

'Do you need help?'

'Piss off,' Violet said. She lowered her voice so only Rose and Joan could hear. 'Dirty bugger.'

They heard him laugh. 'Are you missing anything?'

Rose poked her head around the tarpaulin. 'Yes. One of our trunks, with our costumes. All the Hawaii ones.'

'Then I reckon you'll have to do that number in the altogether,' Reg said. 'Don't you?'

'I'm going to write to Mr Mac,' Rose said. 'We don't put up with that kind of talk.'

'Matter of fact,' Reg said, 'my boys have just got a load of grass skirts they don't know what to do with. Any use to you?'

They could hear him laughing, and the others too. The whole band.

'You did this on purpose, didn't you?' Rose said. 'Give 'em here.'

'Come and get them.'

'You go away first.'

'Okay. Don't be late,' he said. 'Chickety snitch.'

'Bastard,' Rose said.

They could hear the band begin, the first bars of 'Jungle Drums'. The audience grew quiet.

'Let him wait.'

They could see Reg craning his neck for sight of them. They stood, immobile, behind the set so he had to repeat the piece, twice.

'Ready?' Rose said. Clambered up onto the stage, swirling their skirts and swinging their hips, as the boys whooped and whistled and Reg had to play the tune again for the third time. And a fourth. The boys wouldn't let it drop. They'd never had a response like this. 'Well done,' Rose whispered through unmoving lips. They stood, drinking in the acclaim, chests rising and falling, catching their breath.

There was a change of tempo and they felt the mood calm, the men settle. Joan stepped forward, held the microphone stand, waiting for the introduction, for Reg's signal.

'Blue Hawaii', their song of love and yearning and loss. Enough to bring a tear to the eye.

§

She lost track of time. A week here, days there, on the road. Detmold, Gütersloh, Münster. Late August gave way to September. Hamburg, Hannover. October, and with it a cold, eastern wind. Minden, Osnabrück, Paderborn. There was a farewell party in

Berlin, enough champagne to float a ship. Joan and the others didn't bother to change out of the evening dresses they'd worn for the last number, came straight back to the mess.

She was sad the tour had ended. Rose and Violet had taken her mind off things. Was it in Gütersloh that Rose had tied one end of a string to her toe and dangled the other end out of the window so Charlie could tug it with the all-clear? They used to laugh, Rose in bed with her clothes on, sneaking away at the signal, turning up for rehearsals next morning, all butter-wouldn't-melt. Rose was game for anything. There was strength in numbers with the girls.

A fire burned in the grate, the wood smoking and spitting, filling the room with the scent of larch and birch. The logs were too green, she could have told them that.

'Penny for them?' Reg sidled up to her, a bottle of champagne in one hand. He tilted it towards her glass, began to pour, missing so it trickled down her fingers. 'Sorry.' He pulled out his handker-chief, dabbed her fingers dry. 'So, Two Ells,' he said. He picked up his glass, held up his hands, bottle in one, glass in the other. He was slurring his words. 'Truth is, Two Ells is my special name for you. I don't mean any harm by it. Now…' He took a gulp of champagne. His uniform was dishevelled, the top button of his shirt open. He'd taken off his tie, shoved it in his pocket so the tail hung over the flap. Mr Mac would have had a fit. 'It's a bit noisy here for my liking,' he said, squinting round the room. 'Let's go into the billiard room. I've got a proposition to put to you.'

Whatever it was, she didn't want to hear it. She wished he'd go away, pester someone else. If necessary, she'd say goodnight, she had to get up early in the morning, which was true. Still, she followed him. The billiard room was shadowy, dim lights over the green baize of the table. He took another gulp of champagne, topped up his glass, held it towards her.

'Dutch courage.'

She had a horrid feeling he was about to propose to her, even though he was married already. She'd given him no encouragement. She swirled her drink in the glass, watching the tiny bubbles swim to the surface. 'Go on then,' she said. 'Get it over with.'

'Anyone ever said you're an ice maiden?'' he said. 'Hoity-toity?'

'I've had enough, Reg.' She turned to go. He skipped ahead of her.

'I didn't want to say anything before now.' His voice had sobered, become businesslike. 'But we heard today. It's all settled.' He beamed.

She kept her mouth shut. He was frowning at her, bewildered. Good, Joan thought. Don't take me for granted.

'Look, Joan, can we just go and sit over there?' He waved the bottle at two easy chairs by the empty fireplace.

She nodded, walked towards them, the hem of her dress flapping cold round her ankles. She'd be glad to take it off. She hated the feel of rayon, its clutch on her skin.

He placed the bottle and his glass down and pulled the chair close for her. 'Right,' he said, taking out his cigarettes and offering one to her.

She shook her head. *No thanks.*

'The thing is, we get demobbed in a couple of weeks. Me, Charlie, Roy and the boys.'

She raised an eyebrow. Was this all he had to tell her? She'd spent the last few months singing to demob-happy soldiers, she knew what they had to say. 'That'll be nice,' she said. 'See your wife again. You must be looking forward to that.'

Reg shifted in his seat. 'Oh, I am, Joan. I am.' He reached over and grabbed an ashtray from the console table behind him.

'What's more,' Reg went on, 'we're going professional. Me and the lads. The Lancasters. People know us.'

Joan looked at him, not sure why he was telling her that. They'd have to get a new band, that was true, unless Mr Mac had other ideas.

'Does that mean you're done with ENSA?'

'ENSA's finished anyway,' Reg said.

'What?' She breathed in, held her hands to her stomach as if he'd punched her, made a hole in her solar plexus. She'd be out of a job. All of them. The Petal Sisters. She'd thought ENSA would go on and on. There were still soldiers, after all. They needed entertaining. She hadn't given a thought about the future. None of them had.

'Something else will take its place,' Reg said waving his hand as if it were a wand, his voice airy, meaningless. 'The thing is...' He sidled forward so his knees touched hers. 'The thing is, Joan, the boys and I, we'd like to invite you to be our vocalist.'

Joan took a moment to register what he was saying. 'All of us?' she said. 'The Petal Sisters?'

'No.' Reg shook his head. 'Just you.'

'But that would mean breaking us up,' she said. 'I'm not sure I could do that.'

'Perhaps I'm speaking out of turn,' Reg said. He stubbed out his cigarette and a sliver of smoke curled after it. 'But it seems to me that Rose and Violet may not be so loyal to the Petal Sisters if it's a choice between them and marriage. Besides,' he added, 'there's a cherry on the cake.'

She shook her head.

'Richard Parnell. Ever heard of him?' He didn't wait for her answer. 'Biggest music publisher in Tin Pan Alley. He's accepted "Ravens in the Night" and some of my other little ditties.'

'But that is good news,' Joan said, and she meant it. 'Congratulations.'

'What it means is this, Joan.' He had begun slurring again, but Joan thought perhaps he deserved to be drunk now. He'd fought in the war, he'd entertained the men, and now he was going to be famous. 'Parnell feeds material to HMV. That means a record.'

'Even better news,' Joan said. 'You must be thrilled.'

'I am,' he said. 'And I want you.'

'What do you mean?'

'I want you to be the singer.'

'Make a record?' Joan knew she sounded silly, but this was overwhelming, like being caught on the path as a dyke burst its bank.

'Yes.'

She slumped in her chair, playing with the stem of her glass. 'Golly,' she said.

He pushed himself off the table, grabbing the bottle once more. 'Think about it.'

'We're going home tomorrow.'

'I know. That's why I popped the question.' He grinned.

'Yes,' she said. Didn't think. 'What's the record? "Ravens in the Tower"?'

He shook his head. 'The Petals will do it, but without you.'

'Without me?' she said. She grabbed the arms of her chair, stood up, lurching forward. 'They can't. Don't I get a say in this?'

'You're a star, Joan,' he said, signing with his hand, *sit down, calm down*. 'Not a bit-part harmony singer. I've got something far bigger lined up for you.' He fished inside his jacket, pulled out a sheet of music. '"Sweet-hearted Bill".'

She took the music, read the lyrics. Reg had composed this song for her. 'Sweet-hearted Lil', only he'd turned it round, made it a little joke between themselves. The lyrics wouldn't be so hard to learn and they fitted the music, so that made it easier. Mnemonics. That was the word Reg had used once. Music and words, dancing together. The song was light-hearted and serious at the same time. Women in love. Not just frivolity. Happiness depended on the right man. Did Reg understand that? She shut her eyes.

'Solo billing,' he said. 'And we've got a season at the Dorchester for starters. I've listed you as Lillie Pettall,' he said. 'Doubled your Ells and added a Tee.'

She laughed.

'And how does £400 up front sound to you, Joan?'

Four hundred pounds. That was a lot of money. The adrenaline drained from her, knees all wobbly and stomach churning. A fortune. She couldn't imagine it, that much money. She got eight pounds a week with ENSA, and this was fifty times as much. She could buy a little flat for herself and Auntie Win and still send money to her mother for Kathleen. 'Oh,' she said. 'Yes.'

'See,' Reg said. 'A big fat one-off payment, half when you sign the contract, half when the record's released. Share of takings at the Dorchester. That's big, Joan. Big.' He paused, smiled, walked towards her, his lips twisted, sharp canines, a wolf on the prowl.

'There's just one thing.' He smirked, leaning over, lifting her skirt, cold fingers on her inner thigh, walking upwards.

KATHLEEN

Cambridge, Massachusetts: May 1970

Kathleen knew that writing. She picked up her knife, wiped off the butter, slit open the envelope and pulled out the contents. There was a card with a large silvered horseshoe, GOOD LUCK! in pink glitter glued in its centre and inside, in green ink, *To Kathleen. Best of luck. Love, Joan xxx.* There was a slip of paper attached, a typed note.

> *My new address: 47 Victoria Mansions, Maida Vale, West London. Telephone: 01 328 4550.*

Perhaps her sister had settled down finally. Found a good man, a nice place to live. She must have been round the world several times, though she'd never lost her knack for remembering Kathleen at the right occasion. She propped the card on the windowsill for Susan to see and poured herself another cup of coffee, eyeing her dissertation at the end of the kitchen table, her name embossed on its spine.

'How're you feeling?' Susan wore a face pack, talked without moving her lips. She'd worn one every day for the last week, came into breakfast with her face stiff with egg white and cucumber. 'For my skin,' she said. 'It's terrible.'

Susan had had her viva five days ago, passed with flying colours, been offered a tenure-track position in epidemiology at UCLA.

She and Kathleen had prepared together, read each other's theses, staged mock vivas, alternating, good cop, bad cop.

'How am I feeling?' Kathleen said. 'Scared shitless.'

'Flutter your lashes,' Susan said. 'Cross and uncross your legs.' She lifted her hand, kissed her fingers, blew, bedroom eyes, half closed.

'Stop it,' Kathleen said.

'Gloria Steinem was a bunny girl once, you know that?'

'Your face mask is cracking,' Kathleen said. 'And I have to go.' She picked up Joan's card, waved it at Susan. 'From my big sister,' she said. 'I don't believe in lucky omens, but…' She lifted her dissertation from the end of the table. *Inherited Differences in Antibody Production in Mice.* She'd been over it again and again, marked the pages of particular importance and memorised her data. Still, however much she told herself she knew her thesis backwards, the same could also be said of the defence committee, who would have gone over it with a fine-tooth comb, and though she knew all the members, any one of them could prove a wild card.

She tucked Joan's letter into the pages of the thesis and took one final look at herself in the hall mirror. She'd bought a suit for her defence, pale blue with a loose jacket, skirt just above her knees, as Susan had said not to look like a hippy. Or a radical. 'Camouflage,' she'd said. 'Guerrilla feminism.'

Kathleen had tied her long blonde hair into a ponytail and pinned it with a black velvet bow. She made sure her fringe wasn't sticking up, spitting on her fingers and damping it down on her forehead to be on the safe side, and set off, four years and ten months to the day since she'd first enrolled.

§

'Well, *Doctor* Spalding,' Professor Chuck Fryxal said, taking her elbow, escorting her out of the examination room. 'I must congratulate you again, personally.'

Kathleen's cheeks glowed hot, her breath light and airy. 'Thank you,' she said, clutching her thesis tight to her chest. 'It hasn't sunk in yet.'

'For the committee to recommend the award without a single amendment,' Professor Fryxal said, letting out a low whistle, 'is unheard of.'

She was unsure what to say, scared to open her mouth in case she started to cry, tears of relief and happiness. Would it look conceited if she nodded? She wanted to let her hair down, leapfrog over the benches in Harvard Yard, whoop down Massachusetts Avenue, jump into the Charles River and fling her arms wide. *I've done it. Me. Kathleen Spalding. BSc (Oxon), PhD (Harvard).*

'Especially for a woman,' he added. Kathleen was tempted to answer back, but he was a powerful man and she wasn't yet sure of her position, even though she and Susan had vowed to call out sexism at every opportunity.

'I must thank you for all the help you've given me, as my adviser,' she said instead, her voice prim and polite and very English. 'You've been such a support.'

He laughed. Most Americans she knew had perfectly spaced teeth, but his were crooked, slightly yellow. She guessed he was of an age before orthodontics were common. 'You know? When I first saw you in my grad class, the only girl among all those men, I thought you were just here to find a husband. It took me a while to take you seriously.'

Kathleen knew this was a put-down and not a compliment. If he carried on, she'd find it hard to contain a rebuke.

'But once I did, well…' He paused. 'You have a very fine brain there, Kathleen.'

She smiled without opening her mouth. She'd shriek if she did.

'Let me take you to dinner tonight,' he said. 'To celebrate, and to talk about your career. There's a couple of opportunities that might interest you. What do you say?'

She'd been thinking of applying for the position she'd seen advertised at University College, London, but if Professor Fryxal had in mind something at Harvard, well, hell, she'd take that any time. Or perhaps there was a postdoc at MIT.

'I took the liberty of booking a table at L'Escargot,' he went on. 'Corner of Quincy and Cambridge.'

She and Susan had planned to go to Club Passim in the Square, whatever the result of her viva. But her adviser trumped her best friend at times like these. Susan would understand, would do the same if the boot was on the other foot, despite the vows of sisterhood.

'Thank you, yes, I'd like that.'

'Wonderful. There's a couple of articles I'd like you to see too,' he said. 'But I have them at home, not the office. So why don't you call by my house? It's not out of your way. Say five thirty? You remember the address?'

'Yes,' she said. He stopped, held out his hand, and she clasped it.

'You'll go far,' he said. 'Congratulations again.'

He turned towards the subway, back to the Med School in Boston.

Kathleen half ran, half walked to their apartment, swallowing gulps of excitement, wanting to cry and laugh and scream to the world. She let herself in, rushed to the kitchen, hoping Susan would be sitting there, look up, *well?* The place was empty. Susan had left her plate and glass on the table, a cardinal sin they'd both agreed, early on, never to do. 'More room-mates fall out over slovenly habits,' Susan had declared at the start, 'than from any other known cause, including stealing a boyfriend.'

Kathleen checked her watch. Of course. Susan would be at work, waitressing until she took up her post in a couple of months. She must have left in a hurry, wiping off the face mask at the last minute if the soiled pads of cotton wool on the draining board were anything to go by. Kathleen picked up the plate, placed it in the sink, a mundane chore that brought her down to earth, deflating her for a second. She took out some juice from the fridge, gulped it from the carton, not bothering with a glass. Two could be sluts.

She went into her bedroom, slipped out of her suit, pulled off her nylons. It was too hot for them, but the viva was formal and it wouldn't have done to attend with bare legs. She lay back on her bed, letting the breeze from the fan cool her body, the air brush her thighs and stomach. She shut her eyes, reliving the questions, her answers. Thank goodness she'd prepared. She countered every challenge, made some of her own, discussed plans for further research, a publication programme. It couldn't have gone better. She breathed out, smiled and pushed herself off the bed, heading for the bathroom, taking off her underwear and tucking her hair into a shower cap. The tiles were cracked, and mould grew in the grouting. They'd given up complaining to their landlord, and the pump was sluggish but the water was cool as it ran across her shoulders and down her back. She turned, feeling the spray on her face, fine rain on her skin, grabbing the soap and lathering up her loofah, feeling the sweat evaporate, her flesh tingle, scented and clean. She stepped out of the shower, wrapped the towel round her and padded to the bedroom.

Dr Spalding. She should send Joan a telegram. That's all it need say. *Dr Spalding*. Miss Loughton too. She wished Susan would come home. Perhaps she'd have time to call by her work, pop her head through the door, give her a thumbs up. She checked her watch. Susan would have to wait, otherwise she'd run late. She fished out clean underwear, fingered through her clothes hanging in the closet. She'd never been to L'Escargot but it was posh, more than she and Susan could ever afford as grad students. Club Passim was their limit, and then only occasionally.

The little black dress.

'Sure you need one,' Susan had said, turning her nose up at Kathleen's purple Mary Quant frock, which Joan had handed down to her, leading her by the hand into Filene's in Boston on their second day at grad school. 'For all the cocktail parties.'

She'd worn it to every single one, but it was a nice dress, well cut, sleeveless with a scoop neck, short but not too short. The fabric was good, too. Silk dupion, the shop assistant had said, reading the label. Dry clean only. It shimmered, lustres of blue and green, like oil on water. She pulled it on, went back to the bathroom, hanging her towel on the rack, peering into the mirror and reapplying her mascara, mouth open, tongue out in concentration. Perhaps, she thought, a little eyeshadow too. She searched through her make-up bag, pulled out the sky blue, dabbed it on. Perfume? Susan wouldn't mind if Kathleen borrowed a little of hers. She untied her ponytail, shook her hair out, brushed it straight. She'd wear it down, as she usually did, what Susan called her Françoise Hardy look.

Kathleen rummaged at the bottom of her closet, pulled out her smart black platform sandals, slipped them on and stood back from the mirror. Not bad, she thought. At least she didn't look like a student, or not too much like one, smart enough for somewhere swanky like L'Escargot.

She changed her purse to match her shoes. She'd become American, she thought, purse indeed. Returned to the kitchen, found the envelope Joan's card had come in and wrote on the back:

> *So sorry. Going to have to stand you up tonight. Fryxal is giving me dinner to talk about jobs. Can't throw a chance like that up. Sure you understand. Let's do it tomorrow. Kathleen xxx PS I passed! No amendments!! PPS The treat's on me. PPPS Hope you don't mind, borrowed your Estée.*

She checked she had her keys, money, tissues and a small tin of Vaseline for her lips. It was an awful habit that, rubbing on Vaseline to keep them smooth and plump. Her mother had thin, tight lips and Kathleen dreaded hers becoming the same, even though she knew she'd inherited her mouth from the other side of the family. Funny the way genes came out in the wash. Still, you couldn't be too careful. She shut the door, double-locked it and headed off to Professor Fryxal's house. She'd been there several times before. He and his wife always gave a summer party for his grad students, and a smaller party in the winter between Thanksgiving and Christmas for the doctoral students. His wife was an art dealer and the house was full of paintings and ceramics, with exquisite antique furniture too fine and fragile to sit on.

There was something homely about American streets, Kathleen thought, wandering into Hilliard, looking at the clapboard houses and the white picket fences with their tidy front lawns and shady trees. Some of the grass had turned yellow from an unexpected early-summer heatwave where the sprinklers had been turned off, and the leaves of the trees were a dark, rich green, making the most of the season and photosynthesis. Chloroplasts in the palisade cells, drinking in the light, turning it into energy. She still had a love affair with natural science, basking in its beauty, delving into its secrets.

Dr Kathleen Spalding. Miss Loughton would be so proud. Kathleen owed everything to her, taking her in and digging out bursaries and scholarships.

She walked up Professor Fryxal's path, flagstones set in the lawn. She wasn't aware of a postdoc vacancy at Harvard, but he would know of others elsewhere. Johns Hopkins perhaps, MIT. Stanford. A stint in California would be nice. She'd been there once for a conference and liked the campus with its cloisters and palm trees, built like a Spanish monastery. She crossed her bag over her body, tugged down her skirt and rang the doorbell.

Professor Fryxal opened the door. 'Ah, Kathleen.'

'You were expecting me?' He'd sounded surprised to see her. 'You did mean today?' Had she got the wrong day, made a faux pas? The fear hurtled through her mind, plummeting into her stomach.

'Of course, of course.' He beckoned her in. 'I was delayed at the office, I've just got home. Would you mind if I changed quickly?' He crossed the hallway, towards the sitting room. 'Wait in here. I won't be long. I'll bring the articles down with me. I'm sorry Mrs Fryxal isn't here. She's had to go to her sister's unexpectedly. Make yourself at home.'

Kathleen nodded, the heels of her platforms echoing on the polished parquet floor. She'd never been here in daylight. The summer parties were always in the garden, and in winter this room was lit by spotlights trained on the art and the soft glow from the table lamps on the consoles round the wall. There were big, glossy books on the coffee table in front of a sofa and a large crystal ashtray. She was suddenly tired, as if the energy of the day had evaporated. She shut her eyes, breathed long and deep and hard, had a pang of homesickness so sudden and so deep she felt she could never rise again. And yet, apart from Joan, who was there to tell?

She'd never been so happy.

Enough.

She blinked her eyes open and looked around her. She didn't know anything about art, but she was sure everything in this room was original. She'd never really been able to look at it before, there'd been too many people. There was a striking painting over the fireplace, a woman with her body formed like a large letter S, a river of a shape. The face was in profile, but one eye rested above the other. Kathleen peered up at the signature in the top right-hand corner. Picasso. She had no idea people could have Picassos in their own homes. She thought only museums and art galleries could afford them, or should afford them. Wasn't art for everyone? It felt inappropriate, uncomfortable, to be cheek by jowl with privilege like this, and although Mrs Fryxal had never been anything but hospitable, Kathleen suddenly resented her, felt out of her depth.

On the console table to the right of the fireplace were two plates displayed on holders, a bird painted in thick black lines on each, one with a worm in its mouth. She wondered if they were Picasso too, had no doubt they were valuable. Why else display a plate, if it wasn't worth something? She could hear the shower running in a distant part of the house. On the console table to the left of the fireplace was a ceramic head with a large handle on the top, like a fancy hairdo. She wondered whether Mrs Fryxal liked this art, or whether she liked it because she could buy it. None of it was beautiful. She reached over and ran her fingers across its face, feeling the crust of the painted features, gazing at its shape. Someone had sculpted that, moulded the clay and made the indentations, rubbing their thumbs across its surface, taking a brush and choosing the colours, smoothing the skin, and for a brief second she could understand what made art *art*.

'Do you like it?'

She jumped, turned. Professor Fryxal was rearing up beside her. She hadn't heard him enter the room, come behind her, wearing nothing but a bathrobe, standing so close she smelled the soap, saw drops of water glisten on his blonde hair, fair bristles in his nostrils, the lines in his face. She stepped back but the console table blocked her way. She gasped, tried to lift her hands to push him away, but his arms had encircled her, forcing her own tight to her side.

'You're lovely,' he said, pressing himself against her, nuzzling her neck, biting it.

She yelped, felt the firm bulge of his genitals, his fingers rucking her skirt, thrusting their way between her legs. Blood was coursing through her body, she was light-headed, muddled, limbs flimsy as reeds. Her adviser. She breathed hard, mustering strength, shoving and shoving him away, but he was holding her too tight, crushing her, crashing over her, through her. She heard herself screaming. *No, no, no.*

He forced his mouth against hers, his fat tongue rummaging inside. He was tugging at her pants. 'Tell me you want this.' She tried to wriggle free but he had pinned her to his body, lifting her off her feet, throwing her back onto the sofa, smashing on top of her, her cries muffled by his mouth, eyes stinging with tears and fear.

'Chuck!'

He slackened his hold, enough for Kathleen to push him hard to one side. He stood up and she jumped free of him. Mrs Fryxal. Kathleen had only ever seen her in gracious hostess mode, but here she stood like a harridan, her face red and livid. She strode towards her husband, marched past him, raised her arm and slapped Kathleen across the face. 'Slut,' she said. 'Get out of my house.'

Kathleen's cheek smarted, blood rushing to the surface. 'No,' she said. 'No, it wasn't like that. I didn't, I…'

Professor Fryxal stood, his eyes narrowed, glowering, his bathrobe tied tightly around him. Whatever she said, he'd deny it, she could see that, claim she threw herself at him, he was fighting her off, had had to fend off her advances for years. He'd say she'd pulled him on top of her.

She rushed to the door, leapt out of the house, tore down the street, heels twisting as she ran, wiping her mouth with the back of her hand, knees buckling as she staggered down Mount Auburn, into Dunster. She stopped at their apartment building, fumbling for her keys, let herself in the main entrance, down the stairs to the basement apartment. Music. Susan was home. She rushed into the kitchen and spreadeagled herself, face down, across the kitchen table.

JOAN

London: April 2006

Harry had been pressing her to accept his invitation to make the film. She should trust Harry, trust his judgement on the documentary, but some instinct kept her stonewalling, some spectre from her past. Lies, lurking in the shadows, playing dead. *Here I am, Lillie Pettall, this is my front, this is my facade. Hiding in plain sight.*

She hadn't heard anything more from this Steve Kingsman character, though she found herself checking the balcony was clear when she left, or entered, her flat. He'd said he wanted to meet her. Why? Was Queenie ill? Was she dead? She breathed out. *Please let her be dead.* Queenie still had the power to conjure up a night terror, make her sweat in the early hours of the morning when problems became fiery hounds with bloodied fangs. Yet she didn't regret a thing, not a single thing.

She booked an appointment at the hairdresser for two o'clock. Pensioners enjoyed a 15% discount on a Wednesday and although Joan could manage manicures, and she could still reach down and paint her toenails, a cut and blow-dry was beyond her. It was years since she'd been to a salon. Perhaps a new style would suit her, a makeover, a word she'd picked up from *What Not to Wear* on the television. There had been an advert in the local undertaker's for a funeral prepayment plan but what had caught her attention was the model, a woman her age, hair cropped into an elegant pixie cut, short, like a boy. Joan thought that would suit her, make her look younger.

Harry was taking her to the Chelsea Arts Club. He persuaded her that this would be a preliminary chat, a prelude to what to expect if she agreed to do the film. A *business* meeting, he'd stressed. Not a date.

She wore Kathleen's hand-me-down black cashmere jumper over a pair of black slacks, brought it all to life with a rhinestone brooch in the shape of a peacock. It had taken some rummaging in her jewellery box to find it, but it was there along with other signature pieces she'd worn over the years, dress rings, diamante earrings. She touched her hair. It felt strange, light, as if she'd been sheared, but she liked it. What was the word? Gamine. A gamine look. She could tell from the way Harry looked at her that he approved.

The club had hardly changed from the time when she was a member. It looked just as shabby, the oak tables and chairs pockmarked and stained, the walls crowded with paintings. The billiard table was still in the centre of the room, balls and cues resting on its baize, which looked as though it had been recently refurbished. She used to love this place, home from home, safe and secure.

'Now,' Harry said, 'I'm not a youngster. I don't have to prove myself. There's nothing to it. Just relax in the chair and we'll have a little chat.'

'I'm not sure I have anything to say,' Joan said, looking at Harry, this new lover of hers. She'd told him very little about her life, heads on the pillow, *one time, when I was young…* She was seeing a different side to him now, his professional, business side. 'What do you want to know?'

'The low-down on the Petal Sisters,' he said. 'The break-up. Your solo career. Thoughts on the industry, how it changed. Tin Pan Alley. Anything and everything.' He paused. 'I may not use all of it. But I prefer to work with too much than too little.'

She smiled. 'I can understand that,' she said. 'I always had more songs prepared than I could ever use.'

He'd ordered a bottle of champagne and the barman brought it over, two flutes, stems wedged between his fingers. He flipped his hand, released the glasses onto the table and, with a flourish, popped the cork and poured. Joan watched as the bubbles rose and subsided. It was a long time since she'd had champagne, had sat in this bar, louche Sundays when she wasn't working.

'Of course,' he went on, 'it's up to you. No pressure. But the Petal Sisters, and you. So iconic.' He lifted his glass, tilted it towards her. 'To you, Joan.' Added, 'To us.'

She took a sip. She never drank in the day now, was out of training.

'I mean, you were the bridgehead, the first British girl band,' Harry went on. 'From swing to ballads. And then – what? What happened to your career? What turns did it take? That's the sort of thing I want to know.'

She picked up her glass, swirled the champagne, put it back on the table. She could so easily slip, say something she'd regret. She could walk away, should never have agreed even to just this. Harry was too gung-ho about it, and Joan had been caught up in his excitement, didn't stop to think.

'Are you all right?' Harry said. 'You look as if you're about to walk to the gallows.'

'Sorry,' she said. 'I'm just nervous. I don't know whether I can talk sense.'

'Relax,' he said. 'I'll be the judge of that.' He smiled, leaned back in his chair, held up his hands, palms facing her. 'You don't have to tell me anything you don't want. You're in charge here. It's your story.' His voice was soft and smooth, had a reassuring lull about it. 'But I'd like to build up a picture of you, where you came from, what drove you. The *real* Lillie Pettall.' He smiled. 'I'm not trying to trick you, or test you. Or probe into your secrets. But people will be interested in where you came from.' He leaned forward, his knees edging close to her, reached for her hand, brushing it with his thumb. 'You have a big fan club out there. And they'd like to know.'

She shut her eyes, breathing in, seeing again the lie of the fen, the dykes and the wetlands, the treachery of the will-o'-the-wisps, the howls of Old Shuck with his fiery eye. Portents of death, every one.

And Kathleen. She thought of Kathleen.

'Are you all right, Joan?' Harry said, letting go of her hand, brushing her cheek with the back of his fingers, his forehead creased in concern.

'Can you give me a minute?' She pushed herself up from her seat, walked out of the door and into the ladies, bolting herself into one of the cubicles. It was the champagne, made her melancholy. She squeezed her eyes, holding back the tears, overwhelmed by a deluge of loss.

The door of the toilets opened and she heard someone call, 'Joan, are you all right?'

Her knees felt weak. She pulled down the seat on the toilet, sat on it.

Queenie. Dear God. It wasn't Kathleen. It was Queenie.

'Just the collywobbles. I'll be out in a minute.'

Breathe deep. Years of training. She felt the blood that had drained from her head flood its way back, flushing her cheeks. She unbolted the cubicle door, washed her hands, touched up her lipstick, ran her fingers through her new haircut, pulled herself tall, stepped back into the bar.

'Sorry,' she said. 'I don't know what came over me. Where were we?'

KATHLEEN

Los Angeles: April 2006

They were caught in a stampede of heavy freight trucks on the interstate, bellowing and thundering, wedging them in, front, back, either side. Any minute, Kathleen thought, the beasts would heave over and trample them to dust. Susan was driving, her jaw taut, her hands white-knuckled on the steering wheel. It was almost impossible to talk above the din. Not that Kathleen wanted to. She needed time to muster her nerves.

'So you're back with David,' Susan said, her voice raised above the clamour. 'How's that going to work?'

'With difficulty,' Kathleen said. 'Long-distance. Like monarch butterflies.'

The scrub at the side of the highway began to give way to low-rise buildings, eateries with heavy signage, motels, fuel stations. Susan signalled right, manoeuvring the car through the trucks and the roar of their klaxons. Kathleen shut her eyes, opened them once the noise had calmed into the six-lane fast-moving madness of Route 66. Main Street.

'All together now. A one, a two.' Susan clicked her fingers with one hand. 'A one, two, three.' She began to belt out the lyrics, eyeing Kathleen as she sang. 'Come on, honey,' she said. 'It'll get your mind off it. Singing's good for you. It's meditation. Makes you light-headed. Those medieval nuns were on to that with their chanting. Way better than weed.'

Kathleen smiled. Her mind was blank anyway, a numb, white noise of anxiety and excitement.

'From the beginning,' Susan yelled above the traffic. She knew most of the words, *da-di-da*'ed where she stumbled, tapping the rhythm on the wheel.

The song had been a big hit just before Kathleen had started at Oxford, when the horizons she'd dreamed of had become encased in spires which pointed to the stars, a land of innocence and certainty. And now here she was, driving to meet her father in his house in Barstow. He'd 'misreckoned' the dates, he told her, perhaps he could 'assist in her enquiries'. His voice had been husky, but he no longer wheezed. 'Only the doctors have told me not to drive. I'm eighty-five,' he'd added. 'So you'll have to come to me.'

'No way are you doing that by yourself,' Susan said. 'Are you crazy? Meet a total stranger, alone?'

That wasn't the reason Kathleen had agreed Susan could come with her. She needed someone who would hold her hand, hold her close.

'Barstow's a dump,' Susan said. 'Pitsville. Trucks and locomotives and fuck all else. Not a tree in sight.'

Bun Boy Restaurant, Motel 66, Danny's Restaurant, El Rancho Motel, *Vacancy*. There was a sign to the Western America Railroad Museum and another to the Route 66 Museum. This was not a town she wished to linger in, wondered what Michael O'Doyle was doing here. Joan had said he was a singer, wrote poems. She couldn't imagine what could feed his imagination in this place, what would inspire him.

'Read me the directions,' Susan said. 'I printed them off MapQuest. They're in the glove compartment.'

The house was modest, in an arid street of whitewashed bungalows with bare, loose stone yards and chain-link fences. One or two had basketball nets screwed to the walls of the garages, and a couple had trees that grew skewed and stunted. The place was clean, Kathleen thought, she'd say that for it. People in this street cared for their neighbourhood.

A school was opposite the house and next to it was a small park where the grass grew in tufts and the shrubs were grey and dusty. Susan stopped the car. They looked at the house, at the empty driveway, at the barren yard and the telegraph wires that stretched across it. She reached for Kathleen's hand. 'How d'you feel?'

'Terrified,' Kathleen said. 'Angry, too.' She let go of Susan's hand, turned her own over, tracing the lines on her palm. 'I'm telling myself to expect nothing.' She pressed her thumb into her palm, watching the blood drain, the flesh turn white. 'He rejected me.' She released her thumb, observed as the blood flooded back across the plain of her hand. 'But I want him. I want him to love me.'

'He may not be your father,' Susan said. 'He'll need to do a paternity test.'

'What if he won't do that?'

'Let's cross that when we come to it,' Susan said. 'You know, you're under no obligation to like the man.'

'I know,' Kathleen said, taking a deep breath, opening the car door. 'Let's go.'

There was a small porch in the front of the house with a couple of white plastic chairs and a table on which sat a small vase of artificial flowers that had faded in the harsh desert light. Kathleen thought of Joan's flat and its own bouquet of fake blooms, generous and vibrant on the kitchen table.

'I'll wait here,' Susan said. 'Guard the car, and your back.'

Kathleen could hear the muted roar of the freeway and the distant rumble of a train. Trucks and locomotives. She nodded, rang the doorbell, chimes echoing inside as if the house was hollow. Michael was a large man, she was sure, struggling for oxygen to prime his clogged arteries. A slow, clumsy man, fleshy. Would she be able to see herself in him, features reflecting her own? She didn't look remotely like Joan, or any of her brothers. *Uncles.*

The door opened and a small, wiry man reached forward and slid back the screen door. She hadn't been expecting him to look like this.

'Michael O'Doyle?' Kathleen said, searching for a connection.

He smiled. 'Are you Kathleen?'

'May I come in?' Kathleen said. There was a Zimmer frame by the opened door.

'I guess so,' Michael said. 'Who's she?'

'A friend,' Kathleen said.

'I'll just wait here,' Susan said, giving Michael her East Coast smile with its air of gracious condescension.

He turned and entered the house, leaning on his walker. Kathleen stepped behind him. The door entered directly into a sitting room, tidy, airy, a stone fireplace at the far end, two easy chairs against the wall on one side of it and, between them, a coffee table with a lace runner. Opposite, a grey sofa with two ruched cushions. The floor was grey faux wood and the walls a similar colour, their blankness broken by a reproduction Hopper print that sat crooked on its nail and a single wedding photo. A large television was in the corner, images flashing.

'Track and field,' he said. 'Indoor Championships. You interested?'

'I haven't been in America long enough,' she said, not wanting to offend him.

'Don't need to be in America to be interested.' He picked up the remote switch and turned down the volume.

She stood, unsure whether to sit or stand. The room opened into a kitchen, well equipped, with blue cupboards and gadgets on the counters where meals had been prepared, and eaten round the circular table in its centre, covered with a yellow cloth.

'Let me look at you,' he said, manoeuvring his Zimmer closer, searching her face. His eyes were hazel, though now faded and tinged blue with age, his face clean-shaven save for some stray hairs from his nostrils and under his bottom lip. He took another, clumsy step towards her. His breath was sour, the musty smell of uncleaned teeth and phlegm. He made her feel uneasy. She wanted to push him away, *you're too close to me*, but he was an old man, frail, most likely didn't understand about personal space, or had lost the ability to judge it. No, she thought. He's harmless, in his eighties. This is my *father*. He wore baggy jeans held up with a brown leather belt, a checked cotton shirt, frayed around the collar. He had left the top button open and beneath the shirt she could see the top of an old, faded T-shirt with a withered neckline. Was he looked after in this neat, empty house? His wife perhaps, a son or daughter, someone who loved him, shaved him, bathed him, made sure he was well fed, his home clean, his clothes pressed if not replaced? *Nothing wrong with this shirt. Don't waste the money on a new one.* She had never been a part of this home. Other people had shared her father while she had not.

He continued to stare at her. *What do you see?* Kathleen wanted to ask. *Do you see me?* She could recognise no features that were hers, except for the slim build and the thick, silver hair, though hers was straight like Joan's, not wavy.

'Come sit,' he said. 'Would you like something to drink? Some juice. Or would you prefer a Coke? 7 Up?'

'Actually,' she said, 'water would be just fine.'

'Coming up,' he said. 'I'll call you when it's ready. You'll have to go get it.'

She sat on one of the chairs. Its upholstery had the sheen of synthetic, the lace runner on the table, plastic. She looked at the fireplace, at the fake logs and the electric switch by its side, at the furniture pushed against the walls, at the vacant centre in the heart of the room.

'Come and get it.' He was shuffling back into the sitting room, pausing to point at the counter, where two tall blue acrylic glasses sat. She lifted them up, waited until the old man had settled into one of the chairs before she placed the glass on the table and sat on the chair next to him.

He pulled a small inhaler from the basket on his Zimmer, breathed it into his mouth.

'I taught math, at middle school. You'd have thought I could do my sums.' He smiled. A small line of mucus caught his lip, and he wiped it away with the back of his hand.

'My wife had just passed when you rang me,' he said. 'I wasn't myself.' He reached for his glass, sipped the water. 'We'd been married sixty-three years.' He pushed forward in his seat and pointed to the wedding photo on the wall. 'Go look.'

Kathleen went over to the picture. He was wearing the uniform of the US Air Force, and his wife was in a simple, white dress with a short veil. This would be the time Joan had met him, a handsome man with fair hair like her own.

'That's her. Bethany. Then she passed.' He pulled a handkerchief from his sleeve. 'Just like that.'

'I'm sorry,' Kathleen said, returning to her seat.

'Aneurysm. In the brain. She went.' He clicked his fingers, a feeble sound. 'Set my asthma off.' He clutched his chest. 'Acute. Hospitalised. I guess I was kind of breathless when you rang.'

'I'm sorry to hear that,' she said, understanding now the heavy gasping on the phone, his slow, painful suffocation.

'Confused. Lost track of time.' He shifted in his chair again, as if his bony frame was too rigid for comfort.

'You said on the telephone that perhaps you knew my mother, Joan,' Kathleen said.

'She was a mighty pretty little thing,' he said. 'Almost as pretty as my Beth.'

'Were you married to Beth when you met her?'

His face furrowed. 'I guess so,' he said. 'Lady, it was the war. You might say normal rules didn't apply.'

'I'm not judging you,' Kathleen said. He turned and stared at the screen, turning up the volume, as if she wasn't there.

'Tell me more about Joan,' Kathleen said, raising her voice above the sound of the television. 'Where you met her.'

He held up his hand. 'Quiet.' He watched intently, then leaned back. 'He's done it. That's all I wanted to see.' He turned the volume down again, without explanation. 'At a dance,' he said. 'They used to bus us in. What do they call it now? Soft power. Trying to cement good relations, I guess, otherwise there might have been a them-and-us kind of situation.' He laughed. 'If you ask me, it made that situation more likely. You Brits, rationing and all. You had nothing. The girls liked us, yessirree. You know what they used to say about us?' He shook his head, chuckling, went on without waiting for Kathleen to answer. 'Overpaid, oversexed and over here. And you know what we said? Underpaid, undersexed and under Eisenhower. Yessiree.' He breathed his inhaler again. 'Those were the days.'

Kathleen looked at him. He could have picked up any of this information in a book. He was telling her nothing new.

'Was my mother different?'

'Well now.' He paused, leaned back, fumbling to adjust the cushion behind him. 'She was pretty, like I said. And she could dance. But I guess she was a sucker for nylons and cigarettes like everyone else.'

Joan didn't smoke, Kathleen thought, and she'd never mentioned what they could glean from the Americans, though she'd said something about a lipstick once.

'Do you still write poetry?' Kathleen said.

'Poetry?' He laughed. 'Did she say that? Well, well, well.' He looked thoughtful, knuckled hands clawing at his chin. 'Got too busy teaching middle school.' He sniffed. 'Tough job, round here, you know? Most of the kids…' His voice trailed. 'Bad homes. Says it all.'

She looked at him. Had he thought about the kind of home she'd had? Leaving Joan to fend for herself. She wanted to say *I was a war child.* It made no difference that her father was an ally and not an enemy soldier. The loss was the same, the stigma. She wanted to say *Why did you leave? Why didn't you help?*

'I guess you did all right for yourself,' he said.

'My mother struggled,' Kathleen said.

'I'm sorry to hear that.'

She had vowed she wouldn't argue with him, wouldn't challenge him, not this first time, not till she knew him better.

'My grandparents brought me up.' She sipped her water, cold from the ice cubes. 'Do you have children?' Maybe she had brothers and sisters, belonged in a family.

He shook his head. 'My wife and I weren't blessed.'

That's not true, she thought. You had a child, a daughter, who was stillborn. That's who Joan said I was named after.

He smiled. 'It's kind of exciting to think that after all these years, I may have a daughter.' He leaned forward, his hand outstretched. Kathleen hesitated before she took it, squeezed it. The skin was warm and dry.

'Did you try to find me?' she said. 'After the war?'

'I didn't know of your existence,' he said. 'So how could I?'

'Didn't my mother tell you she was pregnant?'

'Not that I remember,' he said. 'But what could I have done? I was a married man. I don't think my Beth would have taken kindly to the news.'

Joan must have dreamed he'd return for her, or believed his lies. Or was lying to herself, deluding herself. She'd been so young.

'Can you remember the dates you were in Lakenheath?' Kathleen said. 'It's important.'

'Now when was it you were born?' he said.

'1944,' Kathleen said. She'd give him that. He might be old, but he could be wily with it.

He held up his hand, gnarled fingers like crooked spires. 'Sometime in the new year,' he said. '"Fraid I can't be more specific than that.'

'You're sure?' Kathleen said. 'Not in October 1943, like you said at first?'

'See,' he said. 'That's where I was confused before.'

'Would you mind, Mr O'Doyle,' Kathleen said. She couldn't call him Dad, not yet. 'If you did a paternity test?'

'Is it necessary?' he said.

'I just want to know,' she said. 'I don't want anything from you.'

He hadn't once asked about her, what she was doing in America, what she had done with her life. Was he still grieving for his wife? Couldn't see beyond the prism of his loss? Or had the shock of her arrival stunted his feelings? He looked small and feeble in the easy chair, his Zimmer by his side, one hand on the remote controls. Indifferent to her.

'What do you do all day?' she said. 'Who looks after you?'

'I have in-home assistance,' he said. 'A lady comes in once a day, cooks my food, cleans me up.' He nodded towards the television. 'And I have that for company.'

'Don't you get out? There's a park opposite.'

'I sit on the porch and watch the world go by,' he said. Kathleen wondered what kind of world that was.

'No company?'

She saw him swallow, his Adam's apple a lump of gristle in his throat. 'Everyone's dead now,' he said. 'Except the priest. He comes once a week, gives me communion, hears my confession.'

What sins could he commit, this puny old man in his frayed shirt and shabby jeans? She had a sudden urge to give him some money so he could treat himself, fished in her bag and drew out two twenty-dollar bills and placed them on the table between them. He was looking again at the screen, his back turned at an angle away from her, his arm and shoulder oscillating. He was breathing heavily, the throaty rumble of an asthmatic.

'Mr O'Doyle,' she said. 'Are you all right? Do you need your inhaler?'

Kathleen heard him groan, saw his shoulder relax, his arm still. He turned his face to her and grinned.

She stood up, put her hand to her mouth and ran towards the door, stepping out into the dry heat of the Mojave Desert. She ran past Susan, into the centre of the gravel yard, and retched. Once. Twice.

§

The lights had come on in the gardens below, casting yellow globes across the pathways, illuminating the palms. Life was lush here, and pretty. She and Susan sat with a glass of white wine on the balcony in shocked, sympathetic silence.

Joan. The urge to see her erupted like magma, without warning. The idea of her as her mother still took her by surprise. It came with, what, a sense of pity? This tongue-tied woman living her lie, too frightened of the world. This tongue-tied woman conquering the world with her voice. What had she seen in Michael O'Doyle? Or was this another delusion, another lie? Well, why not invite her? There was plenty for Joan to do by herself during the day while Kathleen worked, and at the weekends they could take off, drive up the coast to Monterey, Big Sur. San Francisco. It would be a good chance to get to know her, properly. She'd make sure it didn't clash with a visit from David. There is a time for everything, she remembered from her Sunday school. *A time to cry and a time to laugh, a time to grieve and a time to dance.* She wouldn't tell her about Michael. Nor would she ask him to do a paternity test, not now. She'd rather join Joan in her delusion that *her* Michael had died in Normandy. And who's to say he hadn't?

Would you like to come and visit me? she texted. *I'll pay towards your fare.*

The reply came back almost immediately. *Yes, love to!*

Joan deserved a break. *A time to plant, and a time to reap.*

JOAN

London: July 1955

'For passing your eleven-plus,' Joan said, handing a small box to Kathleen. 'Fountain pen and propelling pencil. Matching.'

She'd unhooked Kathleen's arms, kissing her on the forehead, walking away, sunglasses hiding the tears, clown's eyes. Now she sat on the Tube, out of place in dark glasses and a headscarf knotted at the chin. She'd seen a picture in *Woman* of a young Italian actress called Sophia Loren wearing a scarf and glasses and thought, perhaps, people would think she looked like her, chic, glamorous, mysterious.

The Tube stopped at Baker Street and Joan stood up to leave. She was aware of a man trailing her along the platform, up the steps towards the exit. She fished out her ticket and handed it to the collector, snapping her bag shut, slinging it over her arm.

'Lillie?'

She braced herself. She should be grateful for the fans, after all. 'Joan?'

She turned. 'Mr Mac,' she said, pulling off her glasses for a closer look. 'What a surprise.'

'I thought it was you,' he said. 'What are you doing here?'

'I'm just on my way home.' She pointed to the block of mansion flats across the road.

'On the Tube?' he said. 'I'd have thought you'd have a chauffeur-driven car by now. Or at the very least be taking cabs everywhere. You must be coining it in.'

She frowned, shook her head. 'You don't make money from records,' she said. 'You should know that. Not as the singer.'

He clicked his teeth and tilted towards her. 'No?' he said. 'Who's your manager?' Veins threaded his cheeks and nose, there was alcohol on his breath. He'd loosened his tie and it dangled beneath his collar, a white dicky bow, and now she saw he was wearing a dinner suit, the satin lapels shiny in the evening light.

She stepped back. 'I don't have a manager,' she said. 'Reg organises everything.'

'Reg?'

The tone in his voice suggested this was a mistake. She nodded.

Mr Mac narrowed his eyes. 'And what sort of a deal has he got with you?'

Joan shivered, though the summer night was warm. 'I don't think that's any concern of yours, Mr Mac,' she said.

'One-off payment up front, was it?' Mr Mac said, ignoring her. 'Do you get royalties? Foreign sales?'

Reg had said that royalties only applied to the songwriter. She'd checked that out with the Musicians' Union rep in the band and he said the Union only represented professionals and she should be grateful she'd made any money. That had got her mad. She'd come through ENSA, after all. 'Point made,' he'd said, adding that she and the Lancasters were never short of work. Well, not till recently.

'As the artiste you should have a share of the record sales,' he went on. 'Here and abroad. But there's producers who take advantage of young, green singers. Promise them an upfront fee which sounds like a lot of money but is a fraction of what they could earn.'

Joan looked down, nodded. 'I see.'

'I mean, I'm not saying Reg is unscrupulous.' Mr Mac fumbled in his pocket and pulled out a card. 'But there's lots of sharks in this business.' He took her hand and pressed the card into it. 'Come and see me.' He smiled. 'I don't hold grudges.' He turned and walked away, waving without looking back.

Joan peered at the card. MacMannon's Talent and Entertainment Agency. There was a telephone number, and an address in Denmark Street.

§

Reg wasn't home. He'd been staying out of late, coming back in the early hours or not at all. He was never there at the weekends anyway. She'd got used to that. Toddled off to see the wife and kiddies in Chalfont St Giles, always one reason or another why he never divorced them. How long had they been living like this?

At first, it had been a quick squeeze in his dressing room, he'd told her all the big producers were the same, if you wanted a music contract, this was the way to get it. But after 'Sweet-hearted Bill' was a hit in the spring of 1947, he'd gone all amorous, said he loved her, said his wife didn't understand him, him being a free spirit and all, he'd take a flat, install her once she was twenty-one so he could come and go until he got a separation. She'd felt sorry for him, and it had felt good to be loved. That was six years ago. She hadn't thought twice when he found the place in Marylebone. 'Nice and central,' he'd said. 'Convenient.' A hop and a skip from Marylebone Station, non-stop to Chalfont St Giles. There and back in a jiffy. He had no intention of leaving his wife, she'd seen that long ago.

Reg kept the booze on a side table in the sitting room, crystal decanters with plated gold labels round their necks, brandy, whisky, gin. There were small bottles of tonic or ginger ale, and a brand new SodaStream. She picked up a glass they'd chosen in Heal's, a fluted crystal tumbler with matching goblets and champagne coupes. She poured herself a whisky, neat. A stiff drink. She'd have preferred champagne or even a Babycham, sipping it so the bubbles tickled her nose.

Meeting Mr Mac had disturbed her. She'd had seven big hits. What did she have to show for it? She'd bought a little bedsit in Streatham Hill. It hadn't cost much. Auntie Win lived in it now, rent-free. There were some savings, but nothing to flash around, not like the boys with their fancy shoes and fast cars and hard drinking. The last record had been a flop, and Reg blamed her.

She sipped the whisky, swirling it in the glass so the peaty, earthy smells filtered into her nostrils, making her eyes smart. The evening had closed in now, turned to night, but she didn't pull the curtains or turn on more lights. Reg was cheating her, not just with her money but with another woman. Him all dreamy-eyed, smelling of perfume, wrong numbers on the telephone. She walked over to the window and looked out, at the cars and buses on the Marylebone Road, at the dome of Madame Tussaud's. In all the years she'd lived here, she'd never visited. Wax effigies didn't interest her, though, she thought, taking another sip of whisky, she wouldn't mind sticking a pin in one of Reg. There were enough stories of witchcraft in the village when she was a child, best ways to fend it off. Or use it.

She heard Reg's key in the door, a female voice, the flick of a switch, his slurred 'Come in, come in.'

'Reg?'

He walked into the sitting room, slammed on the main light, stood staring at her.

'I thought you were at your mother's.' There was a young woman behind him, scowling, as if this shouldn't be happening.

'Well, you were wrong,' Joan said. She looked at the young woman. 'Would you mind leaving us, please?'

'This is my house,' Reg said. 'I say who comes and goes.' He turned his back to Joan so she couldn't see his face, but she could imagine his expression. 'But perhaps you'd better run along, dear, for now. I'll be in touch.'

The young woman pursed her lips, walked out, slamming the door hard behind her so the decanters rattled on their tray.

'I can explain—' Reg said.

'I knew there was someone else,' Joan said. 'You were cheating on me. I've suspected it for a long time.' She took a gulp of whisky. 'What I didn't know was that you'd cheated me out of money too.'

His lips curled like an angry dog, a look she'd never seen before. 'What are you talking about?'

'Royalties, that's what I'm talking about.' She was sticking her neck out. She only had Mr Mac's word to go on but the whisky was bringing colour to her cheeks, words to her mouth.

'Who do you think pays for this?' Reg said, throwing out his arm to embrace the room and its contents. 'You've lived like a queen for years.'

'I pay my way,' Joan said.

'Pay your way?' There was a sneer in his voice as he spoke. 'What you pay barely covers the doormat. I subsidise you.' He prodded his chest with his thumb. 'And your lifestyle. You could never afford this on your own.' He walked further into the room, pointing to the radiogram and the teak sideboard, toeing the Turkish rug from Liberty's. 'Surrounded by beautiful things.'

Reg had brazenly brought another woman home, to her home. And now he was rubbing her nose in his success, making out this had nothing to do with her.

'And you're asking for royalties,' he said, going over to the tray and pouring himself a brandy. He turned, held the glass at arm's length, wagging his finger at her. 'Well, first you have to earn some money.'

She swallowed, hard. She'd worked her socks off the last ten years, the shows, the tours, the recordings. It wasn't her fault she'd made no money. He couldn't have done that without her.

'Then give me better material,' Joan said, downing the last of the whisky. She'd never answered him back, not like this, but the sight of that woman had put fire in her, made her bold.

Reg leapt towards her, his face close to hers. 'It's not the material that's at fault, my dear,' he said. 'It's the bloody singer.' He snatched her glass away, threw it at the fireplace. She winced as the crystal exploded, shattering into a thousand tiny shards.

'You know what, Reg?' she said. She stood tall, spine of steel. 'I don't have to put up with this.' Droplets of spit flew from her mouth. 'I'm leaving you.'

She walked out of the door, hauled her big suitcase from the box room into their bedroom, flung open the wardrobe door with its creaking hinges. Reg had said he'd oil them, but he never had. She pulled out her clothes, rammed them into the suitcase, hangers and all. He was drunk. Off balance. He hadn't expected to be found out. But she'd had enough of his broken promises, his slurs and insinuations. If it hadn't been for her, he'd be nothing. The band was no great shakes. She was the one who'd lifted it, had made his name along with hers. He'd made a fortune. How else could he afford a house in Chalfont St Giles and a flat in Marylebone? She'd given him the best years of her life, and he'd robbed her of it all, and the money that was rightly hers. Glass clinked as she swept her make-up and perfumes from the dressing table, her nail polish and creams, throwing them willy-nilly into her beauty box. Snapped the case shut, pulled it off the bed so it thumped on the floor, heaved it into the hallway.

'You'll be nothing without me,' he said. He'd poured himself another brandy, stood propped in the doorway, one hand in his pocket. 'I'll make sure of that.' He took another slug of drink, pushed himself upright. 'You've always been petit bourgeois,' he went on, stepping towards her. 'Dragging me down, with your boring little talent and your boring little mind. So yes, clear out now. Clear out of my life.' He grabbed her arm, swung her towards the front door. She held out her hand, stopped her face from smashing into the wall.

'You can forget tomorrow's show,' she said. 'And the rest of the season. I'll send someone for my gowns, my shoes.' They were worth a fortune. There was no way she could afford to replace them.

'Pathetic little tart.' He was shouting. 'Find another sugar daddy.'

Joan lifted her bags, opened the door and dragged her case over the coir doormat with its WELCOME message, bumping it along the stairs.

'And don't think I don't know your dirty little secrets,' he yelled down the well. 'Because I bloody well do. So good riddance.'

She froze in the turn of the stair. He was bluffing. Don't rise to the bait.

'Queenie knew you, she did.'

His words ricocheted after her as she pulled the suitcase down the rest of the flight, a steady thump, thump on the steps.

§

Perhaps Reg hadn't said Queenie. Perhaps it was another word that had sounded like it. Jeannie? She didn't know any Jeannies. More likely she'd imagined it. But she couldn't be sure, couldn't take the risk. Lies played dead, came alive when you least expected them to. *They'll put you inside for life*, Queenie had said. She heard herself as she breathed, light, tight, shallow gulps of air, felt the sweat begin to rise in her armpits and on her forehead. *Life*.

She had to hide, get out of this business, blend into obscurity. Reg was right. Her last release had been a flop. She'd had her day, nobody wanted her kind of music anymore. Bow out, find a job.

But what could she do? Apart from farm labour, which was out of the question, she'd only ever worked in a shop or in the canteen at the NAAFI, and neither of those appealed. She had no qualifications. Not even a school-leaving certificate. Singing was all she knew how to do, the only trade she had. The only work she'd ever truly loved. Damn Queenie. Damn the woman.

She fingered Mr Mac's card. She'd made an appointment with him for eleven o'clock, but she wasn't sure now. Forget it, she told herself. Don't turn up, sign on with the labour exchange, take the first job they offer. Bus conductress. London Transport were short of workers. So were Lyons. Try her hand at factory work. Move out of London.

There was a newsagent's ahead. *Ten Players, please. And a box of matches.* They might steady her nerves. She could smoke now she didn't need to look after her voice. Next door to the newsagent's was a travel agent. Joan stopped, lingering by its window, looking. CROSSING THE ATLANTIC ON THE *QE2*. WHAT WILL YOU DO ALL DAY? She peered at the schedule. Breakfast, lunch, rest. Tea, cocktails, dinner. All right for some, she thought. She read on. DANCE THE NIGHT AWAY. Ray Ellington Quartet in the Queen's Room. Joe Loss in the Double Room. Cabaret. Nightclub.

She pushed open the door, smiled at the assistant. 'I'm enquiring about cruises,' she said.

'Holidays on sea,' the assistant said. 'Very popular.'

'Do you have brochures?' Joan said, pointing at the window display. 'For the *QE2*?'

'Of course.'

'Do they go anywhere else besides America?'

'Oh yes,' the assistant said. 'All over. There's other companies too, if you're interested.' She turned around, opened a filing cabinet. 'P&O, Union-Castle.' She was pulling out brochures, fluttering the pages. 'New York. Sidney. Cape Town. There's also American companies. Delta, for instance. Puerto Rico. Rio de Janeiro. Buenos Aires.'

'I'll take them all,' Joan said, smiling. 'If I may.' The assistant looked at her, eyeing Joan's coat and shoes. 'Cruises are expensive,' she said.

'Oh, this isn't for me,' Joan said. 'It's for my boss. He wants to take his wife on one. I'm just the secretary.'

'That's always the way, isn't it?' the assistant said. 'You need to get yourself a rich husband.'

Joan laughed, taking the brochures, tucking them under her arm.

'The thing is,' Mr Mac said, tilting his chair on its back legs, hands coupled behind his head. Behind him was a poster for the Adelphi Theatre. LONDON LAUGHS, she read. *The New Laughter Review*, with Jimmy Edwards, Vera Lynn and Tony Hancock. 'The liners will kill your career. Talk about backwater.' He laughed. 'In every sense of the word.'

'Ray Ellington's hardly a backwater,' Joan said. 'Nor is Joe Loss. While I've got a name, why not give it a go?'

Mr Mac fingered the brochures Joan had laid out on the desk.

'Music's moved on,' Joan said. 'It's all skiffle, or rock and roll. Lonnie Donegan, Bill Haley. I don't fit in. Where are the women skiffle artistes? Or the British ones, come to that? Apart from Lonnie, that is.'

There was a knock on the door and a secretary entered with a tray and a teapot, two cups. Mr Mac waited while she poured the tea, handing a cup to him and one to Joan. She glanced over at the brochures. 'They look nice, Mr Mac,' she said. 'I've always wanted to go on a cruise. Are you thinking of taking Mrs Mac?'

'This is business, Noreen,' he said, slapping his hand on a brochure, blocking her view. 'Thank you for the tea.'

'Swing,' Joan went on. 'Big band.' She waved her arm. 'A bygone era.' She looked at Mr Mac, narrowed her eyes. 'Except on the liners.'

'Reg may be finished,' Mr Mac said, 'but he was only ever a one-trick pony. But not you, Joan. Not you.' He helped himself to sugar, stirred it into his cup. 'Look at Vera Lynn,' he said, sipping his tea through his teeth with a slurp. 'She's still popular. Always on the wireless.'

'Ah yes,' Joan said. 'But Vera's Vera. She can get away with all that sentimentality.'

'Alma Cogan,' he said. 'Ottilie Patterson.'

'But I'm not really into jazz,' Joan said. 'Or blues.'

'But you could be.' He leaned forward, the spider veins on his cheeks and nose in close view. 'You work hard. You've got the talent. You need to be versatile. We could go far, Joan. You and me.' He rummaged in his filing tray, pulled out a folded sheet of music. 'Take a look at this. It's a Woody Guthrie song.' He twisted his nose as if he was about to sneeze, drained the dregs of his tea and put his cup to one side. 'Go on, look at it,' he said, passing her the music. She felt him watch her as she read the lyrics.

'It's a kids' song,' she said. She shook her head.

'Look what Ella Fitzgerald did with "A-Tiskit-A-Taskit".'

'I don't see myself doing that,' Joan said. 'But I'd really like a job on the liners. Look what they offer for entertainment.' She pulled back one of the brochures from his desk. 'Cabaret. Variety acts. Surely they'd leap at me? Nostalgia.' She smiled. '*The* Lillie Pettall.' She'd never had to sell herself like this, work always came to her, but she needed to persuade him.

Mr Mac twisted in his chair, leaned back, lifted one foot then the other onto his desk. His black brogues were expensive, polished, had steel clips on the heels. 'You're at the top of your career, Joan.' He spoke slowly, like he did to the Petals on tour. *Do. I. Make. Myself. Clear.* His Scottish accent had not softened over the years. 'At the peak of your powers. But you can go higher. Much higher. Why do you want to throw it away? Sink beneath the waves?'

Joan shrugged. 'I just do, Mr Mac,' she said. 'Holiday on the sea and all that. It'd be regular money.' She hadn't had that since ENSA. 'And I'd get to see the world.'

'You'd earn more money making records than on the liners. They pay a pittance, Joan. All right, you get your board and lodging, I'll give you that. No.' He shook his head. 'Forget it. Do that Guthrie song. I've got plenty more for you. World tours. Aim for the skies, Joan. The skies. No limit.'

'I can do a comeback later,' Joan said. 'I could use the time trying out new styles, new songs. How would that work? And if the audience don't like it, there's not much they can do about it, is there?' She laughed. *And if the audience can't go anywhere, nor can my wages.* She could save, build a nest egg. 'Don't you see?'

'Let me think about it.'

'No,' Joan said. 'I'm sure these jobs get snapped up. I'm sure you've got artistes on your books who do this sort of thing. You know the ropes. I don't.'

'What happens after?' he said. 'What then? You could do one season and get away with it. But more than one…' He ran his finger across his throat. 'That's the end of your career as a solo artiste before it's even begun. Do you really want to risk that?'

'Yes,' she said.

'Perhaps we could compromise,' Mr Mac said. 'Between cruises I could look to get you a slot at the Windmill, say, or even the Palladium.' He lifted his feet off the desk, one foot, the other, held the top of his desk, pulled himself forward, the casters on his chair squealing on the linoleum. 'Regions too, working men's clubs, pier theatres. How's your dancing, by the way? You don't want to let that go. The punters like a song-and-dance act. And there's always room for a chorus girl, the Tillers, say, or the Windmill's own.'

'But that's in the nude,' Joan said.

'Oh, but very tasteful, dear, nothing smutty.' He thumped his hand on the desktop, the cup rattling in its saucer. 'Because that's the future you'll have.' He jabbed a thick, lumpy finger at her. 'Think about it, Joan. Do you want to be a has-been, ending up without a penny in some miserable bedsit in Streatham Hill? Or do you want to be a musical legend? Because, Joan, you've got it in you to do that.'

'I want the liners,' Joan said, standing up, straightening her skirt.

Mr Mac blew hard like a whale. 'On your head be it,' he said. 'Any other client, I'd be washing my hands of you. But you're too good, Joan, mark my words.' He sighed, his tone softening. 'What's the real reason, Joan?'

'I just don't want to be in England anymore,' she said. She felt flattened by the conversation, trapped.

'Well, if that's all it is,' Mr Mac said, 'why didn't you say? I can get you a season in Vegas, Buenos Aires. Anywhere you want. Somewhere in the sun, plenty of local colour. Tell you what.' He signalled her to sit down, leaned forward on his desk, the steel elasticated armbands on his shirt glinting. He fiddled with a box of cigars, picking one out, toying with it round his mouth. 'I'll give you the liners, if you give me the concert halls. Is that a deal?'

'Really?' Joan said.

'Really. I'll need a good publicity shot,' he said. 'Alluring, sexy. I know a good photographer, he'll do the job. He'll let you pay by instalments.'

'Thank you,' she said. She breathed in with the relief of it. Safe and secure, travelling the world, port to port, a nomad, leaving no trace.

Mr Mac edged his way round his desk, opened the door for her.

There was a young girl in the waiting room outside. Petite, pretty. Sitting cross-legged, with neat, fragile ankles. Another young hopeful. Joan saw herself in her, smiled as she passed her. 'What's your name?' she said.

'Melissa,' the young girl answered. 'Melissa Balls. Aren't you Lillie Pettall?'

'Yes,' she said.

'Oh, gosh,' Melissa said. 'Imagine. You're my idol.'

Mr Mac opened his office door, the Guthrie music in one hand, beckoning to Melissa with the other. She sidled past him and he shut the door behind them.

KATHLEEN

London: July 1970

Icelandic Airlines may have been cheap, but the flight was long. They had to stop over in Reykjavik, so it was evening of the next day before Kathleen arrived at Heathrow. She went through immigration, collected her suitcases, and left the customs hall, half hoping Joan would be there to meet her. She hadn't replied to Kathleen's letter, but then she'd always been lousy at letter writing.

Kathleen had changed her dollars into sterling and asked for a pound's worth of coins. There was a bank of public telephones across the way and she pushed the luggage trolley over to them, carefully lining up her pennies, poised to insert them as soon as her sister answered. The phone rang and rang. Kathleen checked the number, rang again. There was no reply. Perhaps, she thought, Joan was on her way. She'd give her ten minutes then get a cab. It was extravagant, but she didn't know her way round London, much less to where Joan lived, her suitcases were heavy, and she was tired from the journey, disorientated by jet lag.

She sat on the larger of her two cases, eyes alert, hopes rising and dipping as first one woman, then another, hoved into view and melted into obscurity. Nothing for it. Kathleen pushed the trolley towards the taxi rank, gave the address to the cabbie, loaded her baggage and sat back in her seat.

'Here we are,' he said. Kathleen must have dozed off. She looked up at a block of Edwardian mansion flats. She stepped out of the cab, paid the fare, carried her suitcases one by one up the staircase to number 47 and rang the bell.

The door opened and Joan stood behind it, dressed in a tight blue lamé dress. 'Kathleen?' She stepped out onto the landing, pulling the door to behind her. 'What are you doing here?'

'Didn't you get my letter?' Kathleen said. Exhaustion had made her weepy, and she heard her voice crack. She'd imagined Joan to be excited, to pull her inside, *come in, come in. My clever little sister.*

'Didn't you get mine?' Joan said. 'I'm sorry, Kathleen, it's—'

'Who is it?' a man's voice called from within. 'Get rid of them.'

'It's all right,' Joan yelled through the half-open door. 'Give me a minute.' She turned to Kathleen. 'You can't stay, I'm so sorry.' She tapped her face, her shoulder, bony hand jittery as if she was flustered. 'I'm about to go out. My show.' There was a look of panic in her eyes. 'Hold on.' She slipped inside.

Kathleen had never seen her sister so unsure. They didn't meet often, but Joan was always in command, sophisticated and confident.

Joan came back out, pressed some money into Kathleen's hand. 'Get a taxi,' she said. 'Ask the cabbie to take you to a nice hotel. He'll know what you mean. We're not far from Paddington. There's loads there. Let me know when you've got somewhere to live. I'll make it up to you, I promise.' She folded Kathleen's hands over the money. 'I'm so sorry.' She bit her lip, slipped back inside and shut the door.

Kathleen stood, gathering her wits. She was tempted to ring the bell again, but decided against it. *Well, fuck you, Joan.* She bumped her suitcases down two flights of stairs and dragged them onto the pavement. The street was a busy one, she'd sussed that already, and on a bus route. She didn't have to wait long before she saw a taxi.

The bed and breakfast was cheap and basic. She'd opted for a single room rather than a double or a dormitory. The sheets were nylon, the bed narrow and there was scarcely space for her and her suitcases. The lavatory was down the corridor, and hot water in the shared bathroom ran on a meter. The flimsy curtains were unlined and did little to block the light, casting instead a cold blue shadow across the room.

Kathleen lay on the bed. She hadn't expected to be on her own, not this first night, lying on a single bed listening to the noise of the city, the traffic and the sirens. She hadn't been alone for years. She was a shrunken waif in the centre of other people's laughter, like the first day at school, the first day at university. She had nothing. No home, no job, no friends, no money. And now no sister. This *alone* was different. She wondered what she'd done to make Joan behave like that, to turn her away with no explanation.

She felt the tears build up behind her throat, an unstoppable tide of self-pity pushing hard against the crust of her skin, reducing her thoughts to the soiled froth of a churning river. But she was tired. She'd hardly slept for two nights, and as she lay back on the bed with its lumpy pillow and flimsy blanket she felt the deep wave of sleep roll over and suck her in.

It was morning when she woke. She fished out some clean clothes, grabbed a bowl of cornflakes and a slice of toast and sat in the gloomy breakfast room in the basement of the B & B. The wireless was on, a record request programme. The music was new to her and she realised how long she'd been away. She could hear Susan in her head, *Are you going to sit there and feel sorry for yourself?* It was all right for Susan, she thought. She'd had an easy passage through life, with loving parents and a happy family, the confidence that money and stability and education brought. She'd never had to struggle, wouldn't know what it was like to be on her own.

'Finished?' The serving lady was taking her plate and cup. 'Only we're closing.' Kathleen nodded. She pushed her chair away from the table.

'And here we are,' the broadcaster was saying. 'For Mrs Morell of Basingstoke, Lillie Pettall singing that great Fred Astaire and Ginger Rogers hit, 'Pick Yourself Up'. Kathleen laughed at the sheer, absurd coincidence of it all.

She went back to the bedroom, drew up a to-do list. She'd go to the department at University College to check they'd received her letter to say she'd attend the interview. If Joan's letter hadn't come through to her, perhaps hers had also been delayed.

Now, she needed somewhere to live. The hotel manager said to look in the *Evening Standard*. 'Mind you,' he said, 'they go in an instant. Or there's agencies, if you don't mind paying the fee. They have loads of bedsits, especially round these parts, Bayswater, Queensway…' His voice had trailed off as he turned to greet a new guest arriving in desert boots with the biggest rucksack Kathleen had ever seen, covered in stickers and flags.

Kathleen needed temporary work. Joan's money and the little she'd brought with her from America wouldn't last long. Shop work. Waitressing. Factories. Typing. She had no idea where to start. She'd only been to London two or three times before, when she was at Oxford, and that had been to attend lectures at the Royal Society. She'd been with others then, had followed them onto the Tube, trailed them through the streets without taking in the geography of the city. She had no idea where Paddington even was, or how to get to University College.

First off, a map.

§

She rented a bedsit in Bayswater. It wasn't great, but it would do for the time being, until she could find a flat. She was tempted to write out a slip of paper with her name and address, put it in an envelope and post it to Joan, no explanation, no nothing. Serve her right. Let her stew.

Joan had never been around in their childhood, so they'd never been that close, unlike her brothers, who she'd been brought up with and knew inside out, warts and all. Her older sister had always been an enigma, never really welcome at home. Her mother refused to say why, though Kathleen assumed it was to do with Joan's profession, which in their mother's view was shameless. Their father was kinder to Joan, but not brave enough to stand up for her, not when their mother was having one of her storms. Still, Joan was her sister despite being a stranger.

It was now seven weeks since Kathleen had arrived from the airport. She should stop sulking and let Joan know she was on her feet.

She'd secured a temporary job typing at a law firm in High Holborn. The firm allowed them to use the phone at work for local calls in their own time. Kathleen waited until the typing pool was empty, reached over to the phone and dialled Joan's number. It picked up on the tenth ring.

'Hello?' The voice was bleary, as if she'd been woken.

'It's Kathleen.' There was a pause and Kathleen sensed an awkwardness. She heard the muffled voice of a man, the creak of a door as it opened and shut. 'Can you talk?'

'Not really.' Her voice was soft. 'Meet me later. Ronnie Scott's. Upstairs. Six o'clock.'

'Today?'

'Yes.' The phone went dead.

Kathleen had no idea what Ronnie Scott's was, much less the address.

'Ronnie Scott's?' one of the other typists, a skinny girl called Carol who fancied herself as Sandie Shaw, said. 'You've never heard of Ronnie Scott's?'

Kathleen opened her eyes wide, shook her head.

'It's a jazz club. Frith Street. Why d'you want to know?'

'No reason,' Kathleen said. 'Just a friend mentioned it, so I thought I'd ask.'

Upstairs at Ronnie Scott's proved to be a bar, with lush walls and low lights. It had just opened for the evening, and the tables and booths were empty. A strange night-time world of seedy glamour. It had a forlorn air, like a date who had been stood up, waiting in their evening finery, overdressed, a little shabby even. She looked around. A waiter at the bar was polishing glasses, spotted her, pointed to the far end of the room.

Joan sat alone in the corner in the same blue lamé dress she'd worn the night Kathleen had arrived. She stood up as Kathleen approached, squeezed round the table and threw her arms wide in welcome, embracing Kathleen, hugging her as if she'd been rescued from a nightmare. Kathleen could smell her perfume, the waxy scent of her make-up. The lamé was coarse to the touch, and as Joan released Kathleen there was a subtle whiff of sweat.

'I'm sorry,' Joan said. 'I'm so, so sorry. You know, for the other night.' She took Kathleen's hand and threaded her round the table and to the wall seat opposite. 'I'm so glad you got in touch. I thought I'd lost you forever.'

The barman came over, a round tray tucked under his arm. 'What's it to be, ladies?'

Joan smiled. 'On the house, Kathleen, so have whatever you want.'

What she wanted was a cup of tea, but she could tell this was the last thing available in a place like this. 'A lemonade, please,' Kathleen said.

'Is that all?' Joan's voice rose an octave. 'Bring some champagne, Stefan,' she said. 'For my prodigal sister.'

Stefan bowed. 'My pleasure.'

Kathleen wasn't sure how she was the prodigal sister. More likely the boot was on the other foot, but she didn't quibble.

'So lovely to see you,' Joan said, wriggling in the seat. 'My baby sister. Look how grown-up you are. And so beautiful.' Her eyes glistened tears and she sniffed hard. 'You're a doctor too,' she said. 'I'm so proud. Just imagine…' Her voice trailed off as she rubbed her finger against her nose.

'Thank you.'

'And now what?' Joan said. 'Will you work in a hospital? Meet a nice, handsome surgeon?'

'I'm not that sort of a doctor,' Kathleen said. 'I do research. But yes, I have a job. University College. Starting September.' Added, 'In a couple of weeks.'

Joan twisted her mouth, shook her head, eyes wide. 'Clever you.' She nodded as Stefan brought over the tray, a lemonade in a long glass, two flutes of champagne. 'Thank you, Stefan.' She pushed a glass towards Kathleen, lifted her own. 'Mud in your eye.'

Kathleen took a sip, feeling the alcohol bubble in her mouth and tickle cool and smooth down her throat.

'That's good,' Joan said. 'A job. A steady wage.' She laughed. 'I've never had regular money since ENSA.'

'Not on the liners?'

'They pay by the cruise. No cruise, no money. I do gigs like this on shore.' She flung her hands wide. 'Experimenting. Different styles. Here. Abroad.'

Joan's dress was frayed around the armholes and the lamé had lost its sparkle in places. She'd always seen Joan as glamorous but now she saw how she had faded, how her neck had wrinkled, lines tracing her skin. Her diamante earrings were nothing more than glinting glass and the polish on her nails was chipped.

Kathleen had never had much money, but it had been reliable. An undergraduate grant, scholarships. Now she understood how Joan lurched from one engagement to another, unsure and insecure, had done for years and years. Kathleen could never do her sister's job. She wondered what it must be like to face an audience evening after evening, to lay yourself open, fair game for the cruel, easy prey for the unscrupulous. To bare yourself to strangers. Perhaps that's why performers wore make-up, she thought, why Joan was masked up now, with her false eyelashes and thick eyeshadow, her dark lipstick and plastered foundation. It was all protection, a sham.

Joan uncrossed her legs, tugged her dress so it reached to her knees. She seemed nervous, for all her poise, her air of self-assuredness, calling the waiter by name, *it's on the house.* 'Glad you've got yourself sorted out,' she said.

Kathleen raised her eyebrows, her new-blown sympathy for her sister evaporating. 'No thanks to you.'

Joan winced. 'Look, I know, I'm sorry about that,' she said. 'It's just a bit difficult right now. I can't really explain.'

'Try,' Kathleen said. 'Seems to me, whoever he is, you're frightened of him. Have you been together long? What happened to Reg?'

'Reg? I finished with him years ago,' Joan said. 'Much water under the bridge since him.' She tried to laugh, a skittish *hee-hee*. She went to pick up her glass but her hand caught the bowl and she knocked it over, jumping as the champagne dripped onto her shoe. She righted the flute.

Stefan hurried over, cloth in one hand, champagne bottle in the other. He mopped up the table, gave her the napkin to dry her shoe, poured her some more. She smiled at him, *thank you*, waited until he was out of earshot.

'No,' she said. 'It's just that…' She picked up her drink, held it between her thumb and forefinger. 'Well, you see…' She took a sip of champagne, placed the glass back on the table. 'I shouldn't drink this. I'm singing later. It messes with my voice.'

'Then don't,' Kathleen said, pushing the lemonade towards her.

'It's just that...' Joan paused, and from her frown, the way her mouth was set, Kathleen knew she was summoning courage. 'Promise me you won't say a word.' She leaned forward and grabbed Kathleen's hand, squeezing it hard. 'Because this is all top secret. Nobody knows.'

'I don't know what you're going to tell me,' Kathleen said, 'but I can keep my mouth shut, if that's what you mean.'

'He's a rather prominent man,' Joan said. 'A public figure, and if it got out that I was...' She bit her lip. 'We were, you know, having an affair.' She looked up at Kathleen, her blue eyes clear and steely. 'It would finish him. The end of his career.'

'And yours?'

'In my world?' She shrugged. 'Easy come, easy go. It wouldn't be such a big deal. But for him yes.'

'So who is it then?' Kathleen said. 'Ted Heath? The Duke of Edinburgh? The Archbishop of Canterbury?'

Joan looked around, searching, Kathleen guessed, for imaginary ears in the vacant room.

'Am I close? A politician? A high court judge?'

'I can't tell you.'

'Well,' Kathleen said, relaxing back into her seat, 'whoever it is seems to have you under his thumb.'

'That's not true.' Joan spoke fast, as if her reply was urgent.

'Does he scare you?

'Of course not. Don't be silly.'

She said the words, but Kathleen sensed they had no strength. She raised an eyebrow. Joan was staring into her glass like a moody teenager.

'What would he do if he was found out?' Kathleen went on. She had become the older sister. 'Chuck you out? Make you homeless?' She nearly added *like you did me.*

Joan swallowed and Kathleen saw then how helpless she was, flotsam on the wave of a man's whims. This big sister, whom she had adored and loathed in equal measure but had never known, who she thought had carved a life of independence away from the small-minded cruelty of their home, had become a prisoner in her own. She was a kept woman, Kathleen saw that now, with the vulnerabilities that went with the position. She looked hard at Joan sitting on the upholstered bench, her face sagging as if with the weight of her mask.

'My professor at Harvard assaulted me,' Kathleen said.

Joan flinched, frowned, leaned close to Kathleen and took her hand. 'Poor baby,' she said, stroking Kathleen's fingers with her own. 'That's awful.'

'It had nothing to do with desire,' Kathleen went on. 'But defeat. He wanted to crush me.' She kept her eyes on Joan, unflinching. 'Leave him.'

Joan looked away. 'I can't,' she said. 'He's good to me.'

'So long as you do as he says,' Kathleen said. 'The fate of the concubine throughout history.'

'It's not like that.' Joan was shaking her head. 'You've got it wrong.'

'Have I?' Kathleen said. 'Sometimes it's the outsider who sees most clearly. And I see you cowed. I've never seen you like that before.' She leaned over, took Joan's hand, turned it over in her palm. 'What future is there with him? Do you love him?'

Joan stared down at Kathleen's hand, intertwined with her own. 'You've grown up since I last saw you.'

'That was over five years ago, Joan. What's happened to you in the meantime?'

Kathleen delved into her bag, pulled out her diary and tore out a page. She wrote down her address and handed it to Joan.

'In case you need me,' she said. 'Thanks for the drink.' She stood up, straightened her skirt. 'Men like that are never worth it.'

JOAN

Los Angeles: April 2006

Kathleen had met her at the airport, brought her to the apartment with its tropical gardens and swimming pool. She'd only been here a few days, but she could see already how the rhythm of her day would pan out. Breakfast, swim, coffee, lunch, and a trip out in the afternoon. She lay on the lounger by the pool, yesterday's copy of the *LA Times* folded beside her.

There it was, in black and white. *Los Angeles Times Festival of Books celebrates its 10th anniversary April 23–24 at the University of California, Los Angeles. 380 authors on 96 panels...* Joan's hand was shaking, a flush searing through her body. She folded the newspaper in half to steady it, read again. *Festival highlights include University of California Santa Barbara Poet-in-Residence Michael O'Doyle in conversation with Marius Dines of the UCLA Literature Department. Booking essential.*

There was a number to ring.

And a photograph. It was a publicity shot, she could see that. His hair was white, still thick and wavy, his eyes the colour of autumn. He was smiling in the image, not a broad open-mouthed grin like a toothpaste ad but a small, playful twist that crinkled his eyes and breathed a sensitivity. A sensuousness. She felt that old thrust of desire return, that surge of a love she'd never lost, embers waiting to be fanned into a fearsome burning flame. And that sharp stab of pain, of betrayal and anger that he was alive and hadn't sought to find her. There must have been a reason.

See pages 10–11 for our feature interview with Marius Dines.

Joan scrambled with the paper, found the article.

Dines: First, many congratulations on your residency. You have the dubious honour of being the oldest poet-in-residence in the history of the creative writing department at UC Santa Barbara. I'm curious to know what still drives you, but before we set off on that track, let me ask you about your first narrative poem, 'Joan's Song'. Your use of archaic dialect words such as 'frorn' is one of the devices you employ to conjure the isolation and bleakness of rural life. I remember also that memorable passage: 'The earth bites and gnarls her hands / Her labours bruise her body / Fierce, relentless, season after season / But listen to the wind, Joan said / Listen to its music.' Haunting words. What was in your mind as you wrote them?

Joan tucked the newspaper into her bag, scooped up her sun cream and towel and pulled on the turquoise kaftan Kathleen had lent her. 'You can't go to the pool in your swimming costume,' she'd said. 'Americans can be prudish.'

She slipped her feet into Kathleen's flip-flops and hurried inside, taking the lift up four flights and wending her way along the corridor to Kathleen's apartment. It was large, with two bedrooms, each with a bathroom, two balconies and an open-plan living room and kitchen. The view from the back, where her bedroom was, looked out over LA, a jumble of roofs and parking lots and traffic, but the front of the apartment had a view of the lush, subtropical gardens and the communal swimming pool. For all its grandeur, it was a functional, soulless affair with rented furniture and polyester sheets. There was a temporary air about it.

Joan dumped her bag by the front door, fished out the newspaper, picked up the telephone and dialled the box office.

Please hold, she heard a recorded voice say, *your call is important to us. We are experiencing high demand at present. You are currently fifty-sixth in line.* The Beach Boys, the recording tinny and strained. She held the phone, listening to the music, broken from time to time with a voice giving a countdown.

You are currently forty-eighth in line.

She took the phone into the kitchen and laid it on the counter, filling the coffee maker and spooning out coffee into the filter.

You are currently thirtieth in line.

The machine gurgled and spluttered as the numbers before her came down.

She poured the coffee, went into the sitting room, opening the door to the balcony, welcoming the breeze.

You are currently fifth in line.

She sipped her coffee.

You are currently second in line.

Joan was sweating, her hands damp on the receiver, knew number two was buying up all the available tickets for the event as she sat there waiting.

'Good morning,' a woman's voice broke in. 'This is the Box Office. How can I help?'

'I'd like a ticket for the Michael O'Doyle event.'

'I'm sorry, caller, but that event is fully sold out.'

Joan's hands went cold, sweaty. She shivered. 'It can't be,' she said.

'I'm afraid these events sell out months in advance.'

'But I have to go.'

'Even the rush tickets have sold out.'

Joan knew, if you had the right connections, tickets could be found. 'You don't understand. I'm *Joan*.'

'Hi Joan. I'm afraid we have no tickets for that event. Can I interest you in any others?'

'I'm Joan, from "Joan's Song".'

There was a pause. 'I'm sorry Joan, I don't understand. I'm just the operative and there are no tickets available. Please vacate the line as there are other people waiting to get through.'

'How can I get hold of him?'

'This is the Box Office,' the voice said. 'Have a good day.' There was a click as she was cut off.

The event was that afternoon. Joan had planned to take a sight-seeing bus, Hollywood, Rodeo Drive. That could wait. Michael O'Doyle couldn't. And UCLA was around the corner. No need for a bus. Or a car.

Would Harry mind? She hadn't given him a thought, couldn't think now. She'd waited more than sixty years for this moment. He'd understand, after she'd explained it to him.

For years she'd imagined meeting Michael, had created it in her mind often enough. Sometimes they were alone and she'd sidle up, introduce herself, and he'd study her face and they'd hold a stiff, awkward conversation while her heart thudded and she waited for him to warm to her. On other occasions, they were in company and he'd recognise her, parting the crowds to sweep her up. Fantasies, she told herself, but now, suddenly, they were no more. Meeting Michael was real, and here.

What if he'd forgotten her? Was that possible? It was over sixty years ago, after all, and much had happened to both of them since then. What if he remembered her but wanted nothing to do with her? Their lives had taken such different paths, they'd have little in common. Would he still love her? Their child? He'd be sure to ask about her. She could tell him what a fine woman Kathleen had become, what a success. Could she do that? He'd want to meet her. What could she say?

After all, she'd told Kathleen her father's name was Michael. Michael O'Doyle.

Perhaps she wasn't destined to meet him. The tickets were sold out. He would remain a ghost in her memory. And she in his. A sentimental instant to be cherished but not relived.

No, she thought, because if so, how come she'd spotted him in the newspaper? It was the first time she'd picked up the *LA Times* since she'd been here. Not that she was superstitious, but it had to be an omen. She'd go to the event, see if she couldn't persuade someone at the door to let her in, or find the green room, though she knew from experience that those were closely guarded locations.

Joan rubbed her hair, damp from the pool, combed it through, leaving it to dry naturally. The joy of her new urchin cut. She tiptoed into the bedroom like a nervous cat and studied her wardrobe. She loved the summer, the heat, the casualness and prettiness of it all, the chance for open-toed sandals, pedicures and painted nails. She'd treated herself to some new clothes for the trip, white cropped trousers and a short pink boxy jacket. She held it up against her skin. She'd caught the sun in the few days she'd been here, and the subtle oyster pink offset her tan. She put on her silver wedge sandals, keeping an eye on the time as she looked at herself in the mirror, front, side, back. Was she too old for the outfit, mutton dressed as lamb? No. Not an outfit as classic as this. She dabbed on some foundation and mascara, adding a little eyeliner for enhancement, opening her mouth, applying her lipstick. Checked she had everything in her bag, grabbed her sun hat and her new oversize sunglasses and set off.

The university was a twenty-minute walk away. Kathleen had driven her round the campus, showing her where she worked, the various faculties and departments. 'Four hundred and nineteen acres,' she'd said. 'Bigger than Hyde Park by far.'

They'd walked in the botanical garden and Kathleen had pointed out other landmarks, but as Joan entered the campus she could not recognise a single one. There was a map on a notice-board, a confusing configuration of blocks and boulevards. She had no idea where the Festival of Books was being held, and doubted Kathleen would know, even if she could find her office. She'd left her phone behind, and besides it cost an arm and a leg to ring in America on her mobile. The notice in the newspaper had only said University of California, Los Angeles. It could be anywhere. The event was scheduled to start at two-thirty and it was two o'clock now. Joan looked around for someone to ask, but there was no helpful information centre, not even a security kiosk.

She could take any number of turnings, left or right. The main road appeared to be straight ahead. Her hat was sticky on her head, her skin damp. She could feel her breath come in short gasps, as if she was about to go on stage, the same anxiety, the same terror. She began to walk down Westwood Plaza, her feet scooping up the distance, trying to make speed. A bus was approaching in the other direction. She could get a bus. Maybe the driver would know. She turned round, spotted one coming in her direction, saw a stop ahead. She began to run, holding out her hand, *don't drive past, wait for me.* It overtook her and pulled in ahead. She heard the doors open.

'Wait,' she yelled, waving her hat. 'Please wait.'

Joan caught up, panting, held onto the door rail.

'The Festival of Books?' she said. 'Are you going there?'

'We go to the terminal,' the driver said, reaching for her microphone. 'Does anyone know where the Festival of Books is being held? This lady needs to know.'

'Royce Hall,' a voice from the back called. 'I'll show you.'

Joan didn't think. She stepped aboard, fished for her purse, took out the fare. The driver looked in her mirror, closed the pneumatic doors and pulled out. Joan walked towards the rear of the bus, to a young man signalling to her.

'Thank you,' she said. 'Thank you so much.' Sat down on the edge of a seat, her bag by her side, fanning her face with her hat, blowing air from her mouth, feeling it condense on her nose and upper lip. The young man was wearing earphones, holding an iPod. He was nodding his head to the beat, smiled at her, took out an earphone.

'Daniel Powter,' he said. 'Do you like him?'

'I don't know,' Joan said. He took out the other earphone, handed the pair to Joan.

'Have a listen.' She placed the earphones close to her head. Damned if she was going to stick them in her ear.

'"Bad Day",' he said. 'Wicked.'

The bus trundled, stopping every so often before it came to a halt. It was twenty past two.

'Terminus,' the driver called out. 'Everybody out.'

'Follow me,' the young man said. Joan fed her way through the aisle of the bus, out into the fresh air.

'You going to the festival?' he said.

'Yes,' she said.

'It's supposed to be sick this year.' He paused, pointing. 'Straight down there. Royce Hall.'

'Thank you,' she said. She slapped her waist, either side. 'My bag. I left my bag.' She'd put it on the seat beside her. 'Oh my God.' The bitter metal of fear crimped her mouth. She stared at the young man, then turned, ran as fast as she could, the gristle in her knees shifting with a sharp, stabbing pain. The bus was still at the terminal and Joan rushed towards it, waving her hat. The driver was outside, leaning against it.

'You leave your purse?' she said as Joan drew near.

'Do you have it?'

The driver nodded, opened the door, climbed inside to her cab. 'I was gonna hand it in,' she said. 'And you saved me the trouble. Hang on to it now.'

'Thank you,' Joan said. 'Thank you so much.'

The driver nodded, a knowing half-smile, 'Easily done.' She checked her watch. Joan opened the bag. Her money, Kathleen's keys, everything was there, intact. How could she have been so stupid?

'Thank you again,' she said, turning and walking fast in the direction she'd come. Her heart was thundering and she was sweating more than before, tears misting her eyes. It had passed half past two. The event would have started. She followed the directions the young man had given, breathed out with relief when she saw a large red banner: *Los Angeles Times Festival of Books.* There was an imposing building in front of her with twin towers. It looked Italian, like a Romanesque church. She assumed it was Royce Hall. She walked up the steps, into the foyer festooned with posters and portraits of writers. Stalls had been laid out with piles of books and publishers were advertising their products. She looked around, saw a sign saying TICKETS and another reading INFORMATION.

Joan went over to the desk. 'Michael O'Doyle?' she said.

The attendant pushed a programme towards her. 'Small auditorium.'

Joan nodded, spotted a restroom sign and went in, peering into the mirror and dabbing the sweat from her face with a tissue, wondering how she'd be able to get in without a ticket. She ran her fingers through her hair, took a deep breath, left the toilets and followed the signs to the auditorium. There was a young woman at the door. 'Your ticket?' she said.

'I've done a stupid thing,' Joan said. 'I left it at home, and there's no time to go back. Could you let me in, please?'

The young woman shook her head. 'No ticket, no entry.'

'Not even if I just stood at the back?' Joan said. 'I've come all the way from England.'

'No, sorry.' A couple came up behind Joan, flashed their tickets. Joan peered through the doors as they opened, but the stage was too far away and the doors swung shut before she had time to take anything in. There must be other entrances, Joan thought. She walked around the corridor but the other entrance was manned by a ticket inspector with the same, strict story. *No ticket, no entry.*

She stood, long, slow breaths. *Think.* Michael would most likely have come onto the stage through the wings. He would leave the same way. She knew enough about theatres to work out where the stage door would be, although this was no ordinary theatre but an auditorium in a large building. She walked to the end of the corridor to a pair of double doors, signed No ENTRY. She looked behind her. The corridor was empty. She pushed at one of the doors. It was locked. She pushed at the other and it swung open. Joan slipped inside. The corridor continued and she could hear the sounds of voices. She was close to the stage, too far away to hear anything distinct, but she knew that if she followed the corridor round, she would come to the wings, could watch from there, catch him as he came off.

'Excuse me, lady.' A large man in a blue uniform, UCLA PD emblazoned on his shirt, stood in front of her. 'May I see your pass?'

Joan looked up. 'I'm sorry,' she said. 'I don't have one.'

'Are you lost?'

'I must have mistaken my way,' she said, trying to see past him, to see if she was close.

'Then I must ask you to leave.' He pointed towards a fire door. 'The exit is your friend.' He opened it, waited for her to go through, slammed it shut behind her.

The door led directly outside and the afternoon sun was bright after the shade of the building but, Joan reasoned, this was most likely the exit Michael would come through. As far as she could see, there was no other door. A few yards away there was a bench. She'd wait there for him to come out.

Joan sat, tucking her bag onto her lap. The running and panic of the morning had left her shaky. She'd had no lunch and her stomach gurgled. She looked up to see if there was somewhere close to grab a sandwich, where she could keep an eye on the door. Her hat. Her hat was missing. She must have left in on the information stand. Or in the restroom. She jumped up. If she went to retrieve it, she might miss Michael even though there was still over half an hour of the event to run. What was wrong with her today? She'd do without it. The sun was warm, but not scorching. She settled back down on the bench. She'd collect the hat later.

Would he leave the auditorium immediately? Would people waylay him? Ask for his signature? And what would she say to him? *Michael.* Would he recognise her voice? Or would she have to introduce herself. *It's Joan. Do you remember me?* He would. Of course he would. Silly to think otherwise. Then what would she say? *How are you?* That seemed too lame. *I've thought about you for so long.* That would be too forward. What would he say? *Is it really you, Joan?* Would he say *I searched for you after the war?* Would he say *And the baby? What happened to our baby?*

What would she say? She leaned back on the bench, the afternoon sun bearing down, its warmth comforting. She shut her eyes. *Enjoy the moment.* Opened them. Had she missed him? She glanced at her watch. It was half past three. The event had been scheduled for an hour, according to the programme. He could be out any minute. She could see the door from where she sat. No need to go over and stand by it. It wouldn't do to accost him. There'd be time to walk over, for her to approach him. *Michael, it's Joan.*

The green room would be inside the auditorium. They'd whisk him up there to collect his things before they put him in a taxi headed for— Where? Did he live in LA? Santa Barbara? Had he flown in from some distant place? She should be waiting at the front of the building. If he had a plane to catch, he wouldn't want to be delayed. The pressure built inside, adrenaline churning, unsure whether to stay or rush to the front of Royce Hall.

This was a mistake. She should go home. Forget about him. The door opened and a group of men came out. Which one was Michael? She craned her neck for a better view. And there he was. She didn't think, hooked her bag under her arm, stood up, stepped out.

'Michael.'

She was nauseous, blood tossing and crashing in her head, ears ringing. She saw the ground rise, topsy turvy, heard the roaring din in her mind, and flung out her arms into its blackness.

KATHLEEN

Los Angeles and London: April 2006

Kathleen fetched Joan from the UCLA Medical Center. They'd kept her in three days, for tests.

'I told them I'd only fainted,' Joan said in the car. 'I'd not eaten, I'd been rushing, the sun was hot and I got up suddenly. No need to take all that blood and wallop me with a bunch of scans and what have you.'

'That's American medicine for you,' Kathleen said. 'They're terrified of being sued.'

'And they found nothing wrong,' Joan said, a note of triumph in her voice. 'They thought highly of you, mind.'

'You told them who I was?'

'Sure,' Joan said. Funny how easy it was to pick up those Americanisms, Kathleen thought. Joan hadn't been here five minutes and already her voice had a twang. 'I mean, I know you had all sorts of fancy handles, but imagine them in LA knowing who you were.'

'They wouldn't have asked me over,' Kathleen said, as drily as she could, 'if I was a nobody.'

'All the same.'

They pulled into the parking lot under the apartments, took the lift to their floor.

'The doctors said to take it easy,' Kathleen said. 'So sit down and I'll bring you some tea.' She walked into the kitchen. 'You never told me what you were doing on campus anyway.'

'I read about the Los Angeles Times Festival of Books,' Joan said. 'Sounded interesting, so I thought I'd see if I could get in.'

'Festival of Books? I didn't know you were a reader.'

'There's much you don't know about me.'

Kathleen put a teabag in a mug, poured on some boiling water. 'That's true, *mother*.' She saw Joan smile, a glimpse of sadness too. 'So what did you want to go to?'

'Oh, anything,' Joan said, her voice airy and casual. 'Whatever I could get into. But it was all sold out.'

'So why did Marius Dines visit you in hospital?'

'He found me,' Joan said. 'After I fainted, was checking I was all right.' She looks sly, Kathleen thought, as if she's fibbing. Or fishing.

'Every day?'

'Twice,' Joan said. 'It was easy for him. He teaches here, you know?'

'So I gather,' Kathleen said. 'Supposed to be a big shot. Marius Dines.'

'Dines,' Joan said, turning the word from one into two syllables. Kathleen detected a note of superiority, as if Joan had one over her. Well, Kathleen thought, let her. It wasn't often she could do that. Kathleen winced. That was an awful thing to say about Joan, and there she was, about to make a big comeback album, with a film about her and all. In their own ways, they'd both made their mark.

Kathleen carried in Joan's tea and fetched a cold drink from the fridge for herself, placing it on a coaster on the coffee table. She took a deep breath. 'Listen, Joan, I'm so sorry, but I'm going to have to go back home.'

'What? Why?'

'I got a call while you were hospital.' She shifted in her seat, plumped up a cushion behind her. 'It's David. He's had a massive heart attack.' A lump of grief welled inside her. It was hard to be impassive. She loved him more than she ever thought possible.

'David? Good heavens,' Joan said. 'I thought he was toast.'

'Well,' Kathleen said, 'we had a reconciliation. Long story.' She added, 'Long-distance too at present.'

'Do you have to go back?'

'Of course,' Kathleen said. 'He needs me.'

Joan nodded, a slow, rhythmic movement, weighted with sadness. *I understand*. 'How long will you be gone?' she said. 'Do you want me to leave too?'

'A week or so,' Kathleen said. 'Until he's on his feet. And I don't need you to leave, unless you want to. Will you be all right by yourself? There's lots to do, and I can lend you my car.'

'Of course I'll be fine,' Joan said. 'I'm very happy sitting by the pool all day long.'

'And you have Marius Dines to look out for you,' Kathleen said, looking at Joan, raising an eyebrow.

'As a matter of fact,' Joan said, 'I do.'

She picked up her cup. Kathleen saw her smile before she puckered her mouth to sip her tea. Well, Kathleen thought, why not? Joan was still an attractive woman, deserved some happiness in her life. She wasn't sure how serious this Harry Bowen was anyway. A recipe for trouble, mixing work with pleasure.

§

He was in a stable condition, the doctors said. His bed was surrounded by curtains and he was sleeping when she arrived. His hair was white, changed colour overnight, like a winter hare. He's aged, Kathleen thought, grown old and fragile. She leaned over and kissed his forehead, felt him stir beneath her lips.

'It's you,' he said. She smelled his breath, sickly sweet. 'Thank you for coming.'

'Well, it was a scare,' she said.

'Quadruple bypass,' he said. 'Lucky to be alive.'

'And doubly lucky it happened at work so there was someone on hand.'

He swallowed. She watched his Adam's apple ripple. She noticed how scrawny his neck had become, as if his flesh had withered. 'Did you fly in from LA?'

She nodded. David beckoned with his fingers and she leaned forward, took them in her hand.

'Thank you,' he said, his voice soft and tender. 'Thank you again.'

She'd fallen in love with him, had consumed him, and he her, an unstoppable gale of desire. Feelings like that didn't die. They'd settle into old age, content. Derby and Joan. He'd get better, build up his strength. He'd always been a robust man. She swallowed back a tear as he elbowed his way into a new position on the pillow.

'Nothing like near death to bring a chap to his senses.' He squeezed her fingers, leaned back, the neck of his hospital gown falling open, revealing the pale, translucent skin of his chest, the fine down of white hair that covered it. 'I do love you, Kathleen. I want us to be together.' He closed his eyes, smiling, opened them, looked at her. 'For all times. I'm going to retire. I've made up my mind, do a bit of freelance to keep my hand in. We could live together. What do you say?'

He wouldn't be able to fly to LA for several weeks, and she wasn't sure if she could include him on her medical insurance. Pre-existing condition and all that. And they weren't married and that might affect the insurance, or his residency. The decision might be out of her hands, but she couldn't say that. He'd know it as well as her.

'Let's talk about it when you're better,' she said. 'I've never lived with anyone before. I may be the partner from hell.'

He gripped her hand, shaking his head. He shut his eyes, smiling.

'I'll leave you now to get some rest.' She pulled her hand free of his grip and kissed him on the forehead.

Joan had given Kathleen the keys to her flat. It wasn't ideal, but she'd rented out her apartment and didn't want to stay in a hotel. Besides, she'd wanted time alone, not to make small talk with a hall porter or maître d'. The shock of David. And then Michael O'Doyle. Her father. That was hard to take in. What kind of man would do that to his own daughter? The answer, she was sure, was a fraud. She didn't believe that man was her father. He was posing for some slimy, sinister reason. Sexual gratification. Money. He might have been old, but he was still a scumbag.

She opened the door to the balcony and stepped out into the London air. The evening was warm, the air balmy. The building had once had a swimming pool, Joan had said, and on an evening like now, Kathleen would have given her eye teeth for a dip in it, icy though it might be. She'd never really looked at the flats but could see their elegant modernism, and Joan's bedsit, though poky, was light and airy, with built-in cupboards and art deco tiles. Now Joan had a bit more money, perhaps she could get it decorated, invest in new furniture. It needn't be so dingy. Take away the carpet, sand the wooden parquet beneath, knock down the dividing wall and incorporate the kitchen into the main room with sleek, streamlined cupboards, a wall-mounted oven, a breakfast bar. Here Kathleen was, imagining a future as if the flat were hers. Perhaps, she thought, she and Joan weren't so different now, growing old with little more than the swansong of their careers to look forward to.

The doorbell rang, a sharp, raucous *brrrr*. Kathleen jumped, looked at her watch. It wasn't late, but she wasn't expecting anyone. Perhaps it was a neighbour investigating why there were noises when they knew Joan was away. *It's all right*, she'd reassure them. *I'm Joan's sister. Just using the flat.*

She opened the door. A tall, thin man stood outside, about Kathleen's age, possibly a little older. His hair was thin and spiky, pepper and salt, his skin pink and flaky. He wore glasses which, Kathleen could see, needed a good clean. Indeed, looking at him as he stood there in silence, she could see he was none too particular about his appearance. His jeans were worn and grubby on the thighs, his shirt shabby with a stain on the collar. There was something shifty about him. Down on his luck, perhaps.

All he had to do was push past her and slam the door and she'd be trapped. She was breathing in fast, shallow gulps.

It looked like he was gathering his wits, as if he had expected someone else to be standing before him.

'I'm looking for Lillie Pettall,' he said. 'Or Joan Spalding.'

Did he think they were two people? 'They're not here,' Kathleen said. 'Can I help?'

'They're the same person. Do you know where she is?'

There was an ugly twist to his lip, as if he had one over on her.

Kathleen froze. An instinct kicked in, *give nothing away*. 'I'm afraid not,' she said. 'I'm just using the flat. What's it about?'

'It's a personal matter.'

Joan would never have had anything to do with this unsavoury scruff standing here. She might have been poor, but she was proud and, in her way, a snob. Unless, of course, she'd borrowed money from one of those loan sharks and here was their enforcer, come to collect the debts.

'I can't help. Sorry.' She pushed the door to, but he wedged it open with his foot. He wore sandals. His heels were cracked, his toenails dirty. There was no one around. She could scream, but who would hear?

'Only I've written to her several times,' he went on. 'And knocked on her door.'

'What's it about?' Kathleen said.

He looked at her through his grubby glasses, swallowed, a scrawny Adam's apple rolling up and down. 'My name is Steve Kingsman,' he said. 'Lillie Pettall's a sort of relative. Like an aunt.' He gave a strange, possessive sort of smile. 'The singer. She's famous. I want to meet her.' He peered into the flat, at the shabby, threadbare furnishings, the tired, orange curtains. 'I didn't imagine her living like this. You know, *ordinary*. I'd have thought she must be rolling in it.'

Relative? He must be deranged, Kathleen thought. She knew there were people who preyed on fame, tried everything to get their hands on the money they thought went with it.

'I don't know who you mean,' she said. 'Please leave.'

'Are you her daughter?'

Kathleen looked up, sharp. Too sharp. She'd given herself away. 'Why do you want to know?'

'Are you her daughter, Kathleen?'

He knew her name, knew Joan had a daughter. No one knew that. Thoughts, connections ricocheted in her mind. If Joan somehow was his aunt, though she couldn't see how, then she and this man could be related.

'No,' she said. 'I'm just a friend.'

'Only this concerns her.'

She didn't trust the man, didn't trust what he had to say. Best ask Joan first.

'Will Joan be back soon?' he said. He frowned, his face crumpling with disappointment. 'I only want to meet her. I collect all her records. Got scrapbooks filled with pictures of her.'

'No,' Kathleen said. 'I told you. Go away.' Slammed the door against his bare foot. He yelped, yanked it free. She pulled the bolts.

The visit had been bizarre, the encounter unnerving. Kathleen sat in Joan's chair, unable to make head or tail of it. How had he known about her? Nobody, not even her brothers, *uncles*, knew she was Joan's daughter, apart from her mother, *grandmother*, and she was unlikely to have told anyone. The shame would have been too great. And how could Joan be his aunt? Unless it was by marriage. Had Joan secretly married? No, Kathleen thought, that was preposterous.

She pushed herself up and went into the kitchen, peering through the net curtains to see if he was still lurking on the balcony. He'd gone, as far as she could see. Should she text Joan? Tell her what had happened? Somebody called Steve – oh God, she couldn't remember his name. Steve King? No. King something. Kingston. *Kingsman*. That was it. She should write it down. She wasn't usually forgetful. Was this the beginning of the end, short-term memory loss? Surely not. It had just been a hard day, she told herself, the emotions had taken up all the room in her head, pushed out her thoughts, left no space for remembering. She half smiled. For a scientist, that was a stupid analysis. She wanted to go out for a walk, clear her head, but what if that man was loitering? Waiting for her?

Joan had once told her she kept all her documents in a box, her passport, her insurance, the instructions for her mobile phone, the guarantee for the kettle. She'd even written a will, she said, and that was there.

Why think of that now? Perhaps there were other secrets there. A marriage certificate. Kathleen shouldn't nose around Joan's flat, but on the other hand, why not? Her sister – her mother – would be none the wiser. She delved into the cupboard, pulled out a box file, opened it up. There was a letter at the top, from Steve Kingsman, which Joan had not destroyed. Who knows if she'd answered it? It was from an address in Littleheath.

There were guarantees for everything she had ever bought, some way beyond their expiry dates. There were old passports, council tax bills, hire purchase agreements. Heavens, who had those now, with credit cards? Contracts for performances at venues long closed. She'd love to chuck the whole lot away. It was no possible use to her. There was the agreement with Roxie II, with Music Management Global, another with a record company dated January 2006. Wow, Kathleen thought. She couldn't resist reading it through. A contract for an album, *Lillie Come Lately*. A Nectar card, her library ticket. Spare buttons in a small plastic bag.

She laid the items out on the coffee table in the order in which she'd excavated them. There was a small buff envelope at the bottom of the file, yellowed and brittle with age. She had to claw at it with her nails to prise it away from the floor of the box, where it had stuck. It couldn't have been looked at in years. Kathleen turned it over, opened it up, pulled out a piece of paper folded into four. She opened it up, flap by flap.

> *Mother and Baby Home, Dunsfield Street, London SW9.*
> *Notification of birth details. Top copy.*
> *Instructions to informant: Hand this slip to the Registrar of Births, Deaths and Marriages. It is a legal requirement to register all births, including stillbirths, under the Births and Deaths Registration Act 1894, section 30.*
> *Name of informant: Joan Spalding*
> *Qualifications of informant: Mother*
> *Sex of child: Female*
> *Name of father (if known): Michael O'Doyle*
> *Name of child: Kathleen*
> *Date of birth: 28 June 1944*
> *Condition of child at birth: Stillborn.*

Stillborn. Dead. Kathleen, child of Joan and Michael, had never lived.

The words squirmed and scuttled under her gaze. Nothing made sense. Who was she?

JOAN

Los Angeles: April 2006

The journey to Santa Barbara seemed easy enough. From Kathleen's apartment it was pretty much a line to Santa Monica then up the Pacific Coast Highway, past famous beaches, Venice, Malibu, magic names from California's mythic present. She pored over the map. These were big distances, but the drive looked straightforward. Marius had said he'd drive her, if she preferred, but she wanted to go by herself.

He had been tickled pink when she'd told him who she was.

'Joan?' he said. '*The* Joan? From "Joan's Song"?'

'That's why I was waiting for him.'

'Me and Mikey,' Marius went on, 'we go back some. To think you're Joan, after all these years.' He contacted Michael on her behalf, and Michael replied to his email by return. *Joan? Sure! Send her up to Santa Barbara. We'll have lunch.*

If Joan was honest, she'd hoped for a more enthusiastic response, or something less casual but then, she thought, her approach was out of the blue, the man needed time to collect his thoughts. Marius gave Joan the address and instructions on how to find Michael in his residency at the University of California, Santa Barbara. 'For the spring and summer quarter,' he said. 'Though beats me why he chose those quarters and not the fall and winter. You ever been to Ithaca in the winter?'

Joan shook her head. 'I've been to New York,' she said. 'That was cold enough.'

'Still,' Marius went on, as if she hadn't answered, 'he always was perverse. You sure you don't want me to drive you?'

'I'll be fine.'

It was destined that she and Michael should be in California at the same time, she knew it.

Joan took a sleeping pill the night before, went to bed early to be sure its effects would have worn off by morning. Had a good breakfast, took a shower, dressed. Clean underwear, a blue floral cotton dress with cap sleeves, a flowing skirt and a wide black belt. It had a square neck, low enough to suggest the tip of a cleavage. Not too much. Her skin wrinkled like elephant hide these days when she squeezed her breasts into her bra, nothing to show off about. He hadn't seen her for over sixty years, so he couldn't expect youth, but he could expect alluring, cared for, proud.

She changed her mind at the last minute about driving. She hadn't driven for years and this was in an unfamiliar car, on the wrong side of the road. Took a taxi to Union Station, and a train to Santa Barbara. Another taxi to the University Club and Guest House. Her English accent opened doors along the way. She was grateful for the chit-chat, stopped her from dwelling on the reunion, the impossible, implausible happiness of it.

'Hey, you on vacation? Why you only visiting Santa Barbara for a day? Don't you know it's the most beautiful city in the state?'

'I'm meeting an old friend.'

'That's nice. When did you last see him?'

'More than sixty years ago.'

'My God, I wasn't even born then.'

She was dropped off at the Club, entered the foyer, found the restrooms. Just to be sure, just to check. She slipped her sunglasses on top of her head, touched up her lipstick, combed her hair. She turned to the side, saw herself in the full-length mirror, made sure her dress was not tucked into her knickers, her hands were cool and clean. She might be in her mid-seventies, she thought, but she still had a good figure, and her new clothes were the height of fashion. She smiled at herself, stepped forward. *Michael.* Arms outstretched. *Let me look at you.*

There were several men waiting in the foyer, but none were Michael. She was five minutes early, but even so, she'd imagined him to be the first to welcome her. There were some leather easy chairs by the empty fireplace and she sat in one, positioned to see the doors, monitor who came and went. The busyness of a club, colleagues meeting, sidling off to eat, visiting scholars, checking their watches. Ladies, too, here for lunch. Were they wives? Gosh, no, she told herself. Mustn't *assume.* Most women worked now. These were probably professionals. Look at Kathleen. Look at herself.

He was ten minutes late already. She didn't have any contact details for him. Marius had those, and he'd organised the whole rendezvous. They hadn't given Joan Michael's email or phone number. They hadn't had to spell out why. She knew. *In case you're a fraud.* Perhaps women stalked him, claimed to be Joan, begged him for money. Fame attracted that. Except, she reasoned, he couldn't be *that* famous, otherwise she'd have heard of him, surely?

If he didn't turn up soon, she'd give Marius a ring. Make sure she had the right time and place. The deep worm of despair was burrowing its way into her. She had waited for Michael before, week after week, year after year. Perhaps he had no intention of coming now. She may as well turn round and go straight back to LA.

But there he was, threading his way through the foyer, searching for her. She stepped forward, smiling. 'Michael.'

'Joan?' And it was as she had imagined it would be, arms outstretched, hands entwined. 'I'm sorry I'm late. A colleague—' He broke off, released one hand, waved it in the air. 'You know how it is, "I won't keep you a minute," and ten minutes later, there you are still.' He was talking as if sixty years hadn't passed, as if their reunion was routine, a bi-monthly event of no great import. 'Come,' he said. 'Let's eat.'

The restaurant was crowded. Joan wanted to pull him away, *can't we go somewhere quieter? More private?* Had he chosen this place deliberately? What did those dating agencies advise? *When meeting a stranger for the first time, choose a public place.* There were no quiet niches, no hidden corners where two lovers could meet again, no soft surfaces in the functional furniture, no hiding from the harsh daylight that flooded through the windows.

'So,' he said, as they sat at their table, 'what brings you to this part of the world?'

'A holiday,' Joan said. 'Staying in LA.' She'd keep Kathleen in reserve, for when he asked.

'That's nice.' They needed time, she could see, to bridge the chasm of the years.

'And you? Marius said you live in Ithaca, upstate New York.'

'People think we writers make a lot of money, but we need regular employment too. Hence the residency.' He studied the wine list, signalled to the waiter. 'A glass of chardonnay, please. And you, Joan? Would you care for a drink?'

'Thank you,' she said. 'I'll have the same.'

'When was the last time I saw you? I was trying to figure it out.'

Joan swallowed, a hard gob of saliva. She remembered every second of that meeting. Had he forgotten? Was he fishing for clues, so he could riff on that? Or was he testing her, making sure she was no imposter? 'It was in the war,' she said.

'That's right,' he said. 'It's coming back to me now. Yorkshire.' He pronounced it as two words, *York Shire.*

'No,' Joan said. 'East Anglia.'

'Of course, of course. How could I forget? Tell you the truth, those times were a bit chaotic, my memories hazy. I was posted round so often, and then we were sent to Normandy. That was terrible.' He shook his head, his mouth tight.

He was a good eight years older than her and Joan wondered whether dementia already had a grip on him. That could account for it, his demeanour, distant, unengaged.

'And what have you been doing for the last sixty years?'

'I became a singer,' she said, adding, though she didn't mean to, 'You said never to stop singing. "That way, you'll always be able to hear me." Do you remember?'

'Did I say that?'

'Yes,' Joan said. She didn't think she'd have to prompt him. 'You wrote me a song. You can't have forgotten.'

Was she talking to the same man? A sharp stiletto was needling at the core of her memories, shaving them away, slice by slice. She bit her lip, in case it quivered. This was all so wrong. She could see that now.

'Yes,' she said. She wasn't going to give up, not that easily. She hummed a note, began to sing, as soft as she could, intimate, across the table:

> *'The shadow of her smile, the dapple of her laugh,*
> *The biting of the earth, the blowing of the chaff.*
> *She rises like a phoenix from the ashes.*
> *And calls my name.'*

'That's pretty,' he said. 'Did I write that? I don't recall.' He leaned back, looked at her across the table, eyes narrowed, his thick white eyebrows twisted into a skein.

'"Joan's Song",' she said.

'I wrote a long narrative poem called "Joan's Song",' he said. 'But it wasn't really for you. Or about you, come to think of it.'

This was not how she had imagined the reunion. She wanted to back off, change the conversation. She should never have reminded him. She was angry with him for distorting the memory, squeezing the tenderness out of it.

'You used my words,' Joan said. 'Marius quoted them in his interview. I recognised them. You'd said you wanted to write about working men and women, like you and me. But I said those words.'

'Every writer regurgitates experience,' he said. 'Milling words, processing encounters. It's never raw. Readers see things in a poem or a novel that the author never intended. I think you wanted to see things.'

'You wrote in the first person.' She wasn't going to let him get away with this. 'As if it was your experience, as if you were there.' She realised she was quarrelling, needed to soften her tone. 'Don't worry.' She laughed. 'Singers do the same.'

'No,' he said. 'Singers are merely ventriloquists.'

The waiter placed a glass of wine in front of him, one for Joan. She leaned back in her seat, lifted her glass, smarting from the put-down, trying to hide her hurt. She hated Californian chardonnay.

'Why didn't you come for me after the war?' she said. Her composure was slipping. 'You promised you'd find me, marry me.'

'How could I have done that?' he said. 'I was married. Had a wife and family.'

'I was pregnant,' she said.

'I didn't know that.'

'You did.' Joan raised her voice. 'We were going to call the baby Kathleen if it was a girl.' She closed her eyes. She wouldn't temper her words. 'Kathleen. After your own stillborn daughter.'

'Really?' He blinked fast, a chink in the armour. 'That doesn't sound like me.'

'What are you saying? What are you implying? Michael...' She stopped herself, leaned back in the chair and studied his face. This was not how it had been. She had meant so much to him, and now he was denying everything.

Or was it that he'd meant too much to her, that everything that followed had been a fantasy? She'd made the whole thing up. A foolish child, grasping a dream. Had her life been warped, her memory twisted, by this chimera of a love? Had she lied to herself, all these years? He'd never said he'd come back. He'd given her a two-dollar bill and washed his hands of her. She'd made the rest up, to bury the hurt.

'Listen,' he said, 'I don't rightly know why you've come to visit me after all these years. Sure, it's nice to make your acquaintance again, but what is it you want of me?'

The years had plied his skin with scales, the little fame he had conferred an arrogance. This wasn't the tender, young airman she had fallen in love with but a self-centred, angry old man. And then it came to her. Of course. She'd not seen this before. How could she have done, blinded by infatuation, driven by a pipe dream?

'You took advantage of me, Michael,' she said. 'I was a sixteen-year-old child and you were twenty-four. A grown man. A married man. You abused me. Hung me out to dry.'

'I'm sorry to interrupt.' A waiter hovered by her shoulder, his torso at eye level. 'Are you folks ready to order?'

Joan slapped the napkin on the table. 'Yes,' she said. 'You can stuff him for a start.' She stood up, catching the tablecloth in her skirt, walking away and leaving a trail of shattered glass and tumbling cutlery, a raucous cacophony of broken memories.

Joan had been emptied, the meaning of her life flushed away, reduced to flashes of the California coast, the suburban malls and industrial zones, the traffic on the freeways, a maelstrom of lane changes and blaring horns. She hated this place. She hated the glare, the brashness, the scorched lawns and arid landscapes, the people with their phoney cheer and *have a good day*, their informality and familiarity. She wanted to go home. She wanted her dingy flat in Streatham with its brown moquette chairs and orange curtains, her box of treasures and her scrapbook. She wanted to be alone, content with her life, not chasing a dream of a forever land, a never-never land.

She wanted Harry.

Joan paid the cab driver. It was late afternoon, still hot. She could hear voices from the swimming pool, children playing. It was always quiet in the mornings when she went, sitting in the shallow end, bathing in its coolness, sinking back into that primal element of life.

She turned the key and opened the door. Kathleen's suitcase was in the hallway. She wanted time by herself, not to have to explain where she had been, or why. She wanted Kathleen to go away.

'Right,' Kathleen said, coming out of her bedroom, waving a piece of paper, 'you've got some explaining to do.' She held the paper open, thrust it before Joan's eyes. *Mother and Baby Home, Dunsfield Street, London SW9.*

Joan moved over to the sofa, sat down. She needed time, to collect herself.

JOAN

Mother and Baby Home, London: June 1944

'I said, what did you have?' Joan turned. A young woman in the bed next to her was leaning over, pointing at her. 'Cat got your tongue?'

'What?' Joan said.

'Blimey. I was wondering if you even talked English,' the young woman said. 'I've asked three times now. What did you have?'

Marbled blue, slick with blood.

'A stillborn.' Joan's voice was frail. She'd never get used to that word.

'Oh, that's a shame,' the young woman said, swinging her legs over the side of the bed. She flexed her foot and leaned forward. 'All that work for nothing.'

Joan shut her eyes, waved her hand. *Go away. Leave me alone.*

'They're right cows in here,' the young woman went on. 'Bitter, twisted spinsters, the lot of them. All preachy and holier-than-thou. Don't you listen to a word they say. How long they going to keep you here?'

Joan shrugged. She wished the woman would shut up. 'I don't know. They didn't say. I suppose a fortnight, like everyone else.'

She was tired and the babies in the nursery were crying. Her baby was crying, she was sure of it. How could she be dead? A pale, limp form in the palm of the midwife's hand, wrapped in muslin like a butcher's carcass. That wasn't Kathleen. Her baby, *their* baby. All that love. Joan hadn't seen her, hadn't held her, kissed her goodbye, up with the angels. Not even a lock of hair. Her grandmother had done that, with the babies she'd lost, blonde curls pressed between the fine pages of her Bible.

The young woman heaved herself into the chair next to Joan. 'My name's Irene,' she said, holding out her hand. 'But everyone calls me Queenie. What's yours?'

'Joan.'

'And how old are you, Joan?'

'Sixteen. Nearly seventeen.'

'Just a child.'

Joan shut her eyes, rolled onto her side, away from Queenie.

They didn't need to tell her. The cold metal blades of the forceps grappled as the spasms grew more painful, twisted and tugged, Joan on her back, agony sharp as a sword, the room turning and swaying and the limp blue mollusc taken away without a cry. The baby had been dead for some days. Dead before its time. Joan had screamed and screamed even though her eyes were dry and her chest was tight.

Her baby wasn't stillborn. She was in her cot. Joan wanted to tell the midwives as they marched up and down the ward, *She's not dead, she's alive, can't you hear her?* as they pushed open the swing doors at the end of the ward, letting in the sounds from the nursery, the wails of the newborns. *That's my baby.*

'Do you want to see her?' Queenie was saying.

She must have slept, because it was almost dark in the ward. Joan rolled over. Queenie was standing next to her, holding a baby, its cries sharp and jarring. Joan pushed herself into a sitting position, unsure, her limbs frail and shaky.

'Here you are,' Queenie said, handing the child to Joan, its tongue quivering as it screamed, its fontanelle throbbing. 'It's a girl.'

Joan took the baby, studied her face, pink from yelling. *Kathleen.* She stroked the fair down on her head. *My Kathleen.* She placed her thumb on the baby's dimpled chin, looked up at Queenie. 'Give me the bottle.'

She'd never fed a baby but she guided the teat in to Kathleen's mouth, watched as the infant latched on, began to suck, her lips folded over the nipple, the muscles in her jaw clenching and slackening.

'My husband'll kill me if he finds out about her,' Queenie went on, nodding towards the feeding baby.

'Why?' Joan said.

The woman laughed. 'Why d'you think? She's not his, stupid. It was just a bit of fun, didn't mean anything, night out at the Trocadero, but look where it landed me. You ever been to the Trocadero? You should go sometime. Maybe you and me could go together.'

'The baby?' Joan said.

'Besides,' Queenie said, 'I've got two kids already. How would I feed a third?'

'What will happen to her?' Joan said. Words with a hard echo, for this was her baby and nothing could happen to her.

'Well, once I've signed the papers, they take her.'

'Who?'

'Those busybody welfare workers,' the woman said. 'Put her up for adoption.'

'Strangers?' Joan said. 'You'd let your baby go to strangers?' They'd said they'd take away her baby's body to be buried with someone she'd never met, sharing a grave. Could be a kind person, or a cruel one, no way of knowing. A pauper's funeral, that's what the midwife had said.

Queenie shrugged. 'Why not?'

'No,' Joan said. The baby had finished her feed, lay drunk on the milk, eyelids drowsy, folding over her ink-grey eyes.

'You can't give her to strangers,' Joan said. 'Give her to me. I'll love her and care for her.' Kathleen wasn't stillborn, hadn't died and rotted in the womb. Kathleen was here in Joan's arms, alive and well with her crumpled face and puffy eyes, fine, fair down on her head, traced with blood. She looked at the tiny body in her towelling nappy, at the stump of the cord, at her hands, wrinkled and articulated, the soft, fleshy feet, at her chest rising and falling as she breathed. Joan began to hum, rocking the baby in her arms.

'You're a natural,' Queenie said. 'Even though you're only a scrap of a thing.'

'I'll take really good care of her, I promise.' Joan's eyes had misted but she looked at Queenie as the baby opened her eyes and began to cry again. 'I'll call her Kathleen. I like that name.' And Michael would never know. 'She wants another bottle, I reckon.'

'She'll be lucky,' Queenie said. 'Every four hours, on the nose, bottles made up, handed out. We have to feed them together. I expect she's got wind.'

The baby was crying hard now. Joan propped her over her shoulder, patting her back, swaying. *It's all right*, she wanted to say, *everything will be all right*. She felt a small posset of sick soak through her nightgown, moist and warm on her shoulder. She loved this baby, as sure as if she'd given birth to it herself. How could that be wrong? They did this with the cows, if one lost its calf, they'd give the mother another to suckle and she'd be none the wiser. We're all animals, she thought.

§

Queenie told the welfare workers she'd changed her mind, was going to keep the baby, a little sister to her two boys, Steven and Brian.

'Then I'll hand her over to you,' Queenie said. 'Once we're outside. Now...' She paused, picked her nose. 'We got to register the babies with the Council and that's the tricky bit, because they give you a piece of paper when you leave to take to the registrar with your name and the baby's birth on it, and I expect you'll get the same for your little one.'

Joan tried to take this in. She hadn't realised that you had to register the baby, it had never occurred to her till now.

'So we got to swap the papers, but the names have got to be right. See' – she looked squarely at Joan, her voice barely above a whisper – 'I've thought this out. I'm only doing it for you. Be much easier to let them take care of it, except I'd have to pay for the fostering till it was adopted.'

It was early evening. They'd had their tea, and the babies their six o'clock feed. The ward was quiet. Some of the girls were reading or dozing. One or two were playing patience. Others chatting, two at a time, leaning across the spaces between the beds.

'They write the baby's details on special chits they keep in the office,' Queenie said. 'I've been watching them and seen where they keep them. Top right-hand drawer, sister's desk.' She looked behind her. 'When the midwife leaves to get the feeds ready, go into the office and tear a couple of the sheets off of the pad. From the bottom, mind, so they don't notice.'

Joan had never done anything wrong in her life, but she'd steel herself to do it now. It wasn't a sin, after all, to want a baby, to love it. She lay on her bed, hands damp, her breath catching in her throat, flimsy, airy, waiting for the midwife to leave the ward to make up the bottles, counting the minutes and the hours by the clock, the seconds as they dragged. Eight. Nine o'clock. Nine thirty. Nine thirty-five and three seconds.

'Go on,' Queenie said, nodding towards the empty office. Joan pushed herself up, heart pounding, the sharp taste of fear and excitement in her mouth. What if one of the other girls saw her, raised the alarm? What if she was caught? She'd have to tell a lie, say she was sleepwalking. She sidled off the bed, bare feet on the linoleum, hands clammy. She could feel the sweat in her armpits, the thud of her pulse as the blood churned, tiptoeing through the gloom of the ward, into the office. The desk was directly ahead of her, and on it a fountain pen, a thermometer, a stethoscope. She looked through the glass partition at the rows of beds filled with dozing women. Opened the top drawer on the right. Queenie had done her homework. There was the pad. Joan pulled it out. The name of the home and its address were printed across the top and, beneath it, the lines to be filled in. A sheet of carbon stuck out, its edges frayed. The ward was quiet. She opened the book from the back, tore out the pages, replaced the pad in the drawer, pushed it shut.

'Well,' the midwife said as they stood before her the next morning, 'you two have become chummy.'

'Family friends,' Queenie said, quick as a flash. 'Ain't we, Joan?'

The midwife looked at her, at Joan. Took her fountain pen and wrote in the pad, tearing off the top sheet and giving it to Queenie. 'You need this to give to the registrar.' She turned to Joan, lifting the carbon paper and putting it beneath another sheet, writing the details, handing it to Joan. 'You too. Only yours will be Stillbirth.' She looked at Joan, narrowed her eyes. 'God doesn't like a sinner.' No tenderness in her voice, no sentiment to break its harshness.

Joan and Queenie stepped out of the double doors of the Mother and Baby Home, crossed the front drive, walked into the street. Queenie was holding the baby wrapped in a moth-eaten shawl, which the midwife had given her. 'We'll get a tram to Kennington Park,' she said. 'No one will disturb us there.'

'I'd rather walk,' Joan said. 'The last time I was on a tram a doodlebug hit.'

'Well,' Queenie said, 'lightning never hits twice and it's too far to walk, so either you come on the tram or we forget the whole thing.'

Joan swallowed, climbed on board, sat on the long seat by the doors. Joan took the baby, held her in her arms.

'Little mite,' another passenger said, looking at Joan. 'Is that your baby sister?'

'Pretty, ain't she?' Queenie said, quick off the mark. 'Healthy too. But what a time to be born, eh?'

They got off at the park, found a bench not far from the place where Auntie Win said a bomb had dropped on a shelter and killed almost everyone inside. They'd just put lime on the bodies, Auntie Win said, covered them where they lay. Joan shuddered. Death was all around her. War and death. She wasn't sure how much longer she could take this.

'Come on then,' Queenie said. 'I haven't got all day.'

Joan had hidden the chits in her bra, and fished them out. Queenie delved into the pocket of her frock, pulled out the midwife's pen.

'Where did you get that?' Joan said. 'I didn't see you take it.'

'Nor would you,' Queenie said. 'You've got a lot to learn, Joan.' She nodded at the pages of the notebook. 'You better write it. I can't do joined-up.'

Joan passed Kathleen to Queenie and pressed the pages flat on the wooden slatted bench. 'I'll do yours first,' she said, reading out. '"Mother's name". What shall I write?'

'Irene Mildred Kingsman.'

Sex of child: Female. Date of birth: 28 June 1944. Condition at birth – Joan hesitated. It was such a strong word, *stillborn*, had such a lonely life. She swallowed hard, looked away, because if a tear fell on the paper it would make the ink run and then what would they do? Steeled herself, wrote it out so it looked identical to the chit the midwife had given Joan, except for the name. She took the second page, filled in her name, Joan Spalding, sex, date. Condition at birth: *Healthy*. She replaced the nib in its holder, waved the pages to dry, gave one to Queenie, tucked the other back inside her bra, along with the original the midwife had completed, and held out her hands to take the baby.

'I want something for my trouble,' Queenie said.

'What do you mean?'

'You owe me. For her.'

'I've no money,' Joan said. 'I thought this was from the goodness of your heart. For the baby.' She was close to tears. Queenie going back on her word. What if she took Kathleen back to the home, had her adopted? 'Please, Queenie,' Joan said. 'I love her.' She looked hard into Queenie's eyes, saw steel there, deceit. 'Besides,' she added, 'you said it would save you the cost of fostering.'

'Well,' Queenie said, scowling, 'you can pay me later.' She paused. 'Or I tell everyone how you snatched the baby from me.' She narrowed her eyes, heart of iron. Joan had no doubt she meant it. 'They put you inside for life for that. *Life*.' She waved her original docket from the home. 'I have the evidence.'

Joan breathed in so sharp it made her cough. Her mind had furred, her thoughts tangled. She had to get away, she and Kathleen, go somewhere Queenie would never discover. Where would she get the money to pay her?

'You can find me in the Peabody buildings, Waterloo. Everybody knows Queenie. And you?'

Joan swallowed, spat out her address, only she gave the wrong house number and the wrong street. Queenie nodded, passed the baby to Joan, who took her. Joan ran out of the park, crossed the road, ran and ran. She stopped to catch her breath, glancing behind her. Queenie had gone, was nowhere to be seen. She looked around her, at the bombed-out church of St Mark's, at the sandbags lined up along the Brixton Road, the taped-up windows of those houses that hadn't been clobbered to the ground. She saw a tram in the distance, ran to the stop. She had to get away fast. Clambered aboard and sat down, shutting her eyes. *Please, no doodlebugs*, handing over her fare. She'd register Kathleen on her way home, make it all secure so Queenie wouldn't have a leg to stand on if she made trouble. Joan would make a makeshift cradle from the bottom drawer, place Kathleen out of the draughts. Queenie would never find her, never claw Kathleen back. Joan would make sure of that.

Irene Mildred Kingsman had a stillborn child buried in a pauper's grave and she, Joan Spalding, had a healthy baby girl called Kathleen.

This was true as she stood there that June day in Kennington Park.

KATHLEEN

Los Angeles: April 2006

The doors to the balcony were open. Music drifted in from the pool area, blended with the muted growl of traffic, the clink and tinkle of cutlery and china from the neighbours' al fresco supper, their soft murmurings. It made the silence louder, the space between them cavernous. Kathleen sat on the sofa facing out, watching palm trees silhouetted against a magenta sky, their fronds creaking in the high breeze. The air was warm, sucked dry. She was exhausted from the flight, her body topsy-turvy, her head thick and spinning. But her mind was elsewhere, watching, *listening* as the foundations of her life crumbled and dissolved in the parched California atmosphere.

'Why didn't you tell me I was dead?' she said. 'That I never existed? That the "I" who is "me" is not who I thought I was?' She wasn't sure she made sense. Or would ever make sense. 'How can I believe anything you say?' She curled herself into a ball on the sofa. 'You'd never have told me, would you? If I hadn't found out.'

'Probably not,' Joan said. She paused, added, 'You'd have been happier for it.'

'Living a lie? A double lie? You think that would have made me happy?' What had Joan thought as she handed over another woman's baby to a mother who'd thrown her out, who had no idea she was taking in a changeling, had made Joan swear she'd never acknowledge her as a daughter? *Oh what a tangled web we weave when first we practice to deceive.*

'You didn't know. And what you don't know can't hurt.' Joan shrugged. 'It was what you call this *lie* that brought us together.'

Kathleen looked past Joan to the sunset outside. Her body clock told her it was dawn, not dusk. The sky was turning a deep indigo. If she kept her eye on the king palms, would they stay in her sight forever? Her thoughts were empty, focused on the trees and the darkening heavens, her feelings churning in an inchoate mass.

She was aware of Joan sitting opposite her, a sallow face in the thickening gloom of the room. She should put on the lights, but it was more comfortable in the shadows, disembodied voices, a confessional of sorts. 'Who knew?' she said.

'No one. Only Queenie. She must have told her son.'

If Joan was telling the truth, Steve Kingsman was her half-brother. They shared chromosomes and genes, traits and mutations. She felt nothing but contempt for him. Was his face, in some way she hadn't understood, familiar to her? She had been repulsed by him. Joan had spared her from him, she'd say that for her.

She looked at Joan in the vestigial light from the lamps in the gardens below. Her face was drawn, her mouth cast down. She seemed to have aged in the last hour. Her frame had collapsed, body slumped like discarded skin. Kathleen could contact this Steve Kingsman, own up to who she was, meet her birth mother. That would give her a story, a location for her life. And then what? She had nothing in common with him except the lining of a mother's womb, and those chromosomes and genes. What would she have become, growing up beside him? Which was harder to live with, Queenie's truth or Joan's lie? She didn't know. Nothing was certain.

'What does he want?' Kathleen said. 'What can he do?'

'I don't know,' Joan said. 'I don't even know if what I did was illegal.'

'Of course it was illegal,' Kathleen snapped. 'You lied to the registrar, you fraudulently claimed to be my mother.'

'But I loved you.'

Kathleen snorted. 'Then gave me away? What sort of a mother were you? My grandmother, the person I called Mum, never loved me. I knew that. Children do. They're like animals, they know indifference, resentment.'

'We've been through this before,' Joan said. Kathleen could hear her breathing, knew her shoulders would be rising and falling as her lungs filled and emptied.

'I've had three women now who claimed to be my mother,' Kathleen said. 'How many more are there? And not a father between any of them.'

'Queenie never claimed motherhood,' Joan said.

Kathleen could hear Joan scratching at the arm of her chair, opening her mouth as if about to say something, closing it. She knew she was looking at her, could tell by the way the whites of her eyes were luminous in the gloom. She heard the *putt* of Joan's lips as she opened her mouth again.

'Who do you think made sure you got to the grammar school?' Joan said. 'Who paid for your uniform, and the bus and your dinners?'

'What do you mean?'

'Your mother – our mother – stopped me going to the grammar school, but when you passed the exam I moved heaven and earth to make sure you went. I didn't want you standing by the bus shelter like I did watching your friends go off, knowing you could have been there, *should* have been there, that education was your ticket out and you were denied it.' She paused, took in her breath. 'Who do you think arranged for you to live with Miss Loughton? Paid for you?'

Kathleen turned to face Joan, her head to one side, forehead creasing. 'That was a bursary,' Kathleen said. 'Nothing to do with you.'

'There was no bursary,' Joan said. 'That's what we agreed to tell you.'

Lies on lies on lies. Did enough lies make a truth?

'Miss Loughton knew you were my mother?'

'No,' Joan said. 'She only knew that I cared for your future. She didn't ask questions.'

Kathleen swallowed, trying to take it all in.

'When you got to Oxford,' Joan went on, 'my father refused to fill out the form for your grant, denying you your place.'

'They didn't want me to go, I know that,' Kathleen said. 'They thought university was the Antichrist. Not a place for Christian girls. But I got a grant.'

Joan shook her head. 'I opened a bank account for you and paid money into it at the start of every term. You thought you had a grant.'

'You paid for me?'

Joan sitting there, poker face, nodding.

'I don't believe you,' Kathleen said. 'Why the subterfuge? Why didn't you just give me the money?'

'I didn't want you to be beholden to me.'

'You're lying,' Kathleen said.

Where had Joan got that kind of money? She hardly had two pennies to rub together, working on the liners, touring the clubs. As long as Kathleen had known her, she was on her uppers or living a lifestyle she could ill afford on the whims of men she didn't love. She didn't know when to stop lying. She'd taken a baby, passed her over to someone else to nurture, and now claimed to have been a good mother all along.

'This was the only way I could show my love,' Joan said. 'It's as simple and as complex as that.' She smiled. 'Harvard you did all on your own. I was so proud.'

'And my alleged father, Michael? Is he another lie?'

'Michael O'Doyle fathered the baby I carried and gave birth to as true as I am standing here. And he would have fathered you, had he kept to his word.'

'He's the writer, isn't he? Michael O'Doyle, the writer,' Kathleen said. 'You could have said. You sent me on a wild goose chase, trying to trace him. You could have saved me time and heartache.'

'I'm sorry,' Joan said. 'I didn't think it would mean so much to you.'

'You didn't think, full stop,' Kathleen said. She began to shout, anger and upset catching in her throat. 'This Michael O'Doyle. You'd never have told him the truth either, would you?' She grabbed the cushion, threw it at her sister as hard as she could muster. 'I don't ever want to talk to you again. Or see you. Get out.'

Kathleen pushed herself up, walked to the bedroom, dragging her suitcase behind her. As she shut her door Joan began to sob. *Let her.* Let her weep and wail and gnash her teeth and burn in the fiery furnace of hell.

KATHLEEN

London: December 2006

Irene. Queenie. She'd often wondered why her genes had tumbled differently from the others. Now it made sense.

'She may have given birth to you,' Susan had said, 'but Joan gave you your life. There's a difference.'

'Whose side are you on?' Kathleen had said.

'Sure you're hurt. But nothing really changes. Do you honestly want to meet your birth mother? After what Joan has told you about her? After you met her son?'

But she did. Joan's deception had been a weeping sore at first. It had now festered, had become a livid, purulent wound, its stinking discharge a miasma clouding her judgement. Queenie had become an obsession, an answer to the most basic questions of all: *Who am I? Where did I come from?*

David met Kathleen at the airport and took her back to his flat.

'I've cut down on my drinking,' he said. 'I swim every day. I eat healthily. I have a good pension. Look at me. A picture of fitness.'

'I'm so proud of you,' Kathleen said, folding herself into his arms. She'd seen him four times since his heart attack, twice in LA. He'd flown over as soon as he was fit enough. Twice in London, though they'd spoken almost every day. It was hard, loving someone so far away, needed adjustments every time.

'I have some news,' he said. He was smiling, blue eyes glinting.

'Oh?'

'I've just become the Russell T. Connolly Professor of Journalism at the University of Southern California.'

'What?'

'Couldn't quite face retirement, nor carrying on with you from afar. So I did the next best thing.'

'You'll be in LA?' Kathleen said. 'We'll be together?'

He was nodding, smiling. She laughed. And then they came, words from nowhere, because she had never, ever once thought about it.

'David John Lambe, will you marry me?'

'Yes,' he said. 'I can't think of anything better than marrying you.'

Two days later, coming off the tram link at Littleheath, she clutched her handbag closer to her body, tightened her scarf, checked her *A–Z* and set off for Kennard Close. It was risky to turn up unannounced, she knew, but if he'd had warning, he could prepare himself, and she wanted to catch him on the hop. This conversation could only be held in person, though she had no idea what she'd say to him.

'You sure you don't want me to come with you?' David had said. 'In case he turns nasty?'

'I'll be fine.'

Littleheath was a down-at-heel postwar council estate. The local authority clearly did not think it worth their while sweeping the gutters and pavements, and the litter and detritus had gathered in sordid piles of dirty nappies, plastic bags, cigarette butts, pizza boxes and needles. Some houses were now in private hands, judging from the uPVC front doors and cheap stone cladding.

Most were run-down, overgrown front gardens filled with rusting fridges, washing machines, a rain-sodden sofa with a broken back, buddleias taking root in the foam cushions. Sagging curtains hung at the windows.

Number 49 was not so neglected. The doors and windows were painted and there was an attempt at a front garden, with a small patch of unkempt grass and the dying remains of snapdragons and marigolds in the beds.

Kathleen recalled Steve Kingsman as a sinister presence. Unhinged, almost. She wondered if he was on drugs or alcohol. She shuddered in her coat, a tremble surging like an aftershock through her body. She wasn't ready, she should turn away. Let sleeping dogs lie. Perhaps she was better off not knowing. This could have been her, living in this house. Would she have ever escaped? Perhaps the life Joan had given her was not so bad after all. She twisted, poised to leave. *No. I have to know.* She watched her hand push open the gate, propelling her forward as if she were an automaton, moving without volition. She stepped onto the concrete path. A fox had left its prints when the cement was still wet, and a few straggling leaves from autumn had blown across it and now lay heaped by the doorstep.

She hesitated. Swallowed. Adrenaline had kicked in, she could taste it in her mouth, that sharp cold tang of blood, feel it in her body as her pulse hammered and raced. Fight or flight. It was all the same. Anxiety was compressing her body, squeezing its organs, making her breath shallow, empty. *Calm down. Nothing will happen. A talk, that's all I want.* A talk, a pow-wow, a palaver. She pressed against the doorbell, heard a serrated ring reverberate inside. Waited. She peered through the letter box, her view blocked by thick-brush draught excluders. She looked at the front window, but the flower beds ran up to the house and she wasn't sure she was tall enough to see through it anyway. She rang the bell again.

'What do you want?' A woman had appeared from next door, arms akimbo, a grubby apron tied around her middle, fleshy arms bare despite the December weather.

'I'm looking for Steve Kingsman,' Kathleen said.

'He's out.'

'Do you know where he is? Or when he'll be back?'

'No idea.'

'Is he at work?'

The woman shrugged, turned to go in.

'His mother,' Kathleen said.

'What about her?'

'Is she here?'

'Reenie?' the woman said.

'Reenie? I thought her name was Queenie.'

'I've always known her as Reenie. Short for Irene.'

'I see,' Kathleen said. 'Is she here, Reenie?'

'He put her in a home. When he got hauled up before the beak. Nothing wrong with her but he said it was the stairs. Said he was worried leaving her here by herself.'

'The beak?' Kathleen said. It was an oddly old-fashioned word. 'Why?'

The woman opened her eyes wide. 'Didn't you read about it? It was all over the papers. *Croydon Advertiser. South London Press.*'

'I've been away,' Kathleen said.

'Fancy him doing something like that,' the woman said. 'Dark horse, he was. He's usually out there hugging trees and what have you. Selsdon Wood. Carshalton Beeches.' She nodded towards the half-dead wallflowers. 'Queer fish, but he loves his garden, he does. His plants and all.'

'So what did he do?'

'Well, I'm not one to gossip,' the woman said. 'So can't really say. Not fair to judge him. All a bit murky.'

'What were the charges?'

'The charges?' she said, as if the question was a surprise. 'They said harassment, but who knows? Bit touched, if you ask me. You know, always obsessing. He had it in his head that that Lillie Pettall was related to him. You know who I mean? Bit before my time but she was big like, just after the war. Do you remember her?'

Kathleen bit her lip. 'A bit before my time too,' she said. Steve was right. There was a connection, though it was Kathleen who was the relative.

'Yeah, well, I don't know what hold she had over him, but he was harassing her, it said in the paper. Fixated with her, he was. Collected her records, had pictures of her and all plastered over his bedroom. Plus he took photos of her when she went in and out of her flat, on his camera that had one of those telescopic things. He said he just wanted to meet her. Got a restraining order and a suspended sentence. That means he'll go to prison if he does it again.'

'Oh,' Kathleen said. Had Joan found out? Gone to the police, put a stop to it? She hadn't wanted Joan to intrude, not today.

'Actually,' Kathleen said, the words tumbling out before she could censor them, 'his mother. Can you give me the address? Of the home?'

'Don't suppose the old girl has many visitors,' the neighbour said. 'One of the old-timers. Moved out here when the estate was first built after the war. Most have passed away, the oldies. Mind you, I've been here nearly forty years. Odd man, Steve, her son. Did you say you knew him?'

Kathleen shook her head. The woman made a corkscrew gesture against the side of her head.

'Never did an honest day's work in his life,' the woman said. 'Are you family?'

'Not really,' Kathleen said. 'I'm the daughter of an old friend of hers. My mum asked me to look them up.'

'I mean, a son who still lives with his mother...' The woman stood, unmoving. 'At his age. He must be in his sixties. And then this, what's the word? Preoccupation. With Lilli Pettall. Morbid, it was. Well, has to be a bit touched, don't you think?'

'Or devoted,' Kathleen said.

The woman snorted. 'You'd hear such dreadful rows sometimes. I feared for her, I really did. Like father, like son, I always say. Many's the time I kept my back door unlocked for her sake. You could in them days. Trust everyone. Good riddance when old man Kingsman died, I can tell you.'

For a woman who wasn't one to gossip, she was irrepressible, Kathleen thought. 'So, where is this home?'

'Langley Road. I'd go myself and visit her, but I've got things to do.'

Kathleen's breath quickened once more, every ligament in her body knotting. She hadn't thought about meeting Queenie, not this first time. She hadn't thought this encounter through at all, not properly, hadn't rehearsed what she'd say. 'Thank you,' she said.

'If I see Steve, who shall I say called?'

'He won't know my name,' Kathleen said. 'Just say an old friend of his mum's.'

§

It was a two-storey building with large windows and a facade clad in shiny coloured panels. THE BIRCHES CARE HOME, she read. RESIDENTIAL CARE. NURSING CARE. DEMENTIA CARE. CLOSES FOR VISITORS AT 8 P.M. It was set in well-tended grounds, with rose bushes lining the path to the front door. Only two streets away from Kennard Close, yet it could be in a different world.

She'd not thought about what she was doing. The visit now had its own logic, its own momentum. She opened the front doors, stepped into a wide corridor. A care worker, trousers tight over plump thighs, a pale-blue tunic straining round her hips, came out of a door at the end. 'Can I help?'

'I've come to see Irene Kingsman,' Kathleen said.

'That's nice,' she said. 'Is she expecting you?'

'No,' Kathleen said. 'Well, I don't think so.'

'Only sometimes our residents get a little agitated if people pop in without warning.'

'I'm sure,' Kathleen said. 'But I think she might like to see me.' Kathleen had no idea if this was true. 'Perhaps you could tell her Joan's daughter's here.'

'Righty-ho,' the care worker said, pointing to a couple of chairs propped against the wall. 'Stay here a minute and I'll see if she's awake.'

Kathleen sat down, shut her eyes. When my time comes, she thought, please spare me this, with its shiny linoleum floors, its lingering smell of urine and cheap air freshener. The walls were painted a pale green up to dado height, a sickly peach above. There were framed prints of baby animals cheek by jowl with safety notices invoking the residents to wash their hands, or reminding them where to assemble in case of fire. A large notice, like a hymn board, said TODAY IS: TUESDAY. YOUR NEXT MEAL IS: TEA.

The home was overheated, and Kathleen wriggled out of her coat, rolled it up in a ball and put it on the seat beside her, pushing up the sleeves of her jumper. She pulled out her BlackBerry, scrolled through her emails. Work. She doubted any were crucial. She'd wait until she was home before she opened them and responded. The institute, after all, was closed for the holidays, so there should be nothing urgent.

Joan has sent you a Christmas e-card. Kathleen deleted it. If Joan was putting out an olive branch, she could at least go to the trouble of buying a card and sending it. An e-card was more insulting than no card.

'Mrs Kingsman says she doesn't know you.' The care worker had returned. 'But she said she's happy to see you because she used to have a friend called Joan.'

Kathleen stood up.

'I should warn you, she sometimes gets confused. But she's having a good day today. Would you like a cup of tea? The trolley will be round soon.'

'Thank you,' Kathleen said.

'The lounge is straight ahead. You'll find her there.'

'Thank you,' Kathleen said, adding, 'I'm not sure I'd know her. It's been a while, you see.'

Perhaps she should leave. *I've remembered. I have an appointment. Please apologise to her for me.* Kathleen scooped up her coat, turned towards the front door.

'This way,' the carer said. 'Mrs Kingsman doesn't get many visitors. Sad really. She's got a son, but he hardly ever comes.'

The carer pushed open the doors and ushered Kathleen into a bright, airy room. There were large windows at either end, an oversized television in one corner, a plastic Christmas tree in another. High-backed armchairs upholstered in green imitation leather lined the walls. Kathleen looked around. Would she recognise Queenie? Would there be some primal connection? *That woman is my mother.* She hadn't felt it with Michael O'Doyle, but perhaps a mother was different, a sense echo of her womb.

The occupants were dozing for the most part, or sat chewing their cuds of memory, jaws chomping silently. A couple of the women were knitting and an elderly man was reading a newspaper. Apart from the drone of the television, the room was filled with an apathy, the stillness of the old whiling away their last days.

'Mrs Kingsman is over there,' the care worker said, pointing.

Queenie.

Kathleen stood and stared, trying to square this diminished, emaciated woman, her straight grey hair cut short, shapeless, with the callous ogre she had imagined. Queenie was dwarfed by the armchair, infantilised by it. Her lilac cardigan looked hand-knitted, hung loose on her frame, billowed over the top of brown synthetic slacks. She sat, socks rolled down to her ankles, her feet in cloth slippers which, Kathleen noted as she walked over, had holes cut out for her bunions.

'Are you Queenie?' Kathleen said. The woman turned and looked at her and in those pale, grey eyes and that lank, fine hair Kathleen saw herself. It jarred, that recognition, the knowledge that came with it. She saw Queenie as a young woman with fright in her eyes, knew she'd never had the strength to stand up straight and bold, never thrown off the yoke of victim, never known how, never had the luck. Empathy and contempt sparred in Kathleen's mind for this pitiful creature in her shallow, sallow frame, this servile, abject woman who had traded her own baby to save her skin, who'd infiltrated Joan's mind and terrorised it. It takes a victim to become a bully.

'Who are you?'

Anger bubbled like froth on a cauldron. Somehow Kathleen expected Queenie to know her, that an instinct would have kicked in that recognised Kathleen as her daughter.

'I believe you know my mother, Joan Spalding?'

'Do I?'

The chair next to her was empty and Kathleen sat in it, leaning over to face the old woman. If Queenie's mind was meandering, this would be a difficult conversation. She'd have to tread with care, draw out the memories, one by one, thread them together into a fine crochet. Except there was no end in sight, no pattern for it to follow. Kathleen had no idea of the shape it would make.

'Do you remember her?' Kathleen said. 'It was a long time ago. In the war.'

She didn't want to say *in the Mother and Baby Home*, not yet. That would be too fast. You had to build up a picture, encourage them to talk, she knew that.

'I remember the doodlebugs,' Queenie said, shaking her head. 'And when my Tom came home from the war. He fought in the war, did you know that? They all did. Saw some terrible things, they did.'

'It was an awful time,' Kathleen said.

Queenie was staring at her. 'Do I know you?'

Kathleen smiled. 'Not really. But I think you knew my mother, Joan?'

'Joan?' Queenie reached into her sleeve and pulled out a handkerchief, wiped the corner of her mouth. 'I had a friend called Joan.'

Kathleen could hear the tea trolley, the clatter of cups, the thump of the doors as they were pushed open against the wall. Another carer, a young girl this time, was coming towards them with two cups of tea. Kathleen stood up, took the cups, passed one to Queenie. The tea was milky, had spilt into the saucers, softening the biscuit that had been wedged there. 'I've put two sugars in yours,' the younger carer said. 'If you don't like sugar, don't stir it.'

'Thank you, dear,' Queenie said, picking up the biscuit, dunking it in the tea. She began to drink with noisy slurps. 'Never warm enough,' she said. 'They make it hours ago so it stews.'

Kathleen took one sip of her tea, tucked her cup beneath the seat. She couldn't stand it lukewarm, or with sugar or so much milk. 'You were talking about your friend, Joan,' she said.

'Was I?' Queenie reached for the spoon in the saucer, stirred the tea, took another gulp.

'Joan,' Kathleen said. 'In the war. She was your friend. What sort of things did you do with Joan? Can you tell me?'

'We used to go to the Trocadero.' Queenie leaned back in her chair, the empty cup and saucer balancing in her hands. Kathleen lifted them away, placed them on the floor next to her own. Queenie dabbed her mouth again. 'Such a lovely girl, she was. All-dancing, all-singing.' She lifted her hands, the handkerchief still clutched in one palm, shifted them left, right, as if her hands, too, were dancing and singing, her face lit so it had an echo of her youth, her grey eyes picking up a lustre, her mouth relaxed and smiling. 'All them old-time songs.'

No, Kathleen thought, that was a different time. 'After the war, was that?' she said.

'Oh no, dear. My Tom was home then. He'd never let me out on me own.'

'So you knew Joan in the war?'

'Did I?' Queenie said. 'I can't rightly remember.' Her pale eyes were rheumy and her skin lined and creviced. Kathleen realised with a jolt, as if she'd stumbled on a stone, that she held no warmth or sympathy for this woman, was indifferent to her. She felt no basic attraction, no instinctive affection. A coldness swamped through her, turning up the hairs on her arm, cramping her feet. She wanted to leave, never see Queenie again. She had an unexpected surge of affection for Joan, liar though she was. Perhaps she'd had good cause.

'We met a couple of Yanks once,' Queenie went on. 'Did you know that? Had a really good time with them. I was smitten.' She sank back into her chair, working her jaw. 'Yes,' she said finally. 'I shouldn't have, I know. I was a married woman but he was ever so nice, this Yank. Chuck, that was his name. He was married and all. I said to him, I said *That's a silly name*, but he said it was short for Charles and wasn't silly at all. I'd never heard of it. Have you?'

Kathleen nodded. 'I lived in America,' she said. 'I knew someone called Chuck.' She could say it now, though the anger remained.

'There,' Queenie went on. 'So you'll know. Handsome devil, bit younger…'

Queenie's voice hummed in the background but Kathleen's mind was a steel wrench screwing into her temples, bearing down on her eyes. Chuck was a common enough name. She'd known he'd fought in Europe. He'd told her, at her first supervision, as a way of breaking the ice, *I know England. London. The Trocadero.* It could be any number of Chucks, but the possibility was too much to bear, unfathomable, an eternity of pain, of *what ifs*. She clutched her stomach to hold its agony, the kick of her own history, too large, too immediate to comprehend. She sat staring at Queenie, taking her in, her fragile frame, her cheekbones and jaw, the grey of her eyes and the fine threads of her hair.

'Did he have any other names, this Chuck?' Kathleen said.

'I don't remember, dear,' Queenie said. 'I don't think I ever knew.'

'And the baby?' Kathleen said. She couldn't stop herself.

'What baby?'

'I thought you had a baby.'

'Who told you that?'

Kathleen wasn't sure whether Queenie was confused, or clever. 'Joan,' she said. 'Joan told me that.'

Tears began to well in Queenie's eyes, turning their pale grey pupils into a cloud of unhappiness. 'Yes,' Queenie said. 'I had a baby.'

'Was it Chuck's baby?'

Queenie was nodding, a repetitive jerk, her whole body moving with her head, rocking, rocking backwards and forwards. 'It was the war, you see. We just had a good time. At the Trocadero. It was a revue. She was such a lovely singer. Could dance, too.'

'Joan?'

Queenie's eyes stared into the distance of her mind. 'My friend.'

'Did Joan have a baby?' Kathleen said.

'Oh yes,' Queenie said. 'We was in the Mother and Baby Home together. I expect she told you all about that.'

'Who was the father of Joan's baby?'

'Joan's baby? She never said. She was only a scrap of a girl, a child really, when she had the baby. Yes.' Queenie leaned back, shut her eyes, folded her hands, the translucent skin leathery and liver-spotted, the veins black and still, death hands. You gave me away to a child, Kathleen thought, a child, by your own admission.

How did she ever think Joan could look after a baby? No care for *me*, because you were too cowardly to face the consequences of what you did. Well, Kathleen thought, *well*. At least Joan, child though she was, had had the decency to step in.

The care worker returned. 'I've come for the cups,' she said to Queenie, her voice loud and slow. Kathleen leaned forward, fished them out from beneath the chair, handed them over. 'You didn't drink yours,' the care worker said, looking at Kathleen.

'I forgot,' Kathleen said. 'And it went cold. Didn't want to make a fuss.'

'You should have said, shouldn't she, Mrs Kingsman?'

Queenie looked up. Her eyes had tears. 'Are you talking about old times?' she said to Kathleen, a tone of accusation in her voice. She leaned closer, the cups balancing in her hands. 'She's had a hard life, she has.' She tutted, shook her head.

Kathleen looked at Queenie, wondering how those neurons in her head were colliding and overlapping. Had she ever thought of the child she gave away? Had the memory of that loss become subsumed into the lie she and Joan had colluded in?

'Was that Tom's baby, or Chuck's?'

'My baby? I couldn't keep her, not with my Tom. He wouldn't have put up with that. Would have killed me if he'd known I'd had a fancy man while he was away. She was Chuck's. I never knew what happened to her.' She looked up. 'I think I gave her to Joan.'

Queenie leaned back in her chair again and shut her eyes. Kathleen held the waxy hand, then let it drop. She would never return.

JOAN

London: New Year's Eve 2007–8

Joan stretched out her legs, flexed her feet, making small hillocks under her duvet. She'd been right to spend this money, hire a designer. Her dingy flat was now a highly desirable studio apartment, the single room divided into zones, the kitchen integrated into the living area, the bathroom remodelled as a wet room. She no longer woke up to plastic flowers on a Formica table but instead faced a two-way display case that doubled as a divider full of plants and objects. Harry had given her a polished mahogany bird and together they had scoured the antique shops in Dulwich for art deco lamps and art deco crockery and any number of *objets trouvés*.

The floor had been sanded and limed, the walls painted in shades of grey that toned in to the function of the spaces. Her sleeping area was dark, the living area light, the dining area now lit by a lamp that hung low over a sleek glass and bronze circular table, a tasteful mid-shade that changed its complexion from day to night.

It had taken its time, and Joan had stayed with Harry while the transformations took place. 'Why not? I have the space.'

It felt strange, in another person's home, the tastes of his late wife ingrained in the fabric of the house, the choice of tiles in the kitchen, the wallpaper in the sitting room, the duvet sets in the bedroom.

Of course it had been cumbersome and awkward at first, and they'd both needed patience. After all, neither were spring chickens. She'd been unsure at first about showing her naked body with all its sags and creases, though once she saw how Harry had aged too, she had relaxed. It was a joy and a comfort, sexual attraction no less powerful in old age than it had been in her youth. She knew she'd never die alone, and nor would he, even though, along the way, they'd come to an understanding that both needed to keep their homes, their alone-spaces, being together, living apart.

She leaned over and flipped on the new Teasmade that she kept beside her bed, flexing and contracting her feet, *good toes, naughty toes*. Rose had taught her that at her first dancing lesson. She'd had some good times with the Petal Sisters. Harry had caught some of that spirit in his documentary. The occasion the band hid their hula skirts before the Honolulu number, or played the dance routines too fast, or when their make-up went missing and they had no wet-white and had to use distemper, which cracked. They'd worked together well. Happy times. Light-hearted fun that buried pain and loneliness and hurt. Perhaps she should have stayed with them. Who knows? It had taken her a long time to come into her own. Like little Jimmy Scott who never got the credit in his heyday, until he was plucked out of obscurity and given a new lease of life. Won awards, sang for presidents, hit the charts. A chance encounter.

She sat up in bed, adjusting her pillows. Michael had once asked her what it was like to sing and she'd said it made her feel like herself, as if singing *was* her. But she'd told Harry how music took her over, made her move outside herself. Now, she thought, her voice was a ribbon that connected her to the audience, a breath she exhaled that took on a life of its own, smoke rings that multiplied, absorbed by the ether, adding to it.

Music had a past, had become her history. And her future. She had bookings lined up, money in the bank. She picked up the phone, texted. *Good morning. How did you sleep?* The reply came within a minute. *So-so. All set for breakfast?*

Yes, she texted back. *Give me half an hour to dress. Bring croissants. I'll put the coffee on.*

She finished her tea, flung back the duvet, stepped out of bed and opened the door to the balcony. The late December air was crisp, but Joan relished its freshness. There'd been a hard frost in the night, layers of ice on the windscreens of the cars below, thick even by London standards, sheets of silver flowers and feathers and rime. Hoar frost they used to call it in the fens, and she could see now the mist rising from the frozen land and the rushes and hedgerows sparkle with tiny shards of ice, could hear her mother, harsh as winter, *stoop your lazy back.*

Kathleen. She hadn't opened the electronic Christmas card Joan had sent. It had been over a year now since Joan had been in LA. Not a word from Kathleen since. Joan had sent a couple of texts but had had no reply. She sent a third but it bounced back, 'undelivered.'

'What does that mean?' she'd asked Neal.

'Change of number,' he said.

The rift with Kathleen ran so deep, rawness seared fresh every day. The longing. In a strange way, the fissure brought her closer to Kathleen, to understanding her pain, their connection. The encounter with Steve Kingsman had proved a foil to their bond, though she was at her wits' end in knowing how to bridge the gulf between them.

She'd confessed everything to Harry, from the murky beginnings with Michael O'Doyle, to the provenance of 'Joan's Song', his disavowal of her.

'How could he do that?' Harry had said. 'To you? Why didn't he adore you, like I do?'

'Get away,' she'd said. 'You say that to all the girls.'

She'd told him about Kathleen's stillbirth, about Queenie and the baby. Everything. How that first lie became a truth, the flimsy footings of a life, of every wall and buttress that supported it, every grotesque and gargoyle that defended it, every spire and portal that decorated it, until there was a cathedral of lies, an edifice of glory to nothing. She wondered how it had ever stood the test of time, how insignificant that truth was now, that had to be so hidden then.

'You were in grief,' he said. 'Depressed too, I bet. And so very young.' He pulled her close, kissed her forehead. 'Did no one help you? All alone.'

'There was no help,' she'd said. 'Not in those days, and especially not for single mothers. Single mothers,' she laughed. 'We were called fallen women then.'

'You're a brave lady, Joan Spalding.'

She'd told him about Steve Kingsman and he'd taken her to the police station in Brixton and demanded they arrest the man for harassment. Kingsman claimed Kathleen as his sister, but she showed the duty officer the birth certificate, the original one she'd kept when she'd registered Kathleen with the forged docket from the Mother and Baby Home. Kathleen was her daughter. Mother and daughter. Steve Kingsman had made that clearer to her.

'Mind you,' Harry said, 'it took me all my courage to go into the police station, after the riots.'

'That was years ago.'

'Things haven't changed,' he said, with an edge to his voice.

Kingsman had been up before the magistrates but he'd got off lightly. It was a first offence, suspended sentence. Still, he hadn't bothered her since, and now she knew what to do if he threatened her again. She'd lived her life running from that lie. It had played dead, like a snake, bloated its body to stave off the predators. But when it snapped back to life, it lost its venom, slithered away without a trace.

Harry had a key to her flat and she heard him turn it, watched as he pushed open the door, the newspaper tucked under one arm, a paper bag in his hand. She loved him when he came in as if he belonged here. He placed the croissants and the paper on the table, slipped off his winter coat, his scarf and cap and gloves, put them into a cupboard in the hallway that the designer had discreetly added.

'Smells good.' He sniffed the air. 'But perhaps we could close the door now, before I get icicles on my nose?'

She shut the door as Harry laid the table, two coffee cups and saucers, pots of apricot and cherry jam, butter, plates, knives. Two glasses of orange juice. Napkins.

'And today?' he said, as they sat down. 'Same as always?'

She nodded. 'Practice after breakfast. Vocals. Then down to the studio.'

She had access to a gym for her dancing, one of the many unforeseen perks of her comeback. It took her longer to limber up these days. She knew her routines kept her fit and supple, built her strength and stamina, but some days it was a struggle and she was stiff, so an instructor was useful to have on hand.

'And a quiet afternoon before the show.'

'Yes,' she said. 'I'll stay here, if that's all right.'

New Year's Eve. Old Year's Night, as Harry called it. Star billing. The place was sold out. Once, a long time ago now, she thought, it had been the Dorchester, with its marbled floors and mirrored walls, its glamorous clients who paid no heed to postwar austerity with their billowing frocks and flowing champagne. Yet for all its splendour and prestige, she preferred the intimacy of Roxie's, appreciated its acoustics, which were as good as Ronnie Scott's. She'd been booked there for later in the year, and in the summer she was to go on tour.

'But first,' Harry had said, 'I want to take you home.' After all these years, he still talked about Barbados as home. He had a place there, Pie Corner, in St Lucy, in the north. 'Far from the madding crowd,' as he put it. 'Just you and me.'

She had a good list for this evening, old favourites, new songs, Christmas specials. Auld Lang Syne for midnight. And three new frocks, for before and after the interval, and for the party afterwards. Neal had secured a special license which allowed them to stay open late, but the party would carry on all night at his house.

All the more reason to rest up before the show. She hoped Harry would stay with her that afternoon. She liked to know he was there, to feel his essence, hear his soft, rhythmic breaths as he sat on the chair in her living area, reading or writing. He did it in longhand, in a small exercise book he kept with him. She'd given him a Filofax for his birthday, with a soft kid cover, and a small leather satchel to carry it, as well as his phone.

'Are you all right?' Joan asked. Harry had sat back in his chair, dabbing his napkin over his mouth.

He nodded, smiled. 'It's nothing. Just a little cramp in my leg.' He hadn't touched his croissant.

'Aren't you hungry?'

'Not really,' he said. 'Eyes a little bigger than my belly. I think, my dear, if it's all right with you, I'll stay at my home this afternoon. I didn't sleep so well last night. It's made me a little light-headed so I need to catch up. I'll see you at Roxie's before the show.' He pulled himself to his feet, limped to the cupboard, threaded his arms through the sleeves of his coat. 'I'll be fine later.'

Joan pushed herself away from the table, wrapped his scarf around his neck and handed him his satchel.

'The best present ever,' he said, patting it. 'I never thought I was the kind of man who used a bag.'

'Until you were.'

'Until I was. You saw that potential in me. That's why I love you.' He lifted her chin with his finger, kissed her on the lips, a gentle, tender brush. 'Till later. Take care. I'm looking forward to tonight.' He opened the door, stepped onto the balcony. 'I gone, lady.'

§

Joan made herself a light supper, hopped in a taxi in good time to change and do her warm-up exercises, breathing and yawning, humming and trilling, lips and tongue, vowels and tongue twisters, massaging her jaw. She knew it was a full house, knew everyone would be in a good mood, perhaps already tipsy, a little high. She could hear the talk and laughter from the main body of the club, music from the decks that Neal was DJing until the live show. She could hear the band in the green room next door, loud guffaws and the occasional trumpet blast.

She sat in front of the mirror. She'd put on her make-up before she left, but the lipstick needed another coat and she had to secure the mic.

'Knock knock.' Harry pulled open the curtain. 'How's my diva?'

'Diva,' she said, scoffing at the word. 'I've never been a diva. How are you feeling? Did you sleep?'

'Couldn't be better,' he said. 'Neal says get ready.' He smiled, winked. 'Break a leg.'

She flipped her hand at him. 'Off with you.'

But there it was, that old, demonic churning, the cold sweats, the hot flushes, the vertigo. That familiar brush with suffocation, as if a hefty pillow was being pressed against her nose and mouth, smothering her. She clasped her jaw with her hand, massaging it open, shoving away the terror that was throttling her. She could see the band take their place on the rostrum, hear the applause from the audience, watched as Ted, the leader, nodded to her standing in the wings. She had no muscle left, her tendons flailing strings wrapped round her bones, her bones sticks of plasticine and balsa. She could not walk. Not. One. Step. This time, it was real. She clutched her chest, thinking Neal would have to ring an ambulance.

'Lillie Pettall!'

She stepped forward, her gold-threaded gown glittering in the spotlight. She walked to the centre, picked up the microphone, nodded to Ted, counting the beats, opened her mouth as the audience cheered and whistled, and there was Harry standing up, leading the applause. She hadn't even started. It was going to be a good night, and she'd make it memorable. After all, the punters had paid a fortune to hear her sing. The *legendary* Lillie Pettall.

The club was hot and she doused her face with a cold flannel in the interval, changed her dress, drank some Lucozade and took a bite out of a banana that Harry had brought to her dressing room. 'Onwards and upwards,' he said as the band started up for the second half.

Joan ran onto the stage, no nerves, no shaking, no collywobbles, as Rose used to call them. Sang until one minute to midnight, when the club went quiet as they counted down the seconds and Joan opened her mouth and her deep, ravishing umber voice began as the clock struck midnight. *Should auld acquaintance be forgot, and never brought to mind.* She could hear the audience stand up and sing along with her, a different key so the timbre of her voice resonated below theirs. *Should auld acquaintance be forgot, and days of auld lang syne.* They linked arms, began to thread their way around the tables and chairs, some dancing, some attempting a hokey-cokey. Harry sat, fingering his champagne, looking at her, eyes full of tenderness and wonder. She loved him then, more than any man she'd ever known. Then he stood up and, fetching the biggest bouquet she'd ever seen from beneath the table, walked over to her, stepping up to the dais and presenting it to her.

'I said I'd bring you a bouquet the size of Kew Gardens.' He leaned over and kissed her. She laughed, and her feet began their rhythm. She nodded to Ted, and he struck up a tune. *Shuffle, tap, toe drop, paradiddle, ball change. Ripple, slurp, cramp roll, toe, step, stomp.* Landed in the perfect splits.

The party broke up at around one o'clock.
'I need to close up,' Neal said. 'I'll join you back at the house.'

Joan and Harry stepped out into the clear, frosty night, the contrast between the heat indoors and the icy air making them cough and their eyes water.

'Do you want to join the party?' Harry said. 'Or go home?'

'Let's go home to mine,' she said. 'Wind down quietly, the two of us.'

'We'll get a cab, if we can find one.'

'Or walk?' Joan said. She'd long ago changed her heels for sensible flats.

'A cab,' Harry said. 'It's late, and I feel a little weary.'

They stood by the kerb. Taxis drove past, occupied. It could, Joan thought, be a long wait. Beside her she watched Harry's breath unfurl in the night air, could hear his breathing, light and short. Quicken. Stop. She turned towards him as his knees buckled and he fell, the back of his head crashing on the pavement with a sickening, hollow thud.

'Harry!' she screamed, bending down, cradling his face. He lay still and cold. She looked up, yelled, 'Help.'

She was aware of a man running towards her, calling on his telephone. 'Ambulance, Brixton Road, opposite town hall.'

'Been drinking, has he?' It was a young woman, glittery high heels with peep toes. Another man pushed the girl aside, feeling Harry's pulse. She watched as he opened Harry's coat and pressed the heel of his hand on Harry's chest, another hand on top, interlocking fingers, pushing, pushing, a steady rhythmic pace.

'Harry.' She was whimpering, her fingers feeling for his hand, cold to her touch. 'Wake up. Wake up.'

She could hear the wail of an ambulance, watched as the blue lights drew closer and drew to a stop, paramedics leaping out, straight to Harry, pulling back his shirt, flicking his sternum. She saw Harry twitch. It's all right, she thought, he's alive. They were opening equipment, pulling out a defibrillator, applying it to his chest so his torso jerked with the shock.

'What is it?' Joan said. 'Will he be all right?'

'Are you his wife?'

'Yes,' she said. *As good as.*

She watched as they lifted him onto the stretcher, wheeled him into the ambulance. She climbed in after him, held his cooling hand, stroking his chamois skin.

'I'm sorry,' the paramedic said.

A frail shell of what had once been the man. He'd never wake up now, never call her name. She'd had so little time with him.

§

It was late morning before she arrived home. Neal had come to the hospital as soon as she called him, and they'd sat by Harry's side in A & E, had gone together to collect the death certificate, visit the undertaker. As his nephew, he was Harry's next of kin. They took a taxi back. He saw her to the door, waited while she let herself in.

'Believe it or not,' she said to him, 'I didn't know much happiness in my life until I met Harry.'

He nodded. 'My uncle was a good man.'

'He spoke to me.' Beat a rhythm from the heart of him to the heart of the earth, to the heart of her. 'I loved him, Neal.' He was her element, the air she breathed, the water she drank.

'I know,' he said. There was a flatness in his voice, in hers too, a flatness in the world they'd live in now, a mediocrity.

They stepped into the studio apartment and Joan walked towards her armchair, sat down, staring at the fireplace.

'I'll put the kettle on,' Neal said.

Joan shook her head. 'I'm fine.' Added, 'Thank you.'

'You need to eat.'

'Presently,' she said. 'I just need a little time.' She swallowed. 'The shock.' The nurses at the hospital had talked about him *passing.* But he wasn't passing. He was *dead*, his beautiful body chilled in the mortuary, his presence now a hideous, gaping absence.

'I'll leave you in peace,' Neal said. 'You call me. Any time. Anything you need, just let me know.' She felt his hand press on her shoulder and she reached up and stroked his fingers.

'Thank you.'

'I'll come back this evening,' he said. 'Just to check.'

Joan nodded, stiff automatic movements, words stunned into silence. He flipped on the light in the little hallway as he left, and she heard the soft click of the door as it shut. She reached over and picked up the photograph of Harry that she'd framed and put on the shelf in her new divider, brushing its surface with her thumb. Her last love. Her only true love. She had nothing left for Michael now, but everything brimming over for Harry.

'Why?' She said the word out loud. 'Why did you leave me?' Dry sobs, hard as rocks, hammered inside her, bruises on her heart. She sat looking at the photo, willing him to come alive, hear his walk along the corridor outside, the quiet turn of the key in her door. She thought of Kathleen, her baby, cold and blue in the midwife's hands. Kathleen cried in the nursery, she could hear her, she could claim her. Perhaps Harry was out there too, alive. Grief and lies. They all played dead.

The light began to fade, the street lamps came to life, casting a striped glow which fell between the slats of her shutters, black and orange. She rocked herself backwards and forwards, clutching the photograph, a soft keening parting her lips. Was Harry's death punishment for her lies? Retribution for the misery she'd caused? She'd never known what it was like to receive love, to marry it to her own so it became a majesty, a largess that embraced them all. The only love she'd known before Harry was what had drained out of her with Kathleen. And Michael. A slick of grief she saw floating on a river emptying into the sea.

She could hear her neighbour's television, a ghostly echo of life. She should sleep, crawl into bed and oblivion. In the distance, there was the wail of an ambulance, a screaming siren of pain. Joan shivered, squeezed her eyes shut. She was still wearing her dress from last night, diamantés that sparkled under the glow of the sodium lights outside, soft chiffon that wrapped around her legs. She should take it off, hang it up, pull herself together. Her thoughts were like an anchor that kept her rooted to her chair, the chair Harry used to sit in, looking out of the window, chewing his pencil.

The doorbell rang. She jumped, Harry's picture tumbling to the floor. Steve Kingsman. Please no, she thought, please don't start again. She didn't have the strength, not now, not without Harry. Could he see her? She'd had a draught excluder put on the letter box, which cut out draughts as well as prying eyes, and a spyhole inserted above it. If she sat tight, he'd go away.

The bell rang again. She remembered. Neal had said he'd come later. It must be him. She lifted her wrist so the dial of her watch reflected the hall light. Half past six. She must have slept. She pushed herself up, groped her way to the hallway.

'Joan, are you there? Where are you?' There was an urgency in that voice, an anxiety. Joan quickened her step, flung open the door.

Kathleen.

EPILOGUE

March 2008

Kathleen pressed stop, waited for the player to eject the DVD. She pushed herself off the sofa, retrieved the disk, slipped it back into its cover and placed it onto the shelf with the other DVDs and her CDs. 'It may not have been the film Harry set out to make,' she said, 'but it was the story Joan wanted to tell.'

'I'm glad you were reconciled,' David said. 'What made you change your mind?'

'Queenie. Her son. Joan rescued me, I see that now. Joan told me the truth, after all.' She laughed. 'Finally.'

She picked up her phone, dialled Joan's number.

'All set?'

'All set. See you tomorrow.'

Kathleen smiled at David. 'I've asked her to give me away. She's dead chuffed.'

She walked over to the CD rack, pulled out *Lillie Come Lately*, put it in the player, pressed play. Reached over to David, held his hand as she pulled him up, placing one arm round his waist, the other on his shoulder, nesting her head in the crook of his neck.

> *The shadow of her smile, the dapple of her laugh,*
> *The biting of the earth, the blowing of the chaff.*
> *She rises like a phoenix from the ashes.*
> *And calls my name.*

AFTERWORD

This is a work of fiction, though the issues dealt with are real. Premarital sex has a long history; in the early nineteenth century, for instance, an estimated 20% of births were considered 'illegitimate' and over half of first-time mothers conceived their babies outside of wedlock. Sex before marriage was an accepted part of courtship and continued into the twentieth century, yet illegitimacy and single parenthood for those women who became pregnant and were unable (or unwilling) to marry the father, was socially unacceptable and economically precarious, with no state support and often little family help. Abortion was illegal, expensive and dangerous. In many cases, young women had limited or no understanding of reproduction, or, if they were single, no access to birth control. Until the UK's Abortion Act of 1967 and the USA's *Roe v Wade* judgment of 1973 (which was repealed in 2022), unmarried women who became pregnant and could not secure an abortion had little choice but to carry their babies to term. Many mothers were forced – or chose – to give up their babies for adoption. In some instances, grandparents brought up a child as their own, the child often believing the birth mother to be their sister, as was the case with novelist Catherine Cookson and Nobel scientist Sir Paul Nurse.

During the Second World War, illegitimacy rates rose. Some of these births were the result of affairs with American GIs posted in Britain. The US authorities allowed white GIs to marry their UK lovers, pregnant or otherwise, should they wish to do so, but Black GIs were refused permission to marry whatever the circumstances. Many women were abandoned and their children – effectively 'war babies' albeit conceived by Allied rather than enemy troops – often put up for adoption. In adult life, some of these children have searched for their birth parents, with mixed results.

It is difficult now to understand the silence and shame that surrounded illegitimacy and, by extension, adoption, or the impediments once faced by single mothers to access housing, childcare, benefits and employment. Yet this shift in attitudes is recent. The Finer Report of 1974 recommended that the state should play a major role in guaranteeing a secure income for single-parent families but their proposed reforms were not implemented. Not until 1987 were the old Bastardy Acts repealed and replaced by The Family Law Reform Act, which removed legal distinctions between legitimate and illegitimate children.

ACKNOWLEDGEMENTS

I am immensely grateful to my editor, Jenny Parrott, to Molly Scull and to my agent, Juliet Mushens, for all their help and advice on the road to completion, and of course to the entire Oneworld team, including Paul Nash, Margot Weale, Hayley Warnham, Ben Summers, Laura McFarlane, Julian Ball, Mark Rusher, Lucy Cooper and Deontaye Osazuwa. And a shout-out to my scrupulous copy-editor, Sarah Terry.

Being neither a medical scientist nor a singer, I relied on others for information on medical research, performing and the music industry, so many grateful thanks go to Dr Declan Chard and Dr Victor Tybulewicz, to Sally Alexander and Rick Astley for their insights and corrections – though, as always, any and all mistakes are entirely mine. I have tried to make sure there are no historical inaccuracies, but this is a work of fiction, not research, and in tracing lives and shifting mores over long historical periods some small errors may have crept in.

Huge thanks to Cecilia Ekbäck, Viv Graveson, Laura McClelland and Saskia Sarginson, whose comments and advice along the way were so very helpful and supportive, and to Sara Sarre and Bob and Gill Marshall-Andrews for their astute comments and suggestions on various drafts.

Finally, as always, my husband, Stein Ringen, and my family for their love and support and the fun and the laughter.

I found the following books useful for this novel:

Bland, L. *Britain's 'Brown Babies': The Story of Children Born to Black GIs and White Women in the Second World War* (Manchester: Manchester University Press, 2019)

Holland, I. *Tales of a Tiller Girl: My True Story of Dancing in Wartime London* (London: Harper Element, 2014)

Merriman, A. *Greasepaint and Cordite: How ENSA Entertained the Troops During World War II* (London: Aurum Press, 2013)

Walden, K.B. *Entertaining the Troops, 1939–1945* (London: Shire Publications, 2019)

Walkowitz, J.R. *Nights Out: Life in Cosmopolitan London* (New Haven, CT: Yale University Press, 2012).

© Sean Gannon

Mary Chamberlain is the internationally bestselling author of four previous novels: *The Mighty Jester*, *The Dressmaker of Dachau*, *The Hidden* (Oneworld, 2019) and *The Forgotten* (Oneworld, 2021). She is also the author of non-fiction books on women's history and Caribbean history, including *Fenwomen: A Portrait of Women in an English Village*, the first book published by Virago Press. She lives in London with her husband, the political theorist Stein Ringen.